THE MARK OF CAIN

And Other Tales from the Pulps

THE MARK OF CAIN

And Other Tales from the Pulps

W.C. TUTTLE

"The Mark of Cain" originally appeared in *Giant Western*, Summer, 1948.
"Bad and Mad" originally appeared in *Western Story Magazine*, May 19, 1928.
"The Curse of Drink" This story appeared in *Short Stories*, April 10, 1929.
"When East Met West" originally appeared in *The Blue Book Magazine*, June 10, 1925.
"By Order of Buck Brady" originally appeared in *Adventure*, July 1, 1928.
"The Ranch of the Tombstones" originally appeared in *Adventure*, Dec. 30, 1922.

Contents

THE MARK OF CAIN

CHAPTER I

VERY WELL KNOWN TO the Frontier are the words:

"The Vigilantes are operating in Silver Butte, and have already killed the sheriff."

That statement was repeated in far-flung places in the West—around the camp-fires of the buffalo hunters, at the chuckwagons with the trail herds, and in the hideouts of the outlaw clan. Men, working outside the law, avoided the Vigilantes.

Silver Butte! A booming railroad town. A huge bridge, a long tunnel, miles of cuts and fills would assure Silver Butte of a long-time payroll. Silver Butte had been known as a bad-man's town.

Down along the rough roads, cut deep by freighter's wagons, came "Streak" Malone, tall in his saddle, riding a tall, blue-gray outlaw horse—a horse with the head of a rattler and the disposition of the Devil. Only Streak Malone could touch this brute, which obeyed every signal from its master.

Malone was just over six feet tall, lithe as a cat, ruggedly handsome, his coal-black hair split in the center with a two-inch streak of pure white. His high-crowned sombrero was decorated with a wide, silver-studded band, his vest was beaded in intricate designs, and his shirt was of almost-white doeskin, a present from a Sioux woman. He wore black boots with silver spurs, and his holstered gun was silver inlaid by a master silversmith.

No one knew where Streak Malone came from. He never spoke of his past, and he came into the West several years ahead of the railroad. He was barely thirty years of age, but his face held deep lines, and his eyes were deep under heavy brows.

A hard pair, this streak-haired man and the outlaw horse, but Streak Malone was never outside the law. Horse-breaker, trapper, buffalo hunter, gambler—he never stayed long in any place. Something seemed to lure him on, and now he was riding into Silver Butte. He, too, had heard of the Vigilantes of that part of the Territory, but the Vigilantes conveyed no fear to Streak Malone.

Until the coming of the railroad, Silver Butte was merely a cowtown with one short crooked street, but now it was a booming place of tent-houses, shacks of every description, and more building every day. The main street was ankle-deep in dust, teeming with freight wagons, pack outfits, cowboy riders and a few lighter vehicles.

The biggest building was the Silver Dollar Saloon and Gambling Palace. Less than a block away was another large building, nearly completed, with men working feverishly. A huge sign, ready to swing into place read: EUREKA SALOON AND GAMBLING HALL.

Streak Malone was almost obliged to ride over the wooden sidewalks, in order to avoid the traffic. In front of the stage office a man yelled his name, and he drew up. He vaguely remembered seeing the man in Bismarck a year ago, and waved a greeting.

He found an opening between two freight wagons, and spurred across the street and continued on to a feed-corral. The man in charge said:

"Turn yore horse loose in the corral, stranger, and hang yore saddle in the stable."

"Wait a minute, my friend," replied Streak. "I've got to have a stall for this horse, and I'll take care of him myself."

"Ain't the corral good enough?" The man was inclined to resent Streak's words.

"This horse will try to kill any man who touches him," explained Streak. "Tell everybody to keep away from him."

"I've got an empty stall," said the man. "Much obliged."

Streak walked out of the stable and met the man who had called to him. Streak looked closely at the man, who spoke quietly.

"I own the general store here," said the man. "You're Streak Malone. I'm Jim Buskirk."

"I remember you," said Streak. " Bismarck, a year or so ago."

"Good! We've been lookin' for a man like you, Malone."

Streak's eyes hardened, and his right hand dropped naturally over the butt of his holstered gun. The man grinned and shook his head quickly. "Nothin' like that," he said quietly. "Come to my store at dark, and I'll take yuh where we can talk to other men."

"I don't reckon I understand this deal, my friend."

"Look across the street at that sign on the sheriff's office."

It was painted in big, black letters and read:

CLOSED BY ORDER OF THE VIGILANTES

Streak nodded. "Plain enough," he remarked.

"The sheriff," said Buskirk, "was an honest man. They shot him down in his office."

"The Vigilantes don't usually kill an innocent man," remarked Streak. "I heard they are operatin' here."

"But don't yuh understand?" asked Buskirk quietly. "There's no Vigilantes. I mean, not honest ones. The sheriff was murdered."

"Oh, I see," nodded Streak. "Wolves in sheep's clothing."

"That's it exactly. Will you meet with us?"

Streak smiled. In town ten minutes, and already included in some mystery. He said, "I'll be there, Buskirk—at dark."

The man nodded and crossed the street, while Streak walked up past the feed corral, and stopped to look at the new construction of the Eureka Saloon. They were unloading the sections of a huge, mahogany bar from freight wagons. The dismantled bar had been shipped by steamer from St. Louis, and picked up from a Missouri River boat. A man said:

"The Eureka shore spent a fortune on that stuff. Imagine a mahogany bar in Silver Butte. Pearls before swine, I calls it."

Streak smiled and crossed the street to the one hotel in the town, where he was lucky enough to get a room. The clerk said:

"Are you one of the new Eureka gamblers?"

Streak shook his head. "Do I look like a gambler?" he asked.

"Yuh can't tell about looks. I see they're bringin' in real furniture for the new saloon. Cost a lot of money. Jim Flack is a top gambler, but he'll have plenty of action, buckin' Zero Brant. Brant jist about runs Silver Butte. We wondered why he didn't try to stop Jim Flack from buildin' the Eureka, but maybe he figures to break Flack in one swipe."

"What do you mean by that?" asked Streak.

"Nothin', stranger. Mebbe I talk too much—I dunno."

Streak went back to the doorway, watching the activity on the street. A young cowboy was standing just away from the doorway, and a girl came down the street to meet him. She was pretty, but looked tired. There was so much noise on the street that they did not expect to be overheard.

"I've been watchin' for yuh, Mazie," the boy said. "Near the Silver Dollar."

"I couldn't get away, Joe," she replied wearily. "They wanted me to learn a new song."

"Let's pull out," the boy suggested. "Mazie, I've got folks down in St. Louis. We can get married and go there. We don't have to live in this hell hole."

<hr/>

The girl's smile was as sweet as anything Streak had ever seen, but she shook her head. "Not yet, Joe. We haven't enough money. Mr. Flack offered me more money to sing in the Eureka, but I don't know what to do. Zero Brant heard about it, and he told me I'd better stay with him, if I know what's good for me. What do you think I should do, Joe?"

"I don't know," he replied. "Brant is a bad man and he might do you dirt. Better wait and see what happens when the Eureka opens."

They drifted away together into the dust cloud which hung like a pall over Silver Butte. Streak Malone drew a deep breath. Love in a place like this! He was curious to see "Zero" Brant, the bad-man. He walked toward the Silver Dollar.

Zero Brant was worth more than a passing glance, as he stood at the bar in the Silver Dollar Saloon. There were big men in there, but Zero Brant dwarfed them all. Clad in the raiment of a typical gambler, he looked like the common conception of a cave-man, huge of arm and limb, slightly stooped, a bullet-shaped head on a thick neck, green, predatory eyes, and a face of solid granite.

Gripped in one corner of his gash-like mouth was a frayed-out cigar, while in one huge paw he held a glass of liquor. No man had ever whipped Zero Brant. He and his gunmen ruled Silver Butte. It was a small domain for a king like Zero, but he had ideas. It was a starter—and the West was young. The huge room was overflowing with construction workers, cowboys, buffalo hunters and the usual riffraff which followed the construction work.

A woman came down through the crowded room, and the men moved aside to let her pass. Swishing silks and glittering jewels marked the passing of Conchita. She was a striking figure in that tawdry place, the offspring of a Spanish father and an Irish mother. Someone had once said, "I didn't know that the Devil was Irish."

Rounded, big hipped, small ankles and small feet, she moved with the grace of a tigress. Like the girl in Service's poem—"She knew by heart, from finish to start, the Book of Iniquity."

Zero Brant scowled. He didn't like to have Conchita in the Silver Dollar in the daytime. She was his roulette attraction, and she drew a lot of players. She didn't look so good in daylight. Men stared at her as she came up to Brant and took the glass out of his hand. Neither of them spoke. She faced the crowd and sipped from his glass.

"I have some information from El Chuchilla," she said quietly.

"What?" breathed Zero Brant.

"A man named Streak Malone came today. They say he has the nerve of the devil. They are having a meeting tonight at Buskirk's house and they are going to try and appoint Malone the marshal of Silver Butte."

"What else did El Chuchilla hear?" asked Brant.

Conchita toyed with her glass, a smile on her painted lips.

"They say," she replied, "that Streak Malone will have fifty men behind him—fifty guns."

"I'm bossin' Silver Butte," replied Brant coldly. "Fifty or five hundred—who cares? I'll handle this job."

"What about the Eureka?" asked Conchita. "They're moving in the mahogany today."

"Stay out of this," growled Zero. "This is a man's job."

"They tell me that Streak Malone is a man," she said, as she placed the empty glass on the bar, and walked away, her head high.

Zero Brant scowled. Conchita was his woman, but she was no slave. She would drop him in a minute, if the going got too tough, and he knew it. So they were going to appoint a marshal for Silver Butte, were they? Zero spat out the frayed cigar. All right! Silver Butte would find out that Zero Brant was still the boss.

He found the little Mexican Monte dealer, El Chuchilla, the Knife, and drew him aside. The Knife was a featherweight in size, but notorious for his ability in throwing a blade. He was also Zero Brant's spy. Brant said:

"Listen, you! Be at that meetin' tonight."

"*Por Dios*—no!" gasped the Mexican.

"There's goin' to be a crowd," said Brant. "You can get in. I want information of what happens."

"No," replied the Mexican stubbornly.

"Scared?" queried Brant sarcastically.

"*Si.* My friend, I know Strick Malone, and he know me."

"Yea-a-ah? That's better. Where did you know him?"

"Medora. I am seek for broken bone t'ree month. I have leetle tro'ble een saloon. Malone don't tak' joke. He t'row me twenty feet t'rough a weendow."

Zero Brant grinned. "I'll send somebody else. You keep away from Streak Malone. I need yuh."

CHAPTER II

Silver Butte came to life early in the morning. Or it may be that Silver Butte did not go to bed. The door of the sheriff's little office was open, and the sign was gone. Streak Malone was sitting on a corner of the desk, wondering why he had ever been foolish enough to listen to the pleadings of those men last night and accept the appointment as marshal of Silver Butte. The men represented what was left of law and order. There were men from the construction camps, asking for a square-deal for their men, businessmen, asking protection for their women and for their business. There were other men, too, watching, listening, asking nothing. Streak had said:

"Friends, I appreciate conditions in Silver Butte. No one man can do this job. I have only two eyes. Is there anyone in this room who will stand at my back—act as my deputy?"

Not a person had responded. Streak said, "I reckon it's worse than I thought. I'll find my own deputy. You gents represent the law element of Silver Butte. I want you to vote me the right to shoot first and hold trial afterwards."

The vote was unanimous.

So Streak Malone, a stranger in the town, was appointed marshal. Streak was no fool—he realized the odds. A bullet, a well-placed knife—and, as he had said, he only had two eyes. Leaning against the rough wall of the office was the sign, CLOSED BY ORDER OF THE VIGILANTES. Streak had torn it off the wall. It was his defiance to the killers who masqueraded as the law.

A man stopped in the doorway, and Streak looked up quickly. This man was of medium height, slender, long-haired, hard-faced. He, too, wore his gun. Streak knew who he was. A man had told Streak that this man was Mack Shell, leader of his own outlaw gang, reputed very fast with a gun.

They eyed each other closely, and then Shell's eyes shifted to the sign.

"Opened up again, eh?" he remarked dryly.

Streak nodded. "I'm the marshal," he said quietly.

"Yeah? What do yuh aim to do, Malone?"

"Bring law and order to Silver Butte."

Mack Shell started to laugh, but stopped and began rolling a cigarette. Streak said:

"You're Mack Shell. Are you backin' Zero Brant?"

Shell spat viciously. "Back that wolf?" he snorted.

"He claims that he's the boss of Silver Butte."

"Suits me—I don't live here."

Streak looked thoughtfully at the outlaw. "You've taken over a cattle ranch only a few miles from here, Shell," he said. "This will be your town. When you come here, do yuh want a boss?"

Shell looked coldly at Streak. "Nobody bosses Mack Shell."

"It will be you or Zero Brant some day, Shell. Good folks won't come here—folks with women and kids. There are other kinds of women, Shell, beside the kind at the Silver Dollar. A decent woman ain't safe on the street."

"She shore ain't," agreed Shell. "But that hasn't got a thing to do with me. I ain't got a woman."

"Look at it like this," suggested Streak quietly. "You had a mother—maybe a sister, Shell. They'd—"

Mack Shell flung his cigarette into the street.

"Don't preach to me!" he snapped. "I'm forgettin' things like that. I ain't backin' Zero Brant, if that helps yuh any."

"It doesn't help enough," said Streak. "You're a man with a rep, Mack Shell, and I need yore help."

"My help?" Mack Shell laughed harshly. "I don't understand that remark, Malone. What do yuh mean?"

"I want you to act as my deputy."

For a moment the outlaw stared at Streak, his jaw sagging.

"You—what?" he gasped. "Deputy? Are you plumb crazy?"

"No, I'm perfectly sane."

Mack Shell laughed again and began making another cigarette. It was a preposterous idea. Living for years, only a jump ahead of the law, and now—

"I'd be a bust as an officer," he said. "Mack Shell, deputy marshal—a lawman! What made yuh ask me, Malone?"

"I need an honest man."

"Honest man? Malone, don't you know my rep?"

Streak Malone smiled slowly. "You may be a rustler and horse-thief, Mack Shell," he said. "I don't know. A man told me that you never broke your word. I have my own code of honesty, and maybe it conflicts with the law, too. I don't care about yore rep. I want you to act as my deputy."

Mack Shell didn't smile now. He looked closely at Streak, his brow furrowed. The stage from Whitewater was coming in, ploughing through the dust, pulling up at the stage-depot, only a short distance from where Streak and Mack were standing. Two men got out of the stage, and one of them turned to assist a woman to alight. They exchanged a few words, after which the man picked up the baggage belonging to the woman. They talked for a moment with the driver, who directed them to the hotel, and they came down past the office.

One of the men was tall and swarthy, well-dressed, while the other man was short, long-armed, broad of shoulder, with the face of an ape. His head was rather round, small eyes, deep-set on either side of a broad nose, and with the widest mouth Streak and Mack had ever seen. When he laughed at some remark of his companion, one expected to see canine teeth.

The woman, slightly over-dressed and wearing a huge picture-hat, was beautiful, except that she wore too much paint and powder. The woman turned her head and looked straight at Streak as she walked past with the two men. For a moment her eyes snapped wide in amazement or horror. She stumbled into one of the men and might have fallen had not the ape-like one grasped her quickly.

Then they went on to the hotel entrance. Streak and Mack looked at each other curiously.

"That lady must have known you, Streak," Mack said.

Streak shook his head, his brow furrowed. "I never saw her before in my life, Mack. What went wrong with her? Do I look that bad? She looked scared to death."

"Kind of funny," mused Mack. "Maybe you look like the husband she ran away from."

Streak laughed and shook his head. "It beats me," he said.

"Them two men," said Mack slowly, "are pretty bad characters, Streak. The tall one is Dan Corteen, and the other one is Monk Moore. They're both killers. If you'd like to know, I'd say that the lady is in bad company."

"I've heard of both of them," said Streak. "I wonder why they came to Silver Butte."

"Watch 'em," advised Mack Shell. "You'll find out that they'll go straight to Zero Brant."

"Why would he import gunmen?"

Mack Shell laughed. "You've seen the new saloon goin' up over there. That's Jim Flack's place. A year ago Jim Flack owned the Sundance Saloon. Jim's on the square, and he ran square games. Well, one night his place burned, and Jim Flack was shot. He was laid up for weeks. In the meantime Zero Brant built the Silver Dollar over the ashes of the Sundance.

"The men will back Jim. Because he runs square games and don't doctor his whisky, all the railroad men will come to his place. Zero Brant knows this—knows that if he starts trouble with the new Eureka Saloon, the men will back Jim Flack. That's why Brant is gettin' all the gunmen he can handle. With Jim Flack's place runnin', Zero Brant will go broke—and he knows it."

Streak smiled. "I reckon I bit off quite a chew, Mack."

"Yeah, and I flung in my lot on a bit of hot trouble, too. But I knew what I was doin'. You didn't."

"You mean you'll take the job?" asked Streak quickly.

"Yeah, I reckon I've taken it, Streak. Yuh're right—some day some decent folks might want to live here—folks with good women—and kids. I'd forgotten about things like that."

Streak started to say something, but at that moment Zero Brant stepped into the doorway which was almost too small for his huge bulk. He looked sharply at Mack Shell, but spoke to Streak.

"I'm Zero Brant," he said. "Shell knows me. I understand that you are the new marshal of Silver Butte."

"That's a fact," replied Streak.

"Not that it makes any difference, but what do you intend to do, Malone?"

Streak's jaw tightened at Brant's open sarcasm but he replied civilly, "I'm goin' to try and bring order and decency to this hell-hole of a town, Brant."

"Well!" snorted Brant. "That's a fine way to speak of Silver Butte."

"Has it ever been anything else?" queried Streak.

Zero Brant's eyes shifted to Mack Shell, who seemed just a bit amused over the exchange of words. Brant said:

"Where do you figure in this deal, Shell?"

"I'm the deputy marshal, Brant. Just appointed."

"You? Well, of all the crazy—"

"Your loop's draggin'," warned Shell coldly. "I'm the deputy, Brant, and it might be well to remember it."

"All right," said Brant. "It just seemed—sure, it's all right. Why not? I didn't come over here to quarrel over the job, but I do want to make a complaint. After all, I've got rights."

"Complaint?" asked Streak curiously.

"That's what I said—complaint. Silver Butte ain't big enough for two big saloons. Splittin' the business will hurt my place, but Jim Flack don't want a split—he wants it all. They're lyin' about my place, tryin' to turn the construction crews against me. Flack wants to boss the town—run me out of Silver Butte—even burn me out, if nothin' else works. I demand protection by the law."

"Comin' from you," said Mack Shell slowly, "that's funny."

"Don't say they can't!" snapped Brant angrily. "They burned the Sundance and shot Jim Flack. Almost killed him, too."

"We all know that, Brant," said Shell. "We also know that you was here weeks before that, tryin' to get started. When the Sundance burned, you started buildin' the Silver Dollar Saloon on that same spot, almost before the ashes were cold. Who paid to burn the Sundance has never been proved, but I heard that it was a paid job."

Brant ignored the implication that he had a hand in the burning of the Sundance. He said:

"Do I get the backin' of the law, Malone?"

"When you can show me that you deserve it—yes," replied Streak. "But the law ain't backin' crooked play, Brant."

"Are you accusin' me of runnin' crooked games?"

"*I* do," said Mack Shell quickly. "Malone ain't been here long enough to know what yuh do, Brant."

"I see," muttered the big gambler. "So that's the help I'll get from the law, eh? I thought that the law meant a square-deal for everybody. As far as the Eureka and their bunch of tinhorns are concerned, I'll handle my own case. And as for you two—I don't want yore help. I'll make my own laws, and enforce 'em, too. Malone, you and yore gun-fightin' deputy can stay on this side of the street. I'll handle the other side."

Zero Brant turned and went out into the busy street. Streak laughed quietly. He said, "I wonder if he thinks we'll honor his deadline, Shell."

"He knows we won't, Streak. Brant is no fool. I'm goin' out and find my boys. I won't be goin' out to the ranch for a few days, and there's things I want done. See yuh later, Streak."

It was late in the afternoon when Streak Malone went into the Silver Dollar. The place was about half-filled at that time of day. There were several men at the long bar, and among them were Dan Corteen and Monk Moore.

Corteen was wearing a long, broadcloth coat, patent-leather boots, a wide-brimmed, black hat and the fanciest vest Streak Malone had ever seen. It was a riot of color, with flashing buttons. The tall gambler looked at Streak through narrowed eyes as Streak came in past the bar.

CHAPTER III

Malone did not speak to these men because he didn't know any of them, except by name. Zero Brant was at the far end of the bar, talking with one of his gamblers, and Streak nodded to him. Then he heard Corteen saying:

"So they've got law and order here, eh?"

One of the men said, "Such as it is. They appointed a man as marshal, but one man won't do much."

"The Vigilantes killed the sheriff," remarked Corteen.

Streak stopped short and turned around. Corteen was watching him, and their eyes met.

"The sheriff was murdered, if you want the truth, sir," Streak said.

"That's not what I heard, Marshal."

"So you know who I am," remarked Streak coldly. "We're even, Corteen."

The tall gambler barely moved his lips, as he said, "I don't like the way yuh said that, my friend."

"Could it be that you're a little ashamed, Corteen?"

The gambler's face tightened perceptibly, his hands dropped to his sides. He had two holstered guns under that long coat, the butts close to the front, ready for a cross-draw. The thumbs and fingers of both hands gently touched the edges of that open coat. Then he leaned forward a little.

"This town ain't big enough for the both of us, Malone," he said harshly. "By sundown it'll be too small. We can't both stay here."

"I'll be here—watchin' it shrink, Corteen."

"I hope you have written a will," said Corteen coldly.

Streak Malone smiled slowly. "I'll make yuh a gamblin' proposition, Corteen. We'll both make out our wills, leavin' everythin' to the winner."

"What's the idea?" asked Corteen curiously.

"I'd like to inherit that vest. You probably stole it, but—"

"I what? Why, you streak-haired—"

Corteen forgot the sunset deadline. He went for his crossed guns. Men fell away from behind him, as his hands flashed up, but Streak's draw—they didn't see it. Corteen's guns were still only waist-high, when Streak's forty-five blasted from his hip.

The tall gambler jerked back, his eyes tightly shut. His fingers relaxed and the two guns fell to the floor. Slowly his knees bent and he collapsed.

Streak had stepped back, cocked gun still at his waist-line, his eyes searching the men in the room. Monk Moore's eyes widened a little, but there was no other sign of shock or emotion. Zero Brant had jumped away from the bar, staring at Corteen, flat on the floor.

"Well, there's one gun yuh won't have to pay for, Brant," said Mack Shell's voice, and then he continued quietly: "All right, Streak—I'm behind yuh."

"Thank yuh, Shell."

Brant didn't speak, no matter what he thought. He had seen the deadly efficiency of the new marshal of Silver Butte.

One of the men said flatly, "Corteen reached first." That remark settled any argument as to the aggressor.

Shell said, "Brant, you brought him here—you take care of him."

Streak turned and walked out, but Mack Shell didn't have the same confidence in that gang; he backed out. They met outside and walked over to the office.

As they stopped in front of the office to look back at the Silver Dollar, Mack Shell said, "You spoke a language they understand, Streak. Dan Corteen was fast with a gun but you beat him. Ten minutes ago you was known as the fool who took a dangerous job. Now yuh're Streak Malone, marshal of Silver Butte, who wouldn't wait for sunset."

"I'm sorry," said Streak. "I don't want to kill anybody but he was out to kill me."

"I heard it all," declared Mack Shell. "I was right behind yuh. Dan Corteen started it, thinkin' you'd crawl—and yuh didn't. Forget Dan Corteen. He's had it comin' a long time, Streak."

"I guess you're right, Mack."

"I know this kind of a deal. Corteen was here to get you. The next one won't give yuh a break—yuh're dangerous. I got a good look at the expression on Zero Brant's face, and the sand was spillin' out of his craw. You killed his pet monkey and he don't like it."

It was nearly dark that evening, when Streak Malone ran face to face with the woman who got off the stage that day. She was just leaving the hotel entrance. She stopped short, staring at Streak.

"Who are you?" she asked throatily. Streak smiled slowly.

"I am Streak Malone, marshal of Silver Butte, ma'am."

"Streak Malone?" She shook her head and repeated it again, under her breath.

Streak said, "Ma'am, I'd advise against yuh goin' out on the street alone."

She smiled thinly and said, "I expect to deal faro at the new Eureka and I must see a Mr. Flack."

"No matter what yuh do for a livin', this street ain't safe," Malone declared. "I'll take yuh over there, if I may."

"Thank you, Mr. Malone."

They reached the other side of the street and stopped in front of the Eureka. Streak noticed that she still seemed to look at him in amazement, tinged with disbelief.

"Be careful, ma'am," he said. "Jim Flack is all right, but conditions in this town are very bad."

"Thank you, but I shall do very nicely, I'm sure. By the way, I believe you had a little trouble with Dan Corteen today."

"You knew him?"

"Oh, no, I merely met him on the stage. Thank you for bringing me over here."

"You are very welcome, ma'am."

"I am Clare Ames," she said simply. "Names don't usually mean much out here."

Streak laughed. "Yuh mean—you change 'em often?"

"Not too often. For instance, you were probably not christened Streak Malone—or even Malone."

Streak smiled slowly. "A child has little chance to select a name," he said. "Parents very often give children names that they detest later on in life, so they can't blame us for takin' one that we like better."

"Or one that is safer."

Streak looked at her curiously. "Yes," he said, "I believe that is true, Miss Ames. Good luck to you and your new job."

"Thank you, Mr. Malone."

Streak walked to the edge of the rough sidewalk, his eyes very thoughtful. Why did that woman say, "You were probably not christened Malone," he wondered. Why did she look at him, wide-eyed? He had never seen her before she came to Silver Butte.

There always was a lot of activity in Silver Butte at night. Construction men, off shift, thronged the street, many of them intoxicated. Fights started and ended without interference. The jail was too small to think of starting a crusade against mere personal fights. Tomorrow night the new Eureka would open, which would, no doubt, start trouble. Streak Malone realized the enormity of his job. He had won his first encounter, but he knew, as Mack Shell had said, they would not give him a break next time.

He managed to cross the street to his office where he found Mack Shell, carefully oiling his six-shooter. The little outlaw smiled slowly, and Streak knew that he had seen him taking Clare Ames across the street.

"She's dealin' at the Eureka tomorrow night," Streak said.

"So Jim Flack is goin' to use female bait, too, eh?" remarked Shell. "Yuh know, I'm afraid that Brant is goin' to have plenty competition, Streak. That little singer—the one they call Mazie over at the Silver Dollar—has quit Brant and will sing at the Eureka. The men are crazy about her singin'."

"Have you got a puncher in yore outfit, sort of a kid, named Joe?" asked Streak.

"Yeah. Joe East."

"I heard him talkin' with that singer. He wants her to marry him and go back East."

"He does, eh? Yuh know, one of my boys told me that Joe was shinin' around her but I didn't believe it. Joe's just a kid. He ain't one of my regular gang, Streak. He just works with cows."

"What did yore boys say, when yuh told 'em you was a lawman?"

———◇———

The outlaw hesitated, then shoved back his sombrero and scratched his head.

"Thought I'd gone crazy," Mack Shell grinned. "But I explained the whole thing, and they're behind us. If yuh don't mind, Streak, I'll sleep here in the office tonight. There might be bushwhackers along the road to my ranch and, anyway, somebody might try to put up that sign again on the door of the office."

Streak was in no mood to go to bed and yet he realized the danger of that main street at night. Men were still working at the Eureka when he went over there, polishing the long bar, putting the final touches on the gambling paraphernalia. It cost Jim Flack a pretty penny to have all that shipped to Silver Butte.

He found Flack, a tall, saturnine gambler, watching the men. His greeting to Streak was very friendly. He said: "Glad you came over Malone. I heard about that trouble in the Silver Dollar, and the folks are showing a lot of confidence in you as marshal of Silver Butte."

"Thank you," said Streak soberly. "You've spent a lot of money to build and operate this place. That bar must have cost a small fortune, alone."

"I want to make this place permanent, Malone, but I'm afraid it might not work out that way. You know something of the conditions, and they are not good. I want to operate honest games and sell good liquors, but I don't know."

"I know what yuh mean, Flack—and they're not good prospects."

"A man told me," remarked Flack grimly, "that I'd be serving drinks off a pine table after the opening—if I lived. I don't like things like that, Malone."

Streak looked around the big room. Everything was of the best. He admired the long ornate back-bar, the mirror gleaming in the lamplight, reflecting back the glitter of expensive glassware.

In size, it was smaller than the Silver Dollar, but there was no comparison as to appointments.

"You've been quite a while in buildin' this place, Flack," Streak said. "It took a lot of time and money to get it furnished. Has anybody interfered in any way in the buildin' or haulin' in of all the furniture?"

"Not a soul," replied the gambler. "I've thought of that. It would have been easy to smash the furniture on those wagons, to tear down what I've built. Why did they let me do all this if they objected to me operating here?"

"Maybe it's all talk," suggested Streak.

"I hope it is. I don't want trouble."

Flack walked over to the group of workmen, paid them off in cash and came back to Streak. They were alone in the Eureka now.

Flack said, "I've tried, but haven't been able to find a man to act as watchman. Malone, I believe they are afraid to take the job."

He took Streak to the back of the place and showed him the little office. Off the office was a small room, furnished, with a single-bed, rough table and a chair.

Streak said, "Are you goin' to sleep here?"

Flack shook his head. "No," he said. "I have a room at the hotel. The watchman can use the bed during the day."

"Do yuh mind if I sleep here tonight?" asked Streak.

Flack looked curiously at Streak, but nodded. "I'd be mighty glad if yuh would," he said. "If you want to leave, that front door is on a snap-lock. It will lock behind you."

After a few moments Flack told him good night and went out. Streak kicked off his high-heel boots, and stretched out on the new blankets, smoking a cigarette, trying to figure out just what to do in order to change conditions in Silver Butte. He had finished his cigarette, but not his ideas, when he heard men walking the length of the saloon, their boots sounding hollow in the room. The office door was opened, men came in and closed the door, and he heard them light the lamp.

The partition between the two rooms was thin, and he could hear everything that was said. There was a small window in the little bedroom, but the only door opened into the office. The men in the office were silent for several moments, then one said:

"All right, Flack. You know why we brought yuh here, of course."

"Sorry," replied Jim Flack coldly, "but I do not. When masked men force me at the point of a gun to open doors and go with them, I believe they should do the explaining."

One man laughed harshly. "You ain't that ignorant, Flack. Here is a bill-of-sale, and we want yuh to sign it. Go ahead and read it—we can wait that long. Nobody knows yuh're here, so take all the time yuh want."

Noise from the outside drifted into the place, but there was no sound from the other room, until Flack's voice said:

"Sorry, but I won't sign this, gentlemen."

"Yuh won't, eh? Listen, Flack—you sign it—or die here."

"And if I do sign it, I also die, eh?"

"Oh, shore. But not here. You'll just disappear."

"I don't get the idea of this bill-of-sale."

"Still ignorant, eh? You fool! Why do yuh reckon we let yuh go ahead and build this place, and furnish it? We could have stopped yuh any time we wanted to, but we figured that we'd let you pay all the bills, get everythin' all ready, and then we'd take it over. See the idea, Flack. The bill-of-sale is to Buck Smith. Names don't mean anythin', my friend. Go ahead and sign it."

"No!" snapped Flack. "If you intend killing me, why should I sign it? That would legalize the transfer. Go ahead."

CHAPTER IV

That moment Streak Malone flung the door open. That is, he would have flung it open, but something caught under the door, blocking it half-open.

A man ripped out a curse, and a bullet smashed into the door. At the same moment the other man crashed the lamp, throwing the place into darkness. Streak managed to force his way past the partly-opened door, clawed for the doorway into the saloon. He heard the men racing down the saloon to the door, but he was not able to orient himself enough to shoot in the dark. Then the front door banged shut, and the men were gone.

Streak said, "Are yuh all right, Flack?"

"Yes, I am all right, thanks to you, Malone. That was a close call. Let's get the lamp from the bedroom."

The windows were covered, the door shut, when Streak lighted the lamp, and they looked at each other.

Flack said, "You came just in time, Malone. He was pulling the trigger."

"Glad I did." Streak smiled. "But I'm sorry the door stuck. Do yuh know either of them fellers, Flack?"

Flack shook his head. "They were both masked," he said.

"Do yuh know Buck Smith?"

"Oh, you mean the name on that bill-of-sale? No, I don't. It was only a name. But we know why they let me go ahead with this place. Well, they've ruined their first attempt, Malone, thanks to you. I'll go out the back way and get to the hotel. I don't believe they'll make another attempt tonight."

They went into the dark office and Jim Flack opened the back door.

"I don't know how to thank you, Malone," he said. "Maybe I can make it up to you—some way."

"Forget that part of it," said Streak. "Good luck."

Streak went back to the bedroom and examined the bullet hole in the door. That bullet hadn't missed him by more than a scant few inches. In fact, it had blown splinters onto the blanket. He stretched out again, trying to figure out more angles, but went to sleep quickly.

Jim Flack was over there next morning, before Streak awoke, and they talked things over. Flack said that he had talked with the superintendent of the hard-rock men on the railroad, and that the man was worried. Some of the more intelligent laborers realized that Zero Brant's brace-games were keeping the men broke, and the bad liquor had made several of them unable to work at all. He said that any incident might start serious trouble.

"It's a bad situation," agreed Streak. "But what can be done about it, Flack? You can't make arrests on what people think. Zero Brant has a tough following, and as far as enforcing the law is concerned, who or what is the law? I could put a man in jail, but how could he ever be convicted? What jury could, or would, decide guilt or innocence? Flack, this is a case where Old Man Colt is the only judge and jury."

"I realize that, Malone," nodded Flack. "I realize more than ever now that there will be trouble. Those men, last night, trying to force me to sign this place over to them, proved to me that they will stop at nothing."

Streak found Mack Shell on the street and told him what happened at the Eureka. The little outlaw grinned slowly.

"So that's why they let Flack go ahead with everythin'," he remarked. "If you hadn't been there, Flack would be dead now. Zero Brant is behind all this, Streak."

Streak nodded. "But we can't prove it," he said.

The opening of the Eureka was not auspicious. Zero Brant was furnishing free whisky at the Silver Dollar and the house was packed with half-drunk humanity, mostly foreigners. A half-dozen bartenders were working at top

speed but the games were not being patronized too well. A three-piece orchestra could hardly be heard above the roar of the crowd.

———❖———

Brant was watching the crowd, a scowl on his face. The free whisky was
keeping the crowd away from the games. Streak stood back against the wall,
watching Brant. It was the first time Streak had ever seen Zero Brant without a
hat, and he noticed that Brant's forehead was criss-crossed with scars which
were not too visible under a low-pulled hat-brim.

Chap-clad cowboys, wild as hawks, rubbed elbows with perspiring,
muck-stained laborers, who gulped free whisky and roared songs in strange
tongues. Here and there in the crowd were men in buckskin, bearded,
long-haired, buffalo-hunters and trappers. The buffalo hunters furnished
meat for the railroad crews.

At one end of the room El Chuchilla, the Knife, presided over a
Three-Card-Monte game. This layout was not popular with the rank and file
of patrons, but it placed the knife-throwing halfbreed in a good position to
overlook the room, and flash signals to Zero Brant.

Mack Shell worked his way through the crowd and came in beside Streak.
He said, "There's a storm comin', Streak."

Streak nodded. "It's bound to."

"I mean outside," said Shell. "Wind blowing, and yuh can hear the thunder.
Yuh can't hardly see through the dust right now."

Streak nodded, watching Conchita at the roulette wheel. She was blazing
with jewels, but the wheel was stopped. Shell laughed.

"Free whisky and no gamblers," he said. "Serves him right."

Conchita was looking at them now, and Streak noticed that her eyes were
almond-shaped and almost green.

Mack Shell said, "Some day she'll kill Brant. There's a rattler down along
the Mexican Border, with green eyes—like hers—and they don't always rattle
before they strike."

One of Mack Shell's cowboys forced his way through the crowd and came
in beside them. He said, "If you think Conchita is pretty, take a look at the gal
in the Eureka. She's got this'n beat four ways from the jack. And she's runnin'
an honest wheel. I won forty dollars on one whirl."

The cowboy went on, circulating through the crowd, telling them about the
Eureka. Streak smiled. Flack had probably hired several cowboys to pass out
the good news, and the patrons were already drifting outside.

"Let's go over to the Eureka," suggested Shell.

"These men won't leave free whisky," said Streak.

"The free whisky is over." Shell laughed. "They've just put up the sign."

Slowly the crowd was drifting out of the place, some of them barely able to walk. Streak and Shell went outside. Lights were blotted out in the swirl of dust, and flashes of lightning were frequent now. Just as they found the entrance to the Eureka, a crash of thunder brought the first splatter of rain.

The new saloon was filling fast as they came in. The polished furniture reflected the lamplight, a thing of beauty in that rough, wild country, but the patrons were not interested in that sort of beauty.

Jim Flack, backed against the bar, was watching the gathering crowd, many of whom crowded around the roulette, where Clare Ames was running the layout. Mack Shell circulated among the crowd but Streak stayed near the end of the bar, out of the crowd. Men shoved through the open doorway, most of them drenched with rain.

The building shuddered under the concussion of thunder.

More men shoved in around the roulette, singing, cursing. It was a terrible place for a woman—even for the wrong kind. Flack came slowly over to Streak, tense, hard-eyed.

"I don't like it, Malone," he said. "They tell me that Zero Brant dished out free whisky to this mob. They're all drunk."

Streak nodded, his face grim. "Even free whisky wouldn't hold 'em, Flack. They're like a pack of wolves."

More men surged in, possibly twenty or thirty huge foreigners, singing some sort of a chant. The room filled to suffocation, humming like a giant bee-hive, rank with the smell of unwashed humanity, liquor and strong tobacco smoke.

Somebody deep in the crowd cursed in a foreign tongue, screaming his words against the thud of a pistol shot. Came a babel of oaths, two more pistol shots, and pandemonium broke loose. Men surged toward the disturbance, and Streak caught sight of upraised bottles as the wave of men crushed tables and chairs, trampling drunken men to the floor, yelling like animals.

Suddenly they seemed to split into two factions, fighting each other. Streak knew what this meant. This drunken horde was bent on destroying everything in the Eureka.

Streak backed in against the end of the bar, gun in hand. He lost sight of Jim Flack. Out of the packed mob, like a football player packing the ball, came a huge, bearded giant, carrying a man in his arms. It was one of Mack Shell's men. He dropped the unconscious cowboy and drew back a foot to kick him in the head when a shot crashed out, and the kick was not delivered. The big man went down, and the crowd trampled over him. Mack Shell was there, smoking gun in hand, dragging his cowboy away. Streak tried to help him, but a man crashed into him, and he went spinning against the wall at the end of the bar.

Streak went to his knees but came up quickly. Bottles were whizzing across the room, smashing the lamps, and the smoke-chopped room became a blurred mass of fighting men. Windows were smashed, letting in the wind and storm, and while men battled in the Eureka, nature battled outside, the claps of thunder shaking the building.

Streak fought his way across the room, forcing his way by swinging his six-shooter over-hand, climbing over men, trying to reach the smashed roulette layout. It was like a nightmare, where everything went wrong. Men screamed curses in his face, but he drove them aside and kept on going, while that crazy mob destroyed everything in the place.

He found Clare Ames, pinned under the wreckage of the wheel, unable to escape or protect herself. She was too dazed to know what was going on, when Streak picked her up in his arms. She tried weakly to strike him, but her strength was gone. A man crashed into him and tried to take her away, but he shouldered the man back into the mob.

Streak clawed his way along the wall to a broken window where he shoved her through. Then he crawled after her into the downpour. From inside the saloon came a warning scream, and he looked back. The smashed lamps had started a fire. Someone threw a smashed keg of whisky into the flames and a moment later the place was an inferno.

CHAPTER V

Finally, Streak reached the office with the girl. He didn't dare to light a lamp but the blazing saloon gave plenty illumination. Clare Ames was recovered now. She wiped some blood off her face and looked closely at Streak.

She said, "What is your name?"

"I'm Streak Malone," he replied.

"You are Keith Delmar," she said. "No man could look as much like Jim Delmar and not be his brother."

Streak Malone hunched forward, staring at her in the light of the flickering flames. Keith Delmar! No man in the West knew that he was Keith Delmar—and this woman came out of nowhere to tell him.

"Jim's wife?" he whispered. "How on earth—"

"You look like Jim," she said. "I know the whole story—know that you escaped from a court room, before the jury came back. You should have waited—the jury disagreed. Jim got new evidence. A gambler, who was a friend of your step-father, pawned some of the jewelry you were accused of stealing. It was traced to him, but he was gone. He killed your step-father—not you, Keith Delmar. The law knows it."

"For heaven's sake, keep talkin'!" gasped Streak. "I never knew what happened, after I leaped from that window in St. Louis, ten years ago. Where is Jim?"

"That gambler killed him in Medora two years ago," she whispered. "Jim lived long enough to tell me—it was the same man. In St. Louis he was Tom Hall, but I don't know what name he had in Medora. Jim made him confess to the murder but, in some way, he managed to shoot Jim. Jim told me who shot him, but he never gave me the name."

Clare hesitated, choked, but managed to say, "Jim said to look for the man with the Mark of Cain."

"Mark of Cain?" whispered Streak Malone. "Yuh mean—well, what does it mean—this Mark of Cain?"

"An M, branded on his forehead," said Clare. "It's the only solution I've ever heard. I've kept going, trying to find that man, but I can't find him."

The door banged open and Mack Shell limped in. He saw them and blurted, "Thank God, you're both alive! Streak, I've got our two horses out behind the jail. The devil is dancin' tonight in Silver Butte, and the fiddler ain't been paid yet. There's a lot of people who never got out of the Eureka—drunken workmen, a cowboy or two—that little Mazie, the singer. Somebody said she died in there. That buildin' next to the Eureka is gone, too. Only the wind and rain can save the rest of that side of the street."

Streak Malone said, "You stay here, Clare. Bar that door and don't open it. There's more work to be done. C'mon, Mack."

They went out into the rain and they heard Clare drop the heavy bar into the slots. A man came running, saw them and came back.

He said, "I recognize you now. I'm the superintendent of construction and I want to tell you that the men have gone crazy. A lot of them burned in that building, and they blame Brant. They say he had men start the trouble in the Eureka."

"What are they going to do?" asked Streak anxiously.

"They've got dynamite. It's the one weapon they understand. I can't stop them for they're seeking revenge. Do what you can, but don't take too many chances, because they're a crazy, drunken mob of men, who will stop at nothing."

"We've got to stop 'em!" exclaimed Shell. "I'll see what I can do. Maybe the buffalo hunters can help us. I'll try."

Mack Shell went limping away in the rain. Streak tried to think of some way to halt the mob, but his mind kept hammering:

"You're free again, free again, free again! You're not Streak Malone—you're Keith Delmar. The law knows you didn't kill your step-father. You're free again!"

Streak drew a deep breath and went across the street. Smoke still billowed up from the heaps of hot ashes as the rain hissed down. Streak was hatless, bleeding from several cuts on his face.

He stopped in front of the Silver Dollar. A crowd had gathered in there, but they were not drinking or gambling. Streak shoved his way through the crowd. There was Zero Brant, Conchita, El Chuchilla, Monk Moore and others. Between them and the crowd was Joe East, the young cowboy from Shell's ranch. Joe had no gun, and he had very few clothes. Dirty, torn, bleeding, he stood there accusing Zero Brant, who hunched forward, his evil, little eyes watching Joe East. As Streak shoved forward, he heard Joe say hoarsely:

"You sent one of yore men into the Eureka to start that fight, Brant, you dirty murderer, and they're comin' to get yuh. If I had a gun, I'd shoot out yore black heart myself."

Brant, still hunched, his huge hands opening and closing, came slowly toward Joe East. It was like a gorilla attacking a pigmy. Joe didn't move. He seemed incapable of movement. But before Brant could reach him, Streak Malone stepped out from the crowd and walked between them. Zero Brant stopped as he considered this new enemy, and his eyes blinked. A sudden rage seemed to strike him. His brow furrowed, bringing his brows down over his eyes. There was some sort of a commotion behind Streak, and he heard Clare's voice scream:

"The Mark of Cain!"

Streak leaned forward, staring at Brant, who had lifted his head. Those scars on his forehead, when pulled down in that bestial scowl made a perfect letter M in the middle of his sloping forehead.

It was then that Brant dived at Streak, trying to clutch him in his powerful hands. But Streak was watching and sidestepped quickly, bumping into a man to his left, and Brant almost went into the crowd. Streak suddenly realized his danger and reached for his gun, but the man he had bumped into had taken it.

Brant had swung around, aimed a powerful smash at Streak's head, which he barely avoided. Then he smashed Brant full in the face with a right hand that would have knocked most men down, but it only drove Brant's head back momentarily. Brant was cut and bleeding now.

Men jostled Streak from behind, and he realized that the odds were heavily against him. Then Zero Brant came with a bull-like rush, driving Streak against the crowd, but Streak managed to uppercut him with rights and lefts, sending him off balance. A man threw a shoulder into Streak's back, sending him stumbling ahead, but he recovered and faced Brant again.

Something whizzed past his ear, and he heard a man cry out with pain. El Chuchilla had missed his target and pinned the wrong man. Someone tripped Streak, and at that moment Zero Brant caught one of Streak's arms in a viselike grip. Brant was bleeding from a badly-cut eye, nose and mouth, and he didn't seem to know what to do, now that he had caught Streak.

"The wishbone, Streak!" yelled Mack Shell's voice. "Hit him in the wishbone!"

Streak's right hand was free, and he smashed Brant's nose flat. Again and again he smashed that nose, until Brant released the hold on Streak's left arm, trying to protect himself. Streak drew a deep breath. Brant had flung both hands up, trying to protect his face, when Streak, putting every ounce of power into a right hand blow, drove it deep into Brant's body, just below the arch of his huge ribs.

Zero Brant's mouth snapped wide and he grunted with pain. His stomach was not fortified against such a punch. He sagged, both hands dropping to his sides, and Streak hit him again in the same spot. But Brant merely grunted.

With the agility of a monkey, El Chuchilla had reached the top of the bar, knife in hand, but a pistol cracked, and the little knife-artist was fairly lifted off the bar by the heavy bullet.

"Get out of here!" a man yelled. "They're goin' to dynamite yuh!"

Streak whirled, but at that moment something hit him, and he went reeling against the wall. It was several minutes before Streak could realize what had happened. Clare was trying to help him up, and the place was deserted except for El Chuchilla, behind the bar, and a man sitting against the wall, looking wearily at life. He was the one El Chuchilla had hit.

———◇———

Streak managed to get to his feet on rubbery legs. Gradually the building stopped whirling, and he could recognize her.

"I'm all right," he whispered. "Why did you follow me?"

"I had to come," she said. "I couldn't stay in the office. You saw the Mark of Cain on Zero Brant?"

Streak nodded wearily. "Let's get out," he said. "We've got to help—somebody."

They went outside. There was a crowd further down the street, yelling and cursing.

Streak said, "I forgot the dynamiters. Clare. You go to the office and wait for me." He went at a staggering run down the middle of the street.

"Don't let Brant get away!" he heard someone yell.

A man was running up the street, and Streak called to him. It was Mack Shell, going back to find Streak, panting, swearing.

"They knocked me down and rolled me plumb into the street!" Shell panted. "Brant and his woman got away somewhere."

"The dynamiters?" queried Streak anxiously.

"They ain't got here yet. We've got to find Zero Brant!"

They reached the office and stopped. A revolver exploded somewhere behind the jail, followed by a yell. Shell exclaimed, "The horses!"

Streak had forgotten that Shell had saddled their horses. They hurried down the narrow alley. It was quite dark down there.

Streak heard a voice saying huskily, "I came to get you, Brant. You killed her, so I'll kill you."

A six-shooter flamed so close to a man that the sparks splattered off like water from a hose. A moment later a man was flung almost into them. It was Joe East, but they didn't know it. A horse snorted and they heard Zero Brant's voice:

"Whoa, you devil!"

The fence suddenly splintered, and a horse lunged almost into Streak and Shell. It was Ghost, with Zero Brant on his back. The big gambler had neglected to untie the rope, and the big outlaw was dragging nearly a panel of the fence with him as they went out through the alley. Streak and Mack Shell ran in behind them, and saw Ghost whirl in the middle of the street, that section of fence acting like a scythe.

A crowd of men were coming up the street, yelling, swearing.

"The dynamiters, Streak!" said Mack Shell.

They were almost to the spot, where Ghost had plunged with his swaying rider. With a scream of rage the big gray horse bucked straight into that crowd, the roped fence cutting a swath. They broke for cover and the big gray broke loose from the fence, going into a real bucking frenzy. They saw Zero Brant crash into the street, and the gray whirled, looking for more worlds to conquer.

Streak and Mack Shell were the first to reach Zero Brant. The crowd had been scattered, but they began coming back. The men had the dynamite and right now they didn't seem to remember just what they had intended doing with it. Streak told them, "The man you wanted is dead—here. Pick him up and carry him to the Silver Dollar."

One huge man said stubbornly, "I no carry him—he kill my brother."

"He killed mine, too," said Streak, and without any further word, several of them picked up Brant.

They trooped up to the Silver Dollar. Jim Flack was there, and so was Joe East. Jim Flack looked like he had been sent through a threshing machine, and Joe East looked worse, but Joe didn't mind. He had his arms around Mazie, and Mazie was smiling.

Jim Flack said, "The kid thought Mazie was dead—in the fire—but I threw her through a window. I guess she must have struck on her head, because she's been wandering around in the dark. She's all right now."

Clare Ames had followed the crowd over there, and she went to Mazie. Streak looked around and saw Jim Buskirk. The merchant was carrying a buffalo gun, and he looked as though he had been burrowing in a coal-pile.

"I think this town will be all right now," Buskirk said. "Zero Brant can't run it any longer. I guess the rest of his gang got away, but that's all right. I believe we'll agree that Jim Flack is entitled to the Silver Dollar—since Brant was to blame for wiping out the Eureka. Is that all right with you, Malone?"

"I'm satisfied," replied Streak wearily. "Buskirk, can you and yore wife take in Miss Ames and Mazie for a day or two?"

"You bet we can! I'll take 'em right down there."

"You walk ahead and blaze the trail. I'll take her myself."

Buskirk grinned through his grime, as he said, "What about Mazie?"

"She'll get there," said Joe East huskily, "but she may have to drag me."

Mack Shell drew a deep breath, wiped a grimy hand across his face and said:

"I reckon everythin' is all right, folks. The marshal has done taken over for himself."

BAD AND MAD

"You better put yore hands up, pardner."

The man on his knees at the water hole turned his head slowly and looked at the other man, who was covering him with a rifle. This second man had popped up like a Jack-in-a-box from behind a sandstone boulder. Near the water hole stood a dejected-looking bay horse, head hanging, one hind leg cocked listlessly.

The man at the water hole got slowly to his feet, keeping his hands above his waist. He squinted closely at the other man, his eyes puzzled. Then, with momentarily sagging jaw, he uttered an expression of astonishment.

"Ben!" he exclaimed. "Well, what won't yuh see when yuh ain't got no gun!"

It was a sarcastic expression, because the speaker had a heavy gun in the holster at his right thigh. The other man came closer, but did not lower the muzzle of his weapon. The sun glinted from a badge fastened on the lapel of his vest.

They were as alike as two peas, these two. Both smooth shaven, slightly grizzled, neither of them carrying an ounce of surplus weight. Even their clothes were pretty much the same.

"Well, I'll be darned!" snorted the man with the rifle. "Harry!"

They stood for a while, looking at each other. Then:

"Oh, would some power the giftie give us, to see ourselves as others see us," misquoted the empty-handed man, and then added quickly, "if it would do any good."

"Set down," said the sheriff, indicating a boulder. "But keep yore hands in sight. I don't trust you no more than I ever did."

"You allus was a lovin' brother," grinned the other. "I've heard that twins have queer affections for each other—and it's right. You might lower that cannon, Ben. I know when I'm stopped."

"You robbed the bank in Oro City, yuh know."

"Thasso? How long have you been in this country, anyway?"

"What's that got to do with robbin' a bank?"

"Nothin'. Must have been here quite a while. They don't elect a sheriff in this country until they know something about him."

"I've been here seven years," said the sheriff gruffly. "Where have you been?"

"Oh, around up in the northwest."

"Stealin' horses?"

"That's none of yore business; and if yuh wasn't my twin brother, I wouldn't be that civil."

"Why didn't yuh go straight, Harry?"

"Aw, don't start preachin'! Slip the bracelets on me and take me back to yore jail. Heredity's what ails me, I suppose."

The sheriff smiled grimly. "Heredity! Why didn't it affect me?"

"Don't pull that holier-than-thou, Bennie."

"Don't like to hear about yore sins, eh? Well, it shore is funny to have you pullin' a job in my county. Makes it bad for me, don'tcha know it? I can't let yuh go, and it'll shore reflect on me if I take yuh back. Anybody'd know you was my twin brother."

"Yeah, we do look alike. Everybody used to say that I looked more like you than you do yourself. How far are we from Oro City? I shore traveled in a circle."

"It's only three miles, due south of here."

"Thasso? Yo're thought pretty well of down there, ain't yuh?"

"I'm the sheriff."

"You would be! I 'member you was allus bossin' things when we was kids. Yo're a right big man, I take it."

"I have somethin' to say about things in Oro City."

"You ain't married, I imagine."

A peculiar expression flashed across the sheriff's face.

"No, I ain't married."

"That's queer. You allus was kinda shineful around the wimmin'."

"Where's the money yuh got from the bank?"

The other grinned slowly.

"That's what a lawyer would call a leadin' question."

"Don't be a fool, Harry. I'll make yuh a trade."

"Eh? A trade?"

"Give me that money, and I turn yuh loose."

"Yea-a-ah? On the square?"

"I don't want to take yuh back. If the bank gets its money, they won't howl very loud. I can say I made yuh drop it but that yuh got away on me."

"Brotherly love, eh?"

"Love be dashed! I'd look well takin' my own brother to jail."

"Uh-huh! But suppose I won't tell yuh where it is?"

"Oh, yes, you will! I'll rope yuh tight and leave yuh out there in the rocks for a few days. Nobody ever comes by here; it's out of the beaten trail."

"And then you'll trade me water for information, eh?"

"Yeah—and you'll trade."

The robber threw back his head and began laughing. It seemed to strike him as a huge joke and he shook with merriment. The muzzle of the sheriff's rifle had been lowered perceptibly and his left hand rubbed his stubbled chin wonderingly.

"Trade me water for information! Ha, ha, ha, ha, ha!"

The robber threw back his head and slapped himself on the thigh. It was evidently the biggest joke he had ever heard. Again he roared his mirth, slapped his thigh heavily, and when his hand came up again it was comfortably filled with the butt of a Colt .45, and the muzzle was covering the sheriff.

The man had jerked forward off the rock, head hunched between his shoulders, his eyes glittering. For several moments the sheriff stared at him, realizing what a fool he had been not to take that gun away when he had the chance, and then let his rifle slide to the sand.

"I've done bought out yore tradin' establishment," growled the robber slowly. "Now, you'll trade on my terms."

"I was givin' you the best of the trade," said the sheriff. "What's a few dollars to years in prison?"

"It's jist accordin' to how bad yuh need money. Back away from that rifle, Bennie. Hands up to the shoulders! Oh, shore, I'll take yore six-gun! We may be twin brothers, but we're not twin fools. That's yore part of the heredity."

"What are you goin' to trade with me?"

The sheriff was sullen now, as he measured his brother.

"Trade? I'll tell yuh what I'll trade—me for you? Get what I mean? No? Then here's the idea; I'll be the sheriff, and you lie out here in these hot rocks. I've allus wanted to have a chance to boss things a little m'self. You've been sheriff for so long that it won't hurt yuh to let yore brother handle the job for a few hours or days; it's all accordin' to how yuh stand the heat. I'll come out to-morrow and give yuh feed and water. I can alibi that by the fact that I'm lookin' for the man you *didn't* find.

"Yeah, that's what I said! I never robbed yore bank; never was in Oro City in my life. You trailed the wrong man. I've dodged sheriffs from Laredo to Vancouver, but yo're the first one ever to put the deadwood on me—and for somethin' I never done! But I'm through dodgin' for a while, at least as long as I can keep you under cover.

"I'll jist go down to Oro City and be the sheriff for a while, and what I want you to do right now is to tell me a few things."

"Tell yuh a few things?" parroted the sheriff.

"Yeah. What's the name of yore deputy?"

An expression of animal cunning flashed across the sheriff's face.

"Find out for yourself," he said.

"Meanin' that you won't come through with any information, eh?"

"I'm not tellin' what I know."

"Do yuh think that'll stop me?" The speaker laughed shortly. "I've brought contraband from Mexico under the noses of the rangers, and I've had mounties ride with me on a wagon load of hooch into Alberta. I've run, when the runnin' was good, and I've shot my way through, when it was blocked. I've preached in Seattle and dealt faro in Reno.

"I've lived on my nerve, Bennie; and I'll keep on livin' on my nerve. Yore little penny-ante town don't scare me. I'll go down there and be the sheriff. I'm glad yuh said that few people ever come out here. You'll stay here, while I play sheriff, and after a few days I'll crack that bank for every cent she's got, and then I'll turn you loose."

"You goin' to take my star and my guns?"

"I shore am. C'mon over to my horse while I get a rope."

"Yo're crazy."

The sheriff shuffled ahead and stood there dumbly, while the other man shook out a lariat.

"I'll have to turn my horse loose," he told the sheriff. "I'll cache the saddle and bridle. Whew! that sun is hot. It's a wonder it don't drive all you folks crazy down here. It's a cinch I won't stay here very long, but I'll go away with more than I brought. So yo're a big man in this county, eh? I've never had a chance to be a big man. Mebbe I'll go straight, Ben. It all depends on how you stand the heat out here in the rocks. With you out of the way, I might play a straight game."

"Yo're crazy," said the sheriff in a dull voice.

"Crazy? Ha, ha, ha, ha! Not me, Bennie. Yo're crazy, if you think I am."

"Are you goin' to tie me up?"

"Y'betcha."

The sheriff was standing there dumbly, hands hanging at his sides, while his brother examined the rope. They were several feet apart. Suddenly, without any warning, the sheriff sprang at his brother, the swift leap of a wild cat, slashing as he did so with both hands.

It was so unexpected that the man had no chance to guard himself, except to throw up both hands with the rope, staggering back in the yielding sand.

A slashing fist barely missed his jaw, but struck across his throat, cutting off his breath. Another fist banged against his ear, and then they went down in a heap, clawing, striking, gouging.

There were no rules in this fight. Like two animals, battling to the death, they rolled in the sand, fighting with fists, elbows, knees; berserk creatures of the desert they were, fighting to the finish. There was no conversation, only grunting, choking, panting noises as they fought.

Rolling over and over, they went surging to their knees, only to go down again; digging their feet into the sand, growling, whimpering. Suddenly they fell apart and stumbled to their feet. Without a pause, the sheriff lowered his head and dived for the other, who was clawing at his holster for the gun which had been lost early in the fight. It was out there, shining on the sand, but there was no time to get it now.

Down they went again, but fell apart and got to their feet. Once more the sheriff charged swiftly, but this time the other man was not trying for his gun. The sheriff was coming in low, like a football tackler, and the other man met his charge, jerking up one knee as they crashed together. But the sheriff's clutching hands went limp, as the knee caught him beneath the chin, and he flopped sidewise in the sand, his head twisted at a queer angle.

The other man slumped down in the sand, his head hanging, as he tried to pump air into his tortured lungs. His eyes were filled with perspiration and sand, his nose and mouth bleeding. He looked at the sheriff, blinking foolishly. Then he crawled to the water hole and stretched for a drink. The water was warm, bitter to the taste, but he drank heavily. He washed his face and hands, which dried immediately, and then he rolled a cigarette.

There was no remorse for what he had done. He looked at the inert figure on the sand indifferently. It had been fifteen years since he had seen Ben, and then only for a few days. Their paths had always been far apart. He snapped the cigarette aside and got to his feet. With callous indifference he changed clothes with the dead sheriff.

Then he loaded the body on his horse and took it far back into a little canyon, where he hid it among the rocks. The saddle and bridle he also hid away in a deep crevice, and turned the horse loose to shift for itself.

Back he went to the water hole, where he proceeded to wipe out all evidences of a fight. With a mesquite branch he smoothed the sand, knowing that the first breeze would finish the job. He threw his own gun off among the rocks, shoved his belt beneath a mesquite bush, and put on the sheriff's belt.

Picking up the sheriff's rifle and revolver, he went down to where the dead man's horse was tied to a juniper, and climbed into the saddle. He knew he was playing a risky game, but he was banking entirely on his physical appearance. He had bluffed and stalled his way through life and knew his own ability. For six months, at one time, he had acted as a deputy sheriff in a New Mexico county, which gave him an insight into a sheriff's duties. He remembered that Ben had always been a man of few words, and he intended to keep his mouth shut until he had found out a few things.

It was not difficult for him to find Oro City. It was larger than he had thought. He didn't know where his office was located, and his eyes searched the main street for the court house or a sign which might direct him. He glanced keenly at the bank, as he rode past, and it seemed to be doing business.

"I reckon it didn't get nicked very hard," he told himself. "Just wait'll I get a whack at it!"

A cowboy stopped on the edge of the sidewalk and looked closely at him. The sheriff half waved at the cowboy, who shoved his hands deeply in his pockets and watched him go on down the street.

"Evidently not a friend of mine," the other observed dryly. "I've got to be careful until I get the lay of this thing, 'cause I might make a bad break."

Ah, there it is! Just a little further down the street was the sign: SHERIFF'S OFFICE.

The newcomer smiled grimly. A man was standing in the doorway, but now he turned and stepped back into the office. Boldly, the sheriff dismounted at the little hitch rack, slapped the dust off his sombrero, and walked into the office. His eyes were not very keen, after coming in out of the bright sunlight, and he didn't realize what was happening, except that one man had landed on his back, while two more had grappled him from in front, whirling him sidewise into the wall.

He had no chance to fight back. His arms were twisted behind him, and the handcuffs clicked tightly around his wrists.

"That'll hold him!" panted one of the men.

"Not for mine," protested another. "Soak him in a cell before anybody finds out he's here."

"Good idea! C'mon."

They hustled him through the office, down a corridor to a cell, where they locked him in, still handcuffed. He stared blankly at them—his mind whirling. What was it all about?

Another man came in—the cowboy who had stood on the edge of the sidewalk.

"Wasn't that Ben Allen?" he asked.

"It shore was," growled one of the men, who wore a deputy's badge.

"What did the fool come back here for?"

"*Quién sabe*, Jim? I reckon the jury was right when they judged him crazy. He argued with them that he was sheriff of this county. Bob was to take him to the asylum yesterday, yuh know, but somehow he got Bob's gun away, shot him twice, and made a getaway with Bob's star, rifle, and six-gun."

"And then the danged fool came back!"

"Merely provin' that he *is* crazy."

They moved down the corridor, and the prisoner came up to the bars, his eyes wide, jaw sagging. For a long time he stared into space, licking his dry lips with a drier tongue. Then he rested his hot forehead against the cool metal of the bars.

"Yessir," he said bitterly. "It's the first time in my life I ever agreed with a deputy sheriff. Solomon, in all his wisdom, never made a wiser statement."

THE CURSE OF DRINK

"MAN," SAYS "JUDGMENT" JONES, "is of few days and full of woe."

Well, I reckon he's right. I'm of a cheerful disposition, kinda goin' through life with a wide grin, tryin' to see everythin' in the right light and do well by my feller man; but when Old Man Woe sneaks up behind and swats yuh with his loaded quirt—what'll yuh have?

"Peewee" Parker says that as long as yuh stick to what the good Lord ordained for yuh to do, yo're all right. He picked me and Peewee to be first-class cowpunchers, that's a cinch, 'cause we ain't never goin' to be no good for anythin' else, if for that.

And then there's "Boll-Weevil" Potts, first name Hank. He's about six feet six inches lengthways, and with no width to speak of; bein' built a heap like a single-shot rifle. Hank's all right, but nature was in a playful mood when she laid out his specifications. And he runs to ears so fluently that he has to wear a six and seven-eighths hat on a seven and a quarter head to keep it from wearin' the top off his ears. As a distinguishin' mark, he wears a brown derby.

I don't hold that any man has a right to wear that kind of a war-bonnet in a cow country. It is jist an invitation to those desirin' a legitimate target. But Hank owns the No-Limit Saloon, along with the HP cow outfit, and that kinda gives him the right to look kinda doggy, as yuh might say.

Me and Peewee runs the HP outfit for Hank. Peewee Parker weighs two hundred and fifty on the hoof, and he ain't so awful tall. I'm "Hozie" Sykes, one of the real old Sykes family. My folks was in this country when the Mayflower came over. I've heard paw tell about one of his great, great grandfathers, who was livin' down in Arizona at that time. He heard about this boatload of folks comin' over; so the old man hitched up his oxen and headed for California. He said the damn' country was gittin' overrun with foreigners.

I'm merely tellin' yuh this to prove my pedigree. Peewee don't know much about his family further back than two generations, but that don't hurt his chances to be a good puncher. Owners of cow outfits don't question yuh much, when yuh apply for a saddle-slickin' job.

Hank Boll-Weevil Potts married Susie Hightower. Sometimes I look at Hank and know dang well he wishes it was merely an unfounded rumor. Susie weighs two-twenty, and takes after her pa—and that's takin' quite a lot. "Zibe" Hightower is somethin' for to take after. He ain't very big, but if all the rest of the meanness in the world was give him, you'd never notice the difference in his actions.

Zibe wears flowin' mustaches, two guns and a scowl. He's been in the San Pablo range since long before they built the hills and made the cuts for water to run off in, and he says he'll be here long after it's all flat land again. Nobody knows how old he is, but I've heard him tell how he showed the cliff dwellers how to build their huts.

Everythin' was goin' along all right, except for an occasional fight among ourselves or with the town of Oasis, that sink-pot of iniquity to the south of San Pablo, when along comes Eveline Annabel Wimple. Now, I don't mean any disrespect to a pretty lady. They're necessary, I reckon. Hank showed me her card, and it says, in real pretty gold letters—Eveline Annabel Wimple, D. T.

I got a good look at her, and I says, "Well, they ain't so bad to see."

"What ain't?" he asks.

"Them D. T's. I had an idea they was more serpentine, as yuh might say."

"That D. T. stuff means Dramatic Teacher."

"Pertainin' to actin'?" asks Peewee.

"With flourishes," admits Hank. "She learns yuh stage actin'."

"I've allus hankered to be a contortionist," says Peewee. "Yuh don't suppose she teaches yuh how to bend, do yuh?"

"Does that come under the headin' of dramatic?"

"It shore would, if Peewee ever bent," says I. "He lays on his back now to pull on his boots. But what in hell is a dramatic teacher doin' in San Pablo?"

"It ain't clear to me jist yet," says Hank. "Judgment Jones and her kinda holds several pow-wows, and it's somethin' to do with the church. Judgment has been tryin' to raise money enough to buy himself some fresh pants, or a pulpit or a bell, or somethin' needful for Christianity. He ain't flourished yet, as yuh might say. He said he'd have some news for me in a short time."

"That woman is pretty," says Peewee. "You better keep away from her, Hank."

"I'm a married man—and I'm satisfied."

"Satisfied that yo're married?"

"Thoroughly convinced," said Hank sadly. "Oh, it's all right with me, but when I see a damned old hi-ree-glyphic like Zibe Hightower shinin' around her, grinnin' like a Hallowe'en cat, I git hot. I said to him, 'You ought to have more sense, you danged old shadder of a vanished age.' And he says, 'I'm single, ain't I?'

"I told him he was worse than single—that he was minus one, and he got hot. Said jist because I was happily married, I was tryin' to keep him from marriage bliss. Marriage bliss! And Mrs. Judgment Jones is kinda on the warpath, too. She thinks Judgment is showin' this here D. T. woman too much attention. She told Mrs. Zeke Hardy that she knowed Judgment was smitten, 'cause for the first time in years and years he washed the back of his neck. She said the only reason Judgment faces the devil is 'cause he's ashamed to turn around on account of his neck. Oh, I dunno. The whole town is kinda stirred up ."

"Susie stirred up?" I asks.

"Most always is. She's learnin' to shoot a six-gun. Hurt her arm the last time she threw a flat-iron at me. Them things kinda keep a man active, I s'pose. Some married men kinda git in a rut, but if I ever do I'm a goner. Well, I took her for better or worse, and I shore got it."

———

We left Hank to his reveries of a squirshed love, and has a few drinks at the No-Limit, after which we're unfortunate in runnin' into Zibe Hightower. He's wearin' a clean shirt and he shore smells of perfume.

"Heel-yuh-tripe?" asks Peewee. "Zibe, yuh shore smell tainted. Mebbe it's 'cause yo're so old—kept too long, as yuh might say."

"I smell to suit m'self!" snaps Zibe.

"Exclusive of everybody else. Why all the odor?"

"Ain't this a free country?"

"With certain limits. You ain't learnin' dramatics, are yuh, Zibe?"

"Why not? All the world's a stage."

"And that makes us all stage drivers," says I.

"Yo're funny," says Zibe. "Yuh ought to study comedy. Pers'nally, I've got the physical assets to make a tragedian—voice, carriage—"

"Squeak and a buckboard," interrupts Peewee. "Tragedian!"

"I have so. I could do Shakespeare."

"Shore—in a horse-trade. As far as that's concerned, I ain't never seen anybody yuh couldn't do, Zibe. Yo're in love."

"No such a damn thing!"

"How old is she?"

"I ain't askin' no lady her age. Anyway, age don't make no difference; so—sa-a-a-ay, what lady are yuh talkin' about?"

"The one Judgment Jones is nutty about."

"That old Scriptural scorpion!"

"He's here to save yore soul. Said so last Sunday."

"Well, he don't need to worry about my soul. I don't."

"Yuh would, if yuh had any. Right now all yuh need is one of them little bird whistles to make yuh imitate a flower garden. Man, yuh shore smell like a bed of Sweet Williams."

"Some day, Peewee Parker, I'm goin' to hang yore hide on a bobwire fence."

"Pick yore day, feller, and bring the lady along."

Not bein' interested in dramatic teachin' nor the troubles of married folks, me and Peewee goes back to the HP ranch. We're dependable and as honest as the average run of cowpunchers. Of course, we don't cut down no cherry trees, and then run our legs off to tell folks about it, but we git along. As long as the law keeps away from us, we'll keep away from the law.

That night at supper time, Peewee gits to tellin' me about one time he acts in a play. I figure he's lyin', of course, but a good lie is interestin'. Accordin' to Peewee, he's a pretty good actor. He shot six men in this play—two at one shot. He's one of them pyramid liars—keeps pilin' one on top of the other. I stopped him before he got too good. I ain't never done no actin', but I never seen anythin' a Sykes couldn't do; that is, anythin' that's honest.

"It took me a long time to git as good as I was," says Peewee. "I'll bet I was good enough to git a job in New York actin' on a stage."

"You wasn't a good actor—you was a good shot. All the good actors I ever seen killed 'em with knives."

"Well," says Peewee, "I was a good actor. I wanted to kill 'em with knives, but the boss said, 'You go ahead and shoot 'em, Peewee—knives is too messy.'"

"You never played in Shakespeare, didja?" I asks.

"Nope, only in Dry Lake. This was a home talent show. But I'm good. The stage shore got robbed when I turned my talents to punchin' cows."

"Yeah, and for turnin' yore talents yuh ought to be arrested for cruelty to dumb animals," says I.

The next day Hank Potts showed up, unfolded from his bronc, and sat down with us on the porch of the adobe ranchhouse. Hank looks kinda shopworn, as yuh might say.

"I came out to rest m' nerves," says he. "I'm an actor."

"What kind of a actor?" queried Peewee.

"Good. I'm the leadin' man—hee-roo—gits the fair damsel in the end."

"Who is the fair damsel—Miss Eveline Annabel Wimple, D. T.?" I asks.

"Don't be comical, Hozie ," says Hank kinda sad-like.

"Speak—yo're among friends," says Peewee.

"It's thisaway," sighs Hank. "We held a meetin' last night. Miss Wimple aims to put on a show for the benefit of the church."

"And the meetin' busted up in a fight," says Peewee, bein' somewhat of a prophet.

"A discussion," says Hank. "Miss Wimple has a play of her own, which she desires us to play. Bein' as she is to furnish the play, train the actors, et cettery, and all that, she's to receive seventy-five percent of the profits, the other twenty-five percent goin' to Judgment Jones and his church.

"That started a argument among us. Miss Wimple argues that her play is a dinger, and the only available play in this county, when my wife—"

"She would," agrees Peewee.

"I never knowed Susie wrote a play," confesses Hank. "I never knowed a thing about it, until she steps out and says we can have her play free."

"It would be worth at least that," says Peewee.

"She calls it—" Hank stops to sigh deeplike—"*The Curse of Drink*. And me runnin' a first-class rum shop."

"Mebbe," says Peewee, "she meant sody water or some soft drink."

Hank shakes his head. "I read it, Peewee."

"What's it all about, anyway?"

"Gawd forgive me for sayin' anythin' against my wife, but I don't know what it's all about. Miss Wimple read it. Judgin' from the expression of her face, as she read it, it's a comedy. Even if Susie don't think so. I'm goin' to be Howard Chesterfield, a jockey. I'm the jigger," says Hank sad-like, jambin' his derby down over one eye, "what wins the race, saves the mortgage and wins th e girl."

"That'd be worth goin' a long ways to see," says I.

"That's what Miss Wimple said. But we're short of actors. Susie suggests that we git you two fellers to play with us. But I said neither of yuh knowed the first thing about actin', and Miss Wimple said that mebbe I was right, 'cause, as she read the play, it needed somebody with more brains than an ordinary cowpuncher has to play them parts."

"Lemme tell you somethin'!" says Peewee. "I've done more actin' than you ever seen. I was a actor before you ever knowed there was anythin' but a four-wheel stage on earth; and I never seen any part I can't play."

"I ditto all that and sign my name," says I. "When it comes to play actin', a Sykes jist falls naturally into the part."

"This is a hard play to act," says Hank.

"That's my meat," declares Peewee. "I've shore bit off some hard ones."

"Didja ever see a horse on the stage?" asks Hank.

"Well," says Peewee, "I kinda have, but I never favored 'em."

"This'n has got to have a racehorse for me to ride. Susie said we ort to have a lot of horses to make up the race, but—I dunno."

"Yuh might use Tequila," says I, and Hank kinda shudders. Tequila was a racehorse. I say "was," meanin' the present time. Hank bought him off a horse-trader for a hundred dollars. Fastest horse on earth for a hundred yards, and then crossed his front feet. Always crossed his front feet. Worked himself into a lather, looked like a racehorse, ran like a scared coyote for a hundred yards and then—well, Hank kept him.

"Might use him," admitted Hank. "Got a lotta sense."

<hr>

Hank wouldn't commit himself further, and went back to San Pablo. We don't hear nothin' more about it for a couple days, when cometh "Dog-Rib" Davidson, of Oasis. Dog-Rib almost runs Zibe Hightower a dead-heat, when it comes to bein' mean, and if all the hate in his carcass was laid end to end, yuh could use it for a trail marker from New York to Honolulu.

"I've been laughin' m'self hoarse for two days," says Dog-Rib. "Them there San Pabloers are goin' to put on a play-actin' show, with Hank Boll-Weevil Potts as the big he buzzard of the flock. Calls it *The Curse of Drink*. Haw, haw, haw! Can yuh imagine it? I can't. I've seen shows in my life, I have."

"You look like yuh had seen plenty, but never had none," says Peewee. "You shore look to me like a man who never had a show from the start."

"I've allus got along," says Dog-Rib.

"I reckon all of Oasis will be at the show," says I.

"Oh, shore. Accordin' to their handbills, every ticket will have a number on it, and the lucky ticket will win Hank Potts's racehorse. The tickets are one dollar per each, and no questions asked. Alkali and Oasis has shore invested heavy in them tickets. But it'll be a awful show."

"It's about time they asked us in to learn our parts," says Peewee, after Dog-Rib goes away. "We've got to have a little time."

But by that time the next day there hadn't nobody showed up to tell us; so we saddled up and went to San Pablo. The bartender at Hank's place tells us that the actors and actresses are all over at the San Pablo Hall, where the *Curse of Drink* is to make its showin', and then he gave us a couple of handbills which read:

WORLD PREEMEER
"THE CURSE OF DRINK"
By
SUSIE H. POTTS
A PLAY IN SEVEN ACTS & SOME SEENS

THE CAST:
Eveline Annabel Wimple, D. T. —*Gwendolyn Witherspoon*
Hennery Potts—*Howard Chesterfield Zibe*
Hightower—*Simon Legree*
Limpy Lucas—*Lord Worthington*
Mrs. Thursday Noon—*Lady Worthington*
Zeke Hardy—*Uncle Tom*
Olaf Swenson—*Jason*
SUSIE HIGHTOWER POTTS—LITTLE EVA

Presented by Eveline Annabel Wimple, D. T. under the auspices
of the San Pablo Church and Susie Hightower Potts.
Tickets are one dollar including a chance on winning the racehorse used in this production.

*Don't miss this chance to see Howard Chesterfield win the big DERBY
RACE and see LITTLE EVA go to heaven. Either one will be worth the
price of admission.*

"When is this here show to transpire?" asked Peewee.

"Tomorrow night," says the bartender. "Eight o'clock sharp. She's goin' to be a dinger, gents. I've seen some of it, but from now on, she's private. I tell yuh, they had a hell of a time gettin' Tequila up there. Took him up this mornin'. Built a platform plumb across one end of the hall, and they've been carpenterin' and paintin' up there for three days. If it ain't worth seein', I never seen anythin'. Every danged seat in the house is sold."

"We ain't got none," says Peewee.

"Well, yuh won't git none. They're all gone. Alkali and Oasis shore bought 'em in quantities."

Wasn't that a nice thing to do—sell 'em all out thataway? I shore intended to speak to Hank Potts about it, but he never showed up; so me and Peewee got a gallon of hard liquor and went back to the ranch, brewin' up a hate against San Pablo. We left word with the bartender to tell Hank Potts what we thought of him and his show.

"Two of the best actors in the country—and they left us out," mourns Peewee. "Tha's great. And me, who made Bill Shakespeare turn over in his grave twice in one evenin' in Dry Lake."

I'm kinda hazy about things after that. A gallon of Hank's liquor would make a jackrabbit waylay a lobo wolf. Time don't mean anythin' to yuh, and I thought it was the night before, when I realize that Hank Potts is among us, and with him is a beautiful lady. I remember tryin' to shake hands with her and got Hank's nose in my hand.

"I'm layin' my cards on the table," says Hank. "You fellers said yuh knew how to act, didn't yuh? In two hours we're due to lift the curtain, and we're shy two actors. Zibe Hightower and Zeke Hardy got into a fight, and Olaf Swenson tried to help Zeke, until Susie bent a two-by-four over Olaf's head. Zeke is plumb out of order, too. For the honor and glory of San Pablo, I ask you to help us out. Hozie, you'll be Uncle Tom, and Peewee will be Jason."

"Please, gentlemen," says the lady. "I am Miss Wimple."

"I'll bezzer wife don' know yo're out here with thish woman," says Peewee.

"The curse of drink," says the lady soft-like.

"If you think I'm drunk now," says Peewee, "you ought to shee me, when I'm right."

"Yo're both too drunk to act," says Hank.

"Zasso? Who is? Me and Hozie? Say! Feller, I could play all the parts in yore show, includin' the racehorsh, without any rehearshal—tha's me. Go and git the horshes, Hozie, 'f yuh please."

Peewee bowed to me, hit his head on the corner of the table, and wanted to fight Hank for hittin' him when he wasn't lookin'. Anyway, we got to town an hour before the show is due to commence. I got me a couple more drinks, which I didn't actually need, and then they took me up into the hall. The back of that stage is full of actors and actresses, and I remember Judgment Jones shakin' hands with me and God blessin' me for helpin' 'em out.

"The Sykes fambly never ignores a call for help," I says. "Bring on yore crowd and lemme act."

I ain't never played in a show before, but I thought I had. That's what jiggle juice will do for yuh. I kinda relaxed for a few moments, and when I realized things again, I finds Hank Boll-Weevil Potts and Zibe Hightower workin' over me with somethin' that smells a heap like turpentine.

"Keep yore eyes open, Hozie," says Hank, "they might stick."

<hr />

Bein' in a happy state of mind, I let 'em go ahead, not realizin' that they was paintin' me black as the ace of spades. It don't hurt none, except kinda makin' me stiff around the eyes. They left me in the chair and went about their business, and pretty soon I finds I ain't got no shoes on, and my feet are so black they shine. And by that time my face is so stiff I can't spit and I can't blink my eyes. All I can do is stare at things.

"In the first act, yuh ain't got to say a word," says Hank, "except at the end, where you and Zibe walk out, you say to Susie, 'God bless yore kind heart, Miss Eva.' Can yuh remember that, Hozie?"

I kinda nods. Remember? Shore I can remember. If somebody would crack the paint around my mouth, I might say somethin'.

I can hear Judgment Jones out in front of the curtain, explainin' things, and I hear him tell that me and Peewee has been added to the show. Miss Eveline Annabel Wimple finds me, and she says in a voice what is kinda choked, "Uncle Tom, yo're goin' to be a knockout."

Then along comes Zibe Hightower. He's wearin' an old plug hat, long, black coat, which Judgment Jones uses on Sunday, a pair of striped pants and boots. He's got some big black eyebrows painted up above his scrawny ones and his mustache is as black as ink. In one hand he's packin' a blacksnake whip, and he's seven-eighths drunk.

There's Susie Hightower Potts, wearin' a knee-length white dress, and she's wearin' more paint than a warpath Apache. Susie weighs two-twenty on the hoof, and she ain't over five feet tall. Cometh Hank Potts, ready for the fray, wearin' one of his wife's polka-dot waists, a pair of tight pants made out of a sheet, and a pair of boots, which he has painted with black enamel. On his head is a little speckled jockey cap, with a long beak.

"Limpy" Lucas is almost in-cog-neeto in a boiled shirt, glasses and Hank's old brown derby. Mrs. Thursday Noon is wearin' a necklace of them cut-glass dinguses off a chandelier, a feather fan, and a dress so danged tight that she couldn't set down without havin' an accident.

Then cometh a interruption in the shape of Dog-Rib Davidson, Roarin' Lyons and "Nebrasky" Smith. The two former are from Oasis, and the latter is from Alkali.

"We've been appointed a committee," states Dog-Rib. "We bought tickets in good faith, expectin' to see a show, but we finds that you've done fired two of yore best actors—Zeke Hardy and Olaf Swenson—and we know why yuh ditched 'em. It's 'cause Zeke used to live in Oasis, and Olaf used to hibernate in Alkali. We hereby demand our money back."

"No, yuh can't do that," says Hank. "We're ready to start the show."

"Money or scalps," says Roarin'.

"Let us arbitrate," suggests Judgment Jones. "We've got two better actors to take their places, and the show will be much better."

"That's what you say," grunts Dog-Rib. "Where's the proof?"

"How's it better, I'd crave to know, that's what I'd crave," says Roarin' Lyons.

"Brother, you've got a cravin'," agrees Nebrasky, "and so have I."

"Well," says Hank sad-like, "the only way to prove it is to go ahead and play her out, boys."

"I'll tell yuh what we'll do," says Dog-Rib. "I'm a fair man and I'll allus do the right thing. Us, as a committee, will judge. We'll watch yuh do this here play-actin', and if we decided it ain't as good as Zeke and Olaf could have played her, you give us back our money."

"My Gawd!" groans Hank. "In yore opinion! Well, I reckon it'll be all right, Dog-Rib."

"We'll be on the front row," warns Dog-Rib, "and yuh better give us plenty show for our money. We'll be especially watchin' Peewee and Hozie."

And me without a voice in the matter. I'd quit right now, if I could talk enough to resign. The rest of the outfit gits around me, and they shore told me a lot I didn't know about actin'.

"You two jiggers ain't the leadin' parts in this here drammer of the Sunny South," says Hank, "but right now yo're prominent as hell. On you depends about five hundred dollars; so act. San Pablo is watchin' yuh."

"I'll do my bes'," declares Peewee, "and if it comes to the worsht, I can lick about three of that committee. How about you, Hozie?"

I don't say nothin'. Peewee takes hold of my face and squeezes it a little. It left my nose out of line and my lips open, as though I was goin' to whistle.

"Hank, that paint hardened on Hozie," says Peewee. "He can't talk."

"All right. Mebbe it'll be better. There goes the openin' music."

It's the three-piece orchestra—bull fiddle, accordion and drum, playin' "My Old Kentucky Home," with variations.

———————————

After that, the show started, and Hank led me and Peewee around to where we can see what's goin' on.

"This first act is the drawin'-room of the Witherspoon mansion," whispers Hank. "Watch Susie and Miss Wimple; they do this well."

I reckon I got some paint in my ears, 'cause I don't hear so awful good, but I hears Susie sayin', "—since my darlin' pappy died—"

And then Dog-Rib stands up and says, "Wait a minute, will yuh. Lemme git this straight. Is Zibe Hightower dead?"

"That's worth the price of admission," says "Kansas" McGill, "if she gives the right answer."

Old Judgment Jones steps out and says, "This here is all actin', and Zibe ain't dead. Now, we don't want no more interruptin' from nobody. Amen."

"You shore act cheerful while givin' bad news," says Kansas, and the show starts in ag'in.

I can't git head nor tail to any of it. Mrs. Thursday Noon comes on, and the audience gives a big whoop. She shore sparkles, but forget what she came out there for, and proceeds to knock over a table and hit her chin on the edge of the sofy, where Miss Wimple is settin'. Her necklace got up around her ears and the dress busted between the shoulders, but they got her propped up on the sofy. The thing seems kinda deadlocked out there, so Hank Potts goes on. They gave Hank three cheers, but he don't mind. He's got somethin' to say, and he's sayin' it.

"When yore daddy died he called me to his bedside and he says to me, 'Howard Chesterfield, everythin' I own has been swept away, except my two daughters and my racehorse, and I—I—'"

Hank goes bug-eyed and forgets the rest.

"The horse was too fast and one daughter was too heavy, eh?" suggests somebody from Oasis.

"Go on, Howard; go on," begs Miss Wimple, and Hank mumbles for a minute.

"You are goin' to ride Thunderbolt in the big race?" asks Miss Wimple.

"That's it," grins Hank. "Thunderbolt will win, and you'll all git back yore fortune."

"But we haven't money enough left to enter the horse."

"I—I've saved my salary," says Hank. "I'll enter the horse."

"But we can't afford to hire a jockey."

"I'll ride him," says Hank, hammerin' himself on the chest. "I'll wear the glue and bold of the Witherspoon stables. I—I mean the bold and glue."

"Oh, you hero!" explodes Susie. "I knew you'd be loyal."

Old Zibe has come around where we are, and now he hammers on a loose board with the butt of his whip. From the other side comes Peewee Parker, all dressed up in a funny lookin' blue suit.

"Someone at the door, Jason," says Miss Wimple. Peewee goggles around, and Zibe motions him over to us. When he's out of sight of the audience, Zibe grabs me by the wrist, and the next thing I know I'm out there in the middle of the stage, with Zibe bangin' onto me. He takes off his hat, bows to the ladies and then takes a look at Hank.

"So yo're the jockey who is goin' to ride Thunderbolt, eh?" says Zibe. "Well, go on back to the stable—I want to talk with highgrade folks."

Hank hops his arms like he was sad all over, but goes out. Zeke grins at Susie and Miss Wimple.

"I'm Simon Legree," says he, "and I want to sell yuh a negro."

Susie takes one look at me, jumps up and throws up both hands.

"Uncle Tom!" she yells. "Uncle Tom! What have they done to you?"

Jist then my mouth busts loose, and I says, "They got me drunk and painted me with black enamel, and I can lick any damn' man —"

Zibe kicked me on the bare ankle and hisses in my ears, "Shut up, you danged fool!"

"Haw, haw, haw, haw, haw!" roars Dog-Rib. "That's actin'!"

"O-o-o-o-oh!" wails Susie. "They sold you, Uncle Tom."

"Somebody got gypped," says Nebrasky Smith.

"I got him in that boatload of negroes down at Nashville," says Zibe. "I recognized him right away, and I knowed you'd like to buy him back."

"Oh, I'd love to buy him back," says Susie, "but we ain't got no money, Mister Legree."

"Lotta good work left in that negro," says Zibe. "How about tradin' me yore racehorse for him?"

Zibe kicks me in the ankle and whispers, "Beg her not to. Go ahead and beg."

"Ma'am," says I, tryin' to work my face into shape for talkin', "don't let this jigger make any trades with yuh. He's a —"

Whap! Old Zibe steps back and wraps that bullwhip around my legs.

"Git back!" he roars. "Git back, or I'll cut yore legs off!"

I ask yuh if that wasn't a dirty trick. I didn't like Zibe, anyway; so I took a wild swing at his jaw, knocked him silly with one punch, took him to my bosom and pitched him headfirst into the committee on the first row.

"The negro wins by a knockout!" yells "Greasy" Easton, and somebody cut the curtain loose, with the *Curse of Drink* outfit haulin' me back by the slack of my overalls.

Well, I got told all about myself, while old Zibe manages to get around to the back, where he got his gun and wanted to assassinate me, but they took his gun away. The committee comes up and says that the show begins to look like it was worth the money, but they've got to see it all first.

While they're tryin' to fix the stage for the next act, Hank explains the show to me.

"In that first act, the father of them two girls has just died, leavin' 'em nothin' but that racehorse. I was their father's jockey, and this horse is to win a big race. That's the climax. Legree owns a horse in that race, but he knows it can't beat our horse; so he schemes to git our horse. Legree is the villain, yuh see. Yo're an old negro, which was owned by the old man, who went broke and had to sell yuh, along with other slaves. Legree buys yuh. He knows Susie is crazy about yuh, and he figures to trade you to her for this racehorse. She won't trade the first time; so he beats yuh up—"

"He tries to, yuh mean," says I.

"That was all in the play, Hozie. You ruined it. There won't nobody know what it's all about now. We've got to go ahead with the second act. This act—"

Comes a lot of racket, and I thought the audience was goin' to assault the stage, but it was merely female against female. Judgment Jones comes back and kinda tearfully explains that Susie Hightower Potts and Eveline Annabel Wimple has had a battle, and Susie swears that Eveline and Hank ain't goin' to do no love scenes, except over her dead body.

Hank said he'd talk with her, but he came back pretty soon, nursin' a black eye. The audience is plumb impatient, and the committee comes back to see what's keepin' us.

"We'll give yuh five minutes more," says Dog-Rib, "and if yuh ain't actin', we declares this here show null and void. We come here to see actin', and we'll see it to our fullest capacity or take our money back."

Then they single-files out again. Judgment Jones flops his arms and his face registers ashes-to-ashes, even unto the last ash. Hank rubs his black eye and ponders deeplike. Pretty soon he says, "There's jist one thing to do and that is to jump this show to where them snake-hunters will see plenty action. We'll put on the last act and them three scenes—the kidnappin', the death of Little Eva and the finish of the race."

"But they won't know what the show is all about, unless we act it all."

"Let 'em guess at it—that's what I've been doin'. C'mon."

I've decided that I've had about enough and starts to walk across the stage to where I can get out, but all to once I starts walkin' faster and faster, but don't get nowhere. The floor is goin' out behind me, and all to once I lands on my chin and rolled over against the wall.

I fans a few stars out of my eyes and looks at Peewee, who humps down beside me.

"I was wonderin' if that thing worked," says he, "and I see it does."

"What works?"

"That treadmill jigger they made for the horse race. They explains it to me that we're all in there, playin' we're watchin' the race, and at the finish Hank rides Tequila onto that treadmill and the audience can see everythin', except the horse's feet. Then they drop the curtain."

Oscar Tubbs, "Burlap" Benson and "Fetlock" Feeney, the blacksmith, show up, and I wonder what they're the committee for. They talk with Hank, and then climb up on a two-by-six, which extends across above the stage. I don't sabe their idea, unless they want to git above all trouble. Hank comes to me and takes me up front again.

They've got the same room fixed up a little different, and there is Limpy Lucas settin' at a table, with a bottle of liquor.

"You go in there," says Hank. "All you've got to do is fool around. In a little while Zibe will come in with me as his prisoner. You won't have a thing to do, until Susie asks yuh to rope both Limpy and Zibe. There's ropes back there on the floor. This will be easy for you. Now, go ahead and we'll lift the curtain."

Well, all fools ain't dead yet; so I went ahead. The curtain went up and I said, "Limpy, I'm as dry as a lost match in Death Valley."

"Fellow," says he, "don't speak to me. I am Lord Worthington, a scion of British aristocracy."

"I dunno what a scion is, but the rest of it's a lie. You was born down in Cochise County and yore father was a squawman. Gimme a drink."

"That's the stuff!" yells Dog-Rib.

"That's real actin'."

Jist then in comes Hank and old Zibe.

Hank's hands are tied behind him, there's a handkerchief around his eyes, and Zibe is proddin' him with a gun. He makes Hank set down in a chair, and then he turns to Limpy.

"So yo're here, eh? Playin' the game my way, eh?"

Limpy begins to wipe his eyes and beller.

"I have been a proud man," he states emphatic, "but likker brought me to this. I have bited the hand that fed me. I sold my soul for gin, Simon Legree. Yes, I will go in with you, even to the depths of hell."

"Ah, ha-a-a-a-a!" sneers Zibe. "Well, we win, Lord Worthington. Without Howard Chesterfield that horse never can win—and there sets Howard Chesterfield. We hold him until after the race. He will be disgraced in the eyes of his sweetheart, who will marry me. Ah, ha-a-a-a-a!"

I swear I never did see Susie, until there she was on the stage, with a two-barrel shotgun in her hands, pointin' it at Zibe.

"Hands up, you foul beast," says she, and Zibe puts up his hands.

"You think his sweetheart will marry you, Simon Legree? Bah! If you was the last man in the world, I wouldn't marry you. Uncle Tom, will you take ropes and bind these foul vultures?"

Well, I shore tied 'em up tight. Susie took the ropes off Hank and he stood up straight and looked down at her.

"Thank yuh, Little Eva," says he. "I heard what yuh said to Legree, and I hate to disappoint yuh. I'm a fair man, and no falsehood ever passed my lips. I don't love you—I love Gwendolyn."

Susie takes a deep breath, points her nose toward the ceilin' and says, "Oh, woe is me, I am undone!"

And then she let loose all holts and went down so hard that she busted two boards in that floor. Hank puts one hand over his eyes and kinda staggers around sayin' "I've broken her heart, I've broken her heart!"

"Yo're right!" yells somebody in the audience. "I heard it break, Hank."

Hank flops his arms and turns to me.

"Uncle Tom, I believe I have killed her. I'll have to carry her home."

Hank tried three different holts and they all slipped.

"Damn it, Susie, help yourself a little, can'tcha?" he whispers.

"I'm supposed to be swooned," she whispers. "Pick me up, you idiot."

"Git her by the legs, Hozie," whispers Hank.

"You touch my legs, and I'll kick yuh loose from the surroundin' country," hisses Susie.

Hank straightens up and turns toward the audience.

"Ah, I cannot touch her," says he. "She looks so peaceful in death."

Susie took a kick at me and I got away fast. She turned over and got to her feet, as Hank lifts up both hands and says real loud, "I'll leave her here for the angels, while I go to ride for love."

But he didn't. Susie socked him one on the back of the neck with a right swing and he went off the stage into the three-piece orchestra, with both legs in the air, while the committee stood up and whistled through their fingers, and somebody had sense enough to yank down the curtain.

The committee brought Hank back with them. He was smiling sweetly, but as an actor he's a total loss.

"This here show," says Dog-Rib, "is kinda jumpy, it seems to me. We've been tryin' all along to find out what it's all about. That there last act was plenty actful, as yuh might say, but we dunno what it was about."

I didn't wait to listen to the argument. Peewee got that bottle they used in the last act, and we emptied it together. We're leanin' up against a black curtain at the back of the stage, and all to once somethin' hit Peewee and knocked him plumb up past the treadmill, where he landed on his hands and knees.

"Yuh better git away from there, Hozie," says Limpy. "That racehorse is behind the curtain."

We stretched Peewee out on the floor in a corner, and the rest of us are asked to come out on the stage. They're all inquirin' for Miss Wimple.

"She's gone down to the hotel to git the money," says Judgment. "She said, bein' as the play turned out like it did, she wanted the money out of her hands; so I told her to bring it up here for a settlement. Her and Susie had a fight over them love scenes, and she was through up here."

"We don't need her," says Susie. "If she was actin' for saw mills, she wouldn't git a sliver in her finger. Is everythin' all set?"

Susie laid down on the floor and Zibe fastened a belt around her. She's all dressed in white, with a couple things that might be mistaken for wings. We all squats down around her. They've got a heavy wire ownin' up from that belt. Somebody pulled the curtain, and the three-piece orchestry begins playin' "Nearer My God to Thee," kinda soft.

"Uncle Tom," says Susie, her voice kinda cracked, "I'm goin' to leave yuh. I'm goin' to my place beyond the skies."

Mrs. Noon begins to blubber.

"Don't cry," says Susie. "It's better this way. Tell Howard that I forgive him for everythin'. Ah. I hear the angels callin'. Can't you hear 'em, Uncle Tom?"

"She's dyin'," wails Mrs. Noon.

"Git yore feet braced, Burlap," says Oscar Tubbs, up there, on that two-by-six.

"Angel voices," says Susie. "They're callin' me home."

"Pull, you damn' fools!" yelps Oscar.

And Little Eva starts on her long trip, as yuh might say. Up and up she goes, head and feet down, them spangled wings straight up. I've allus had my own idea of an angel, and Susie didn't fit that idea.

Then the angel stopped and kinda hung there, swingin' around.

"Keep her goin'!" hisses old Zibe from the side of the stage.

"The angels are takin' her away," wails Mrs. Noon.

Cra-a-a-ack!

That two-by-six snapped by too much weight, and down comes the hand-made heaven. Susie lit on her head, and here comes Oscar Tubbs, Burlap Benson and Fetlock Feeney, follered by that busted two-by-six. Oscar lit on his feet, busted plumb through where Susie had already cracked the boards, and stopped with only his head in sight.

It shook the whole stage and also the whole danged house. One of Burlap's boots hit me in the head, but as my lights went dim, I heard somebody yellin', "Three angels gone to hell a'ready, and the fourth one dropped for reasons knowed to all of us!"

I woke up with Zibe and Zeke Hardy moppin' me head with cold water, and I can hear Dog-Rib arguin' at the top of his voice, "I don't care a dang if Hank is still knocked out—we'll have that there hoss race, or our money back. You've done advertised a race, and we crave a race."

"But there ain't no jockey to ride that race," pleads Judgment. "You can see for yourself that Hank Potts ain't fit to ride nothin'."

"Suit yourself. I've done sent a couple men down to the hotel to set on that safe, where yuh keep the money. Oasis and Alkali towns crave that horse race; so it's shore up to you."

They go stompin' out, while the crowd out in front makes all kinds of noise. I sabes them people, and if we don't give 'em what they want, they'll take the hall apart.

"Are you loyal to San Pablo, Hozie?" asks Zeke.

"Look at me and answer yore own question."

"You're a good rider. Hozie: ride for the honor of San Pablo. Never let Oasis say that we didn't make good. Yo're the man of the hour—the best rider in the San Pablo range. Think of poor old Judgment Jones and the starvin' cannibals he aims to help with that money. Will yuh, Hozie?"

I said I wouldn't—and swooned. When I woke up, I've got on Hank's jockey clothes, and they're helpin' me on Tequila, that big, cold-jawed, leg-crossin' sorrel. The horse is blindfolded, and it takes three men to hold his head down. The boards are crackin' under his feet, and the blamed brute is scared stiff.

To the right of me is a thing like a big window, and in that window is Susie, Zeke, Zibe, Mrs. Noon, Oscar Tubbs, Burlap Benson and Fetlock Feeney, and they're all yelpin' their heads off, as though they're lookin' at a race, yellin', "C'mon, Thunderbolt! Come on, Thunderbolt!"

"Let go!" yelps somebody, and they turned Tequila loose.

"Spur him straight ahead, Hozie!" snorts somebody else.

Spur nothin'. The next thing I knowed I was back on his rump, and he was climbin' through that window affair, and the next thing I knowed I was out on his head, with both legs wrapped around his neck, and we're on the edge of the stage, facin' the stampede. The air is full of sombreros, all sailin' at us, men are yelpin', "Whoa! Whoa!"

I got one flash of the committee goin' out the door on the heels of that stampedin' mob, when somebody threw a chair, which landed on my head like a crown. It shore made me see a lot of stars, but I kept my presence of mind, as Tequila whirled around and went buck-jumpin' straight to the back of the stage, knockin' down everythin' in sight, with me still out over his ears—and then we hit that treadmill.

Did we go? Man, that Tequila horse never ran so fast in his life. Why, he never had time to cross his legs. We wasn't goin' no place, but we was sure goin' fast. Out from a pile of busted lumber I sees Peewee raise up, his eyes wide at what he sees.

"Can'tcha stop this?" I yells at him. He picks up a busted two-by-four, staggers over and shoves it down in the treadmill. They told me afterward that it throwed Peewee plumb against the back of the buildin', but it shore stopped the machine.

I'm only about ten feet from the rear of the stage, which is covered with a black cloth, and this rear of the stage is the front of the room.

Wham-blam! We went off that treadmill like a skyrocket. I hears the crash of glass, the rippin' of a cloth, and there I am out over the main street of San Pablo, two stories high, with nothin' but air above, below and on all sides.

I spread my arms like the wings of a turkey buzzard, turned over once and landed settin' down on a buckboard seat, which smashed like an egg under the impact. It also knocked me a little colder than I was, but I knowed the team busted loose and was runnin' away. But I didn't care. What was one little runaway beside what I'd been through? The rush of night air was coolin' to my fevered brow.

And all of a sudden we went high-wide and handsome. *Rip-pety-bing-bang-boom!* There's a bell ringin', somethin' roarin', and then I landed on the seat of my pants on the depot platform and almost skidded into the train, which was ready to move. The team and buckboard was just leavin' the other end of the platform.

I'm knocked kinda silly, but I heard a woman scream, as she ran past me and onto that train. The depot agent's boots are stickin' up from behind a trunk, where the runaway knocked him. I sets there and watches the train go out of sight. Beside me is a lady's handbag, jist a little one with a white handkerchief stickin' out of it. I put the thing in my pocket and got to my feet. I say "my feet" merely because they was hooked onto me. I didn't have no feelin' in 'em.

Then I wandered back down the street, stoppin' now and then to get my toes pointed right, and finally got to the No-Limit Saloon. For a while I ain't recognized, even if I have got most of the enamel knocked off my face. There's Judgment Jones, talkin' with Dog-Rib, and they come over to look me over.

"It's all right, Hozie," says Judgment. "Oasis and Alkali are satisfied we done our best. Dog-Rib says they expected more action, but I been tellin' him it was jist a little rural play. Next time we'll do better—I hope. But, take it all in all, we got our money's worth—but no money."

"No money," says he sadly. "Miss Eveline Annabel Wimple, D. T., took it all and pulled out durin' the play—we think. Anyway, she ain't here, and the money was given to her in the hotel. The hotel keeper said she was in a big hurry, and she put the money in her handbag. Now, we're goin' to raffle the racehorse—if he's still alive."

I found Peewee settin' on the sidewalk, and we went home. He's so bent out of shape that his saddle don't fit him, but we got back to the HP ranch and found the horse liniment. After the first or second deluge, I said to him, "Peewee, that Wimple woman got away with the money."

"Did she? Good for her."

"You don't believe in stealin', do yuh, Peewee?"

"Not stealin'—takin'."

"If somebody happened to find her handbag and kept the money, would that be stealin'?"

"Finder's keepers."

I tosses the handbag on the table, and Peewee goggles at it. He don't ask no questions. That's what I like about Peewee. After while he blinks one of his purple eyes, the other one bein' shut tight, and says, "Thinkin' it over, Hozie. I'm wonderin'."

He opens the bag and there's an envelope, folded in the middle, and we can feel the money inside—paper money. On it is written: *Funds of The Curse of Drink*. It's Judgment Jones's writin'. Peewee shakes his head.

"We can't do it, Hozie. Old Judgment is the most honest man on earth. He needs that money for the heathen. I could never look him in the face again. He wouldn't do wrong to anybody, and he needs that money. He trusted that woman, jist like he trusts everybody. Why, he'd even trust me and you."

"That's right," says I. "We'll give it back."

But I wanted to see how much money they took in for that show; so I steamed the envelope open and dumped it out. I looked at Peewee and he looked at me. Money? Nothin' but a lot of old newspaper, cut to the size of bills. We sets there and does a lot of thinkin', and after while Peewee dumps the whole works into the stove.

And as far as we know, the heathen are in jist the same shape they were before we put on this show. Peewee wanted to be a contortionist, and for once in his life he got tied in a knot. Peewee's satisfied. Hank's satisfied, but Susie ain't; she wanted to go all the way to heaven. I'm satisfied—that a cowpuncher ought to keep off every kind of a stage, except one with four wheels.

Susie says it's too bad we were obliged to miss the moral of her play, but I said I didn't.

"What was the moral?" she asks.

"Don't kill yore jockey before the race starts," says I.

And I'm right, too.

WHEN EAST MET WEST

Some poetical person once wrote:

For East is East and West is West.
And never the twain shall meet.

He was all wrong, that feller—all wrong. And I'll tell you how I know he was wrong.

I ain't no pessimist. Not by a danged sight, I ain't. If a little kid burns his fingers on a red-hot stove and keeps away from the fire from that time on, you don't call him a pessimist. That's me—burnt to a caution.

All the Harper tribe, as far back as I can figure out, was cautious. We bred more runners than we did fighters. Of course there ain't as many of us as there is Smiths. Smiths predominate, as it were. Anyway, the Smith tribe ain't got nothin' to do with this.

I ain't been in Piperock for several weeks. Me and "Dirty Shirt" Jones has been prospectin' back in the Whisperin' Creek hills, with our usual good luck—of gettin' back before all our food was gone. And we finds my pardner, "Magpie" Simpkins, settin' at the table in our shack, wearin' his Sunday clothes.

Magpie is so danged tall that it takes him all day to find out whether a certain pain is indigestion or inflammation of the kneecaps. He's solemn, Magpie is. And when that elongated, pious-faced cross between a scientific lecture and a — fool statement gets pouches under his eyes and droops his eyelids like a blood-hound—caution cometh to me.

Magpie is writin'. He's got ink plumb to his elbow and the floor is plumb littered with paper. Does he welcome us effusively? Like — he does. He just looks at us, kinda reprovin'-like, as if we should 'a' knocked.

"Well, you old cattywampus, howdy!" greets Dirty Shirt.

Dirty has one eye that kinda oscillates, as it were. Not bein' what an astronomer would call 'a fixed orbit,' it does a lot of jigglin' before it picks up what Dirty's lookin' at.

But it don't noways affect Dirty's aim, bein' as he shoots with both eyes open, and most of the time with both legs workin'. Magpie looks him over solemnly and says—

"Mr. Jones, I give you good afternoon."

Dirty spits in the general direction of the stove.

"I'll take it," says he.

"Mr. Harper," says Magpie dignified-like.

I kicks the door shut, slides my gun around where I can get it real quick and looks my old pardner over. He's shaved. Yeah, you can always tell when Magpie has shaved, because he's got so danged many wounds. He's got on a celluloid collar—one of them kind that it ain't safe to smoke in. I can smell stove polish, which Magpie has used on his boots.

Take it all the way around, Magpie Simpkins is a dude.

"You ain't got yore days mixed, have yuh?" I asked.

"Days mixed?"

He speaks like an actor—kinda runnin' the scale in G flat, as yuh might say.

"This ain't Sunday," says I.

"I am well aware of it."

"Then what's the idea of dressin' up thisaway?"

"The idea? Hah!" He kinda swells up with importance. "I'm the president."

I looks quick at Dirty, who is starin' at Magpie with his mouth wide open. Then he looks at me and shakes his head.

"Ike," says he hoarse-like, "I knowed it. By —, the human brain can jist stand so much. He's been feeblin' up in the head for a long time. I've seen it comin' on by degrees, and I ain't a mite surprised. There ain't nothin' yuh can do, except to hopple 'em so they can't hurt nobody."

Magpie looks at Dirty kinda funny and Dirty edges toward the door.

"Better git a rope, Ike," advises Dirty, backin' agin' the door. "Them high-minded first symptoms is apt to degenerate into vi'lence, and we don't want him to hurt nobody."

"Set down, you — fool," says Magpie. "I ain't crazy."

"Proves it on himself," declares Dirty nervous-like. "They all swear they ain't. Look out for his first rush, Ike."

But I holds firm. To me he's always been crazy so I ain't scared of an extra degree.

"Democrat or Republican president?" I asks. "We didn't git back in time for the convention, you remember."

"Don't try to be smart, Ike," says he. "I plumb forgot that you fellers has been away. Since you was here, Piperock has advanced by leaps and bounds. Right now I am writin' a biography of our fair city for all to read and appreciate how we have advanced. It is marvelous."

"What is? The biography?" asks Dirty.

"No—our advancement. Gentlemen, we are on the threshold of a wonderful era for Piperock. No more shall the rest of the world point a finger of scorn at our community. No more shall they say that Piperock is uncivilized, unbalanced. From this day henceforth we shall blossom like the rose. Our ideals shall and will be realized to the fullest extremity. How is that, Ike?"

"Fits in with what we've just heard," says I.

"And with the dawnin' of a new day—" Magpie squints at his paper—"all these—that's as far as I've got."

"And that's a — of a long ways, if you ask me," said Dirty Shirt solemn-like.

"Now about bein' president," says I. "Yuh hadn't ought to go that far, Magpie."

"Hadn't I? Huh! That's who I am, Ike. Look upon me. I am the first president of the Piperock Chamber of Commerce."

"What the — kind of a thing is that?" asked Dirty.

"Chamber of Commerce? Dirty Shirt, I'm surprised at you. It is an organization."

"It's the same thing as the Chamber of Horrors," says I, "only they deals in commerce mostly. This one will prob'ly have horrors as a side-line."

"Nothin' of the kind, Ike," protests Magpie. "Piperock is past the age of swaddlin' clothes. We has emerged into the sunlight and it will be well for all other cities to look to their laurels. I wouldn't be surprized to see Piperock one of the big cities of the world. We have everythin' to make it big."

"Yeah, we've got a lot of country," admits Dirty Shirt. "Me and Ike came across twenty miles of it today, and there was more beyond where we started from. If you want to go east, west, north or south from here yuh can find a lot of open country. We've got room to build, that's a cinch."

"But what would bring anybody here?" I asks. "Folks won't even come from Paradise, except to a dance; and then they come to pick a fight. We ain't got a — of a lot to offer—except to somebody that wants trouble, Magpie."

"We will have, Ike. The idea was started in Paradise originally. Me and Wick Smith was down there last week and we went to see a tent show. It wasn't much good and it wasn't doin' no business. Me and Wick got to talkin' to the feller that owned the show and he told us all about his hard luck.

"He says that a circus is a drug on the market now, and that animiles ain't worth nothin', except in a zoo. He says that he's really surprised that some of our towns don't have no zoo. He says they're all puttin' 'em in in the East, and that no town can ever be an attraction unless it's got a zoo.

"Well, me and Wick has a few drinks with him and got to talkin' it over with him. He says he's got the ingredients of a first-class zoological menagerie, and that he's got a idea of puttin' the proposition up to Paradise. He's got a elephant. Of course it ain't no first class elephant, bein' as it's kinda run down from travelin' so much.

"The camel is—well, it ain't noways in full plumage, but it's a camel. The tiger seems to be as good as tigers go. He says he'll take a thousand dollars for the whole bunch. 'Course he tells us how much we'd have to pay if we bought them animiles at retail price; but he kinda lumps 'em together and gives 'em to us at cost.

"Wick Smith is public-spirited, and after I tells him what we'll do about organizin' a Chamber of Commerce, he ups and buys them animiles on the spot. The feller throws in the cage free gratis for nothin'; so that saves us quite a lot. I figures that we can pick up a grizzly and a wolf and mebbe a mountain lion to kinda add to our zoo. Folks will come a long ways to look at wild animiles, Ike—a long ways."

Me and Dirty looks at each other and goes out to unpack, while Magpie goes ahead on Piperock's epitaph.

<hr>

It's been quite a while since we put our foot on the rail; so we hurries up to Buck Masterson's saloon, where we runs into Wick Smith and "Mighty" Jones. Mighty and Dirty Shirt ain't no relation. Mighty is a little jigger, who thinks he's big enough to hold his own. That's one reason why Mighty is mostly always on crutches. He swears in a tenor voice and chaws his tobacco.

Buck greets us gladly, but Wick don't seem so happy.

"You fellers been prospectin' again?" asks Buck.

"Yeah, and we're goin' ag'in," says Dirty Shirt. "This here town is gettin' too danged effete to suit me and Ike."

"It is effete," agrees Mighty. "Ain't been nobody killed for two weeks."

"Cheer up, brother," says Wick solemn-like. "There's allus a lull before a storm."

"You preparin' to massacre?" I asks.

"Well, I ain't been treated right," says Wick. "I done paid a thousand cold dollars for some jungle insects, and I'm wonderin' jist how I'm goin' to cash in on said contraptions. Magpie Simpkins got me drunk and talked me into bein' a public benefactor, dang his hide.

"Got me to procure the ingredients of a zoological garden, that's what he done. Got the whole — town heated up over a thing he calls the Piperock Chamber of Commerce, and then goes out and gits himself elected president. That's a — of a way to do, ain't it?"

"You wanted to be president, eh?" I asks.

"Well, —, why not. I bought the — thing, didn't I? Magpie said that Piperock would pay me back for it. How'll they do it, I'd like to know. Mebbe I'm supposed to raffle 'em off, eh?"

"I won't buy no chances," says Buck. "I've been down to the livery-stable and got a look at them there animals, and I'm free to state that I don't want none. Magpie orates that we'll have 'em to attract more folks to Piperock. My —, that bunch will drive away what we've got."

"If I had that elephant," said Mighty, "I'd shore take a reef in him. His hide don't fit him no place. He ain't no attraction—he's a disgrace. From the rear he looks like 'Polecat' Perkins in his Sunday pants. Wick, you ort to give him a belt to take up the slack."

"That's why he's an attraction," declared Wick. "The feller I bought him from said that Gunga Din was a rare species of elephant. His name's Gunga Din. My —, he ort to be good. I paid three hundred and thirty-three dollars and thirty-three and one-third cents for him. That camel and the tiger cost the same."

"I think that Magpie's crazy," say I.

"How about me?" wails Wick. "I paid for 'em myself."

"Yore wife's callin' yuh, Wick," observed Buck.

Wick squints toward the door and nods sadly.

"Yeah, I left her to run the store while I talks over my sorrow. Now I've got to go back and git — agin'. She don't believe in Chambers of Commerce, she don't; and I'm commencin' to wonder if she ain't right."

Wick pilgrims across the street, while me and Dirty goes down to the livery stable to see what Wick bought. "Hassayampa" Harris is runnin' the stable.

"Howdy, Hassayampa," says I. "How are you?"

"Liver trouble," says he, diagnosin' himself. "Spots before m' eyes, dizziness and kinda sluggish-like."

He does look kinda pale and walks antegodlin'.

"How comes you to git them there symptoms?" asks Dirty.

"Ignorance," says Hassayampa. "I tried to take a bale of hay away from Exhibit A of the Chamber of Commerce."

"Meanin' Gunga Din?"

"That accordion-skinned thing," says Hassayampa painful-like, kinda pluckin' at his Adam's apple. "I ain't jist right in m' mind yet. It grabbed me by the slack of the pants and took m' pants plumb off while I'm still in the air. Them kinda shocks ain't noways good for the human form. Then the — thing slapped me across the face with my own pants and knocked me plumb across the stable and into the oat-bin. I ain't been right since."

"You ort to read up on things like that," says Dirty.

"Read? What in — can a man read at a time like that?"

"Wasn't there no directions with 'em?" I asks.

"No. Direction don't mean nothin' to a thing like that, Ike. Do you want to gaze upon 'em?"

"Yeah, we'll look," nods Dirty.

"Cost two-bits per each," informs Hassayampa. "Magpie says they're worth it—and they are. My —, there ain't no questions about it."

"That's a — of a idea!" snorts Dirty. "Two-bits to see a elephant. I'll tell you what we will do, Hassayampa; we'll pay the two-bits to see you try to take another bale away from Gunga Din."

"You never will," sighs Hassayampa. "I'm cured. Anyway, I'm about half out of hay. I've got a bill of seven dollars agin' them critters right now. By golly, that tagger c'n go plumb to —. Meat costs money."

We left Hassayampa talkin' to himself and went back up town, where we leans on Buck's bar.

We ain't been there long when Mike Pelly, Ricky Henderson and "Old Testament" Tilton rides in from Paradise. Mike is the saloon-keeper and Ricky runs the barber shop. The third member of this here trio represents the other element of Paradise.

Testament looks a heap like some old buzzard that had been disappointed in love. He wears one of them beetle-backed coats, a pair of pants that sure follers the contour of his skinny legs and a pair of boots that sag a heap at the top and shows that Testament don't noways pinch his feet.

Mike parts his hair on one side, slicks one side down until she almost reaches the bridge of his nose, where it retreats some sudden-like. He smells a heap of heel-yuh-tripe perfume.

Ricky is a barber. He looks, smells and acts like one. When he gets excited he applauds, like he was stroppin' a razor. Testament used to think that he had snatched Ricky and Mike from the burnin'. When Testament first comes to that country he has an idea that there was a lot of brands to snatch from the burnin'; but he got scorched a few times and let things go as they lay.

Them three angles up to the bar, shakes hands with us, just like they cared to meet us, and asks us to drink. Testament has his usual lemonade and a wink, and then we discusses conditions.

"How is everythin' in this village of iniquity?" asks Testament kinda offhanded.

"Iniquity, —!" snorts Buck. "There ain't no iniquity in Piperock. We're clean-minded and antiseptic of condition. If there's any infection in this city it's brought here from Paradise. By golly, some day you'll be glad to be knowed as bein' a suburb of Piperock City."

"Haw-haw-haw-haw!" says Ricky. "Suburb of Piperock. Paradise will be a mee-trop-polis when Piperock goes back to the prairie-dogs."

It's difference of opinion that makes horse races, wars and so many kinds of whisky—all out of one barrel. Me and Dirty Shirt are plumb full of civic pride, and we're willin' to fight for our fair city—if we had one—but Piperock and Paradise ain't worth no supreme effort; so we slides out kinda graceful-like and pilgrims back to our shack.

Magpie is just goin' away, carryin' complete dignity and a lot of stationery. I tells him about the three men from Paradise.

"The word has reached," says Magpie, swellin' his chest. "We shall not hide our light under a bushel."

"Then you better hide yore carcass behind a wood-pile," says Dirty Shirt. "Them three antagonizers didn't jist ride up here to git a drink of liquor."

"We are a peaceable aggregation," says Magpie. "No more shall the war-cry sever, nor the runnin' rivers be red. We are about to shed the things that have held us back. Uncivilization must bow to the tread of wisdom. The wheel of progress is turnin', and woe unto him who gits under the tire. The people of Piperock have risen in their might, unleashed the bonds which have held them in darkness and are comin' out into the light of a new day."

"And," says Dirty kinda awed-like, "if that ain't a — of a lot to say all in one bunch, I'll eat the garment that made me famous."

Magpie snorts and pilgrims on up the street. In spite of the mighty proclamation he emits to us, I notices that he's got a six-gun shoved into the waistband of his pants. Me and Dirty stretches out on the two bunks and rolls up a little sleep.

———◦———

In the course of human events some queer things happen. And the queerest thing I can think of is the fact that Jasmine Greenbaum came to teach school at Piperock. Jasmine ain't the kind you'd imagine would take a job like that.

She's plumb decorative, if yuh know what I mean. I ain't goin' to describe her, 'cause I ain't got words enough. Her eyes would make a man lift his head when somebody is shootin' at him. She lives with Wick Smith's family while she's teachin' the young of Piperock to not shoot at each other.

Me and Dirty runs into her that evenin' after we've been stationary at Buck's bar for an hour or more. Dirty's active eye jiggles convulsive-like for a while, and he seems to be wearin' about six too many hands.

"I'm sure you remember me," says she, smilin' at us.

"If I lives to be a million, I won't forget," pants Dirty.

"I am Mister Harper," says I. "And the Harper fambly has the longest memories of any fambly on earth."

"Outside of the Jones's," says Dirty. "My old pa could remember before they started puttin' aces in the decks of cards."

"Memories don't figure," says I. "We're glad to meetcha, Miss Greenbaum. What can I do for yuh, ma'am?"

"Same here," says Dirty, kinda elbowin' me aside.

"I told them that you were always willing to do anything for the public good," says she, smilin' sweet-like.

"To whom did yoo tell this, ma'am?" I asks.

Somehow I kinda gets a hunch that everythin' ain't just right.

"Mr. Simpkins, the president of the Chamber of Commerce," says she. "He and Mr. Smith seemed to think—"

"Since when did they start thinkin'?" asks Dirty. "That shore is a novelty to my ears, ma'am."

"Mr. Simpkins is a very brilliant man," says she. "He has some wonderful ideas."

"With parts missin'," says I.

"Perhaps you do not appreciate what he is doing for Piperock, Mr. Harper," says she. "I have just come from a meeting of the new Chamber of Commerce, where Mr. Simpkins presided and read us some wonderful plans for the betterment of this town.

"As you know we already have the nucleus of a zoological garden. Mr. Smith, who is heart and soul in the advancement of Piperock, purchased these three jungle animals. Our meeting this afternoon was to decide upon a plan to reimburse Mr. Smith and to acquire the animals for the city.

"Next Monday is Labor Day. I have been led to understand that Piperock has never celebrated Labor Day."

"They've sure celebrated everythin' else," says Dirty Shirt. "My —, ma'am, don't let 'em celebrate. You don't know Piperock."

"It will be a harmless celebration. I spoke about having you two gentlemen assist, and Mr. Simpkins and Mr. Smith assured me that neither of you had any civic pride. They said that both of you were uncivilized, unprogressive and not at all in accord with any movement that would curb your savage tendencies. I'm sure it is prejudice on their part."

"Yo're danged right!" says Dirty. "Them pelicans sure did lie to you in fine shape, ma'am. Piperock don't mean a whole lot to either one of us, but I'm willin' to do anythin' yuh say."

I'm cautious, as I said before. This here idea of havin' a pretty school teacher come to us and hoodle us into doin' somethin' that our hearts tell us is dangerous don't set so good. I've heard this same kind of stuff before, and so has Dirty; but any old time a pretty girl smiles at Dirty, it's just another old Garden of Eden and a lot of apples.

She don't tell us what we're supposed to do, but she does ask us to promise to help 'em out. Well, what can yuh do in a case like that? Me and Dirty goes back to Buck's place, where we massages our insides with Buck's Best.

And lemme tell you somethin'—Buck's liquor sure tempers the wind to the sheared sheep. Ten years ago he bought a barrel of it. He sells on an average of two or three gallons a day, and that barrel is still over half-full. It has never weakened, as far as we can taste.

After while Magpie and Wick comes into the place. Dignified? My —, they act like a pair of royal flushes.

"Greetin's, Mr. Masterson," says Magpie lofty-like. "How goes things this day and date?"

"Well, all right," says Buck, bein' kinda dazed. "How did the meetin' go?"

"Perfect," says Magpie. "The die is cast. The ladies' auxiliary is in complete accord with us and we all feel that it will be a day to date time from. Piperock will emerge from her shell and take her place among the cities of the world."

"The ladies' what?" asks Dirty.

"Auxiliary," explains Wick. "My wife is president. It is an a-ad—uh—"

"Adjunct," prompts Magpie.

"I know it," says Wick. "There's my wife, who is president, and the followin', to wit: Mrs. Wick Smith, Mrs. Pete Gonyer, Mrs. Yuma Yates, Mrs. Mighty Jones, and Miss Hilda Hansen. Of course the list is not complete, as it were, and we expect more. However, we have a quorum, et cettery, *ad libitum*."

"I s'd hope sho," says Dirty, gettin' dignified. "What 'bout Mish Jasm'n Greenbaum? Ain't she invited t' j'in?"

"Miss Jasmine Greenbaum is actin' in an advisory capacity," explains Magpie. "It kinda makes her feel free to do as she wishes. We're leavin' a lot of it to her imagination."

"What was Testament and Ricky and Mike doin' up here?" asks Buck.

"Kinda gropin' around," says Magpie. "They heard that we was due to progress, and of course they had to come and see what it was about. I told 'em about Piperock acquirin' a Chamber of Commerce and three jungle cu- riosities. They don't *sabe* the idea of the Chamber, but they offers to take the animals at a slight advance over what Piperock paid."

"What did you say?" asks Wick anxious-like.

"I told 'em to go to —. Them animals ain't for sale."

"Ain't they?" asks Wick. "At more'n I paid? Magpie, I'd like to have the say-so over them critters myself. I own 'em, don't I? They ain't Piperock's animals until Piperock has a bill-of-sale for 'em. I sure as — don't thank yuh for what you've done to me."

"Where's yore public spirit?" asks Magpie.

"Thassall right," complains Wick. "I've got more public spirit than most folks, I reckon; but a thousand dollars is a thousand dollars. If Paradise wants to pay me more'n I paid—they git 'em, by gosh!"

"You'd make a fine president for the Chamber of Commerce," says Magpie.

"All right," says Wick. "If you can think of anythin' else that's funny, I'll listen."

"Yore livestock are eatin' up dollars," says I.

"Yeah, and that's another thing," wails Wick, pawin' at Magpie's sleeve. "Who's goin' to pay their board?"

"Gunga Din eats a bale of hay every fifteen minutes," offers Dirty Shirt solemn-like.

"He—he does?"

"He—he do," nods Dirty. "The last bale was two pounds short; so Gunga Din ate Hassayampa's pants for dessert. Them there tigers will eat a whole cow for a meal and you know what cows are worth right now."

"Magpie—" Wick is almost cryin' by this time—"Magpie, I asks you as a friend—what'll I do?"

"Have patience, Wickie."

"Have —! I'll go down there and massacree all three of them monstrosities, that's what I'll do, by gosh!"

"And lose yore thousand dollars, eh?" Magpie shakes his head. "Wick Smith, you ain't hardly fit to help us build up Piperock."

"It's for the glory of our fair city," says Buck.

Wick turns around and walks out. He's kinda all choked up, but I know danged well it ain't emotion. Me and Dirty feels that the fair city of Piperock ain't so badly in need of our assistance; so we saddles up our rollin' stock and goes to Paradise town.

Paradise runs a dead heat with Piperock, as far as city is concerned. When P. T. Barnum said that a fool is born every minute, he might have added that they were all pointed toward Yellowrock County.

We finds several of the above in Mike Pelly's saloon, and among them is "Chuck" Warner, "Muley" Bowles, "Telescope" Tolliver and Henry Clay Peck. These four disgraces are from the Cross J ranch, but claims Paradise as their native haunt. Also we finds "Liniment" Lucas and "Tombstone" Todd and "Hard-Pan" Hawkins.

Tombstone is so tough that he can wear tight boots on his bunions, and "Hard-Pan" Hawkins keeps books on his crimes. Tombstone draws me aside and gnaws on one end of his mustache, while he cuffs his sombrero plentiful.

"Ike," says he hoarse-like, "what's this I'm hearin' about the hamlet of Piperock? Somebody was a-tellin' me that they've convened up there to re-spectablize the town somewhat."

"It's kinda hard to per-fume the rose," says I.

Tombstone gnaws a little more and fights his hat.

"Yeah, I s'pose that's right, Ike. Are you and Dirty Shirt part and parcel of this here movement?"

"Not knowin'ly, Tombstone," says I. "You can speak to me with perfect confidence and go away feelin' that I won't exaggerate what you've told me."

"There has been braggin' goin' on," stated Tombstone. "If there's anythin' Paradise hates it's braggin'. Piperock orates that she's leapin' ahead like a bee-stung bear. She ain't, Ike. It jist ain't no ways possible for her to leap thataway. She ain't active like Paradise. We're able to do things.

"Whereabouts in — does Piperock compare with Paradise, I asks yuh to answer honestly? She don't. We've got spirit, climate and brain power. We've got courageous men, wimmin and children. Why, our offspring are equal to two grown men of Piperock. We've got everythin', Ike."

"Except a elephant, a camel and a tiger," says I.

"What's them amount to?"

"And a Chamber of Commerce, Tombstone."

"Mm-m-m, yeah. Well?"

"Well—right back at yuh. I never started this argument."

"It ain't no argument, Ike," he explains. "Paradise is the legitimate place for them things. We could do it up right."

Tombstone invites me back to the bar, which I accepts. Dirty is arguin' with the Cross J outfit and Liniment Lucas, and from Dirty's talk I'd gather that he's body and soul with Piperock.

"From this day henceforth, Piperock shall rossom like a blose," orates Dirty Shirt. "The people of Piperock have rosin in their might, and we are comin' out into the dight of a lew day. And if that ain't a — of a lot to say at once, I'll eat the garment that made me what I am today."

From that time on things get kinda hazy. Mike Pelly peddles a brand that would make a cotton-tail rabbit grow fangs in his mouth and rattles on his tail. I'm led to understand that Paradise is jealous of Piperock, and that Paradise hankers for them three animals, like a calf hankerin' for its ma.

Me and Dirty balances on the edge of the sidewalk in front of Mike's place and begins to cheer for Piperock, when some careless son of a gun moved a heavy chair plumb out of Mike's doorway and it hits me and Dirty Shirt at the same time.

And when we woke up we finds ourselves in jail. Hank Padden, our estimable sheriff, tells us that we're in jail for disturbin' the peace.

"You be—!" wails Dirty Shirt. "Paradise never had no peace to disturb. I can prove it to any judge, jury or collection of folks which has two ideas above a monkey."

"I done my duty," says Hank firm-like. "I was hired for this kind of work. You'll prob'ly git six months apiece."

This was sure cheerin' news. The Paradise jail don't feed none too good. We had a idea that Piperock would arise in its wrath and come down to drag us forth—but they didn't. I sent word to Magpie, and he answered it.

I sent him this word—

Me and Dirty Shirt are in jail for upholdin' Piperock.

And this is what he sent to me—

Good for you. We appreciate yore civic pride.

He didn't sign his name, but he didn't need to. I *sabe* that *hombre* like a book. Dirty gets kinda gloomy over it all and swears that he's all through with Piperock. Right there and then I adds my voice to his.

"If that's patriotism," says Dirty, "gimme death. Our own town has turned us down, Ike Harper. I didn't think they'd do it. And they wouldn't, if they wasn't gettin' civilized."

A little later on cometh Chuck Warner, Liniment Lucas and Testament Tilton.

"You can take the preacher back," says Dirty. "We ain't in for murder, you know."

"I'm not in my clerical capacity," says Testament. "Be ye both of good cheer."

"— of a fine chance, the way Hank runs his place here," snorts Dirty.

"I've been up to Piperock," says Chuck, wigglin' his ears. Chuck's got flexible ears and he can wiggle 'em like a mule.

"And nobody shot yuh?" gasps Dirty. "My gosh, they're sure gittin' forgivin', Chuck."

"They ain't no friends to you two," says Chuck seriouslike. "They're glad yo're in jail down here."

Chuck Warner is the biggest liar west of the Atlantic Ocean—but this time I believed him.

"Magpie and Wick Smith hope yuh stay in jail," says he.

"It kinda looks like they'd git their hopes," Dirty acts kinda mournful.

"It kinda does," agrees Liniment.

He's got one of them long, wet-lookin' noses and sad eyes. I reckon his folks intended him to be a undertaker, but Old Lady Fate had "horse-thief" marked after his name in the Big Book.

"Is this here a party of condolence, or did yuh come to gloat?" I asks. I hate like — to have folks lookin' at me through the bars.

"Condolence and good cheer," says Testament, hitchin' up his pants. "You might call it a parley. I will go now, as it would not be meet for me to be party to it. Not that I ain't in accord with it entirely, you understand."

"It sure must be a tough proposition to drive you away," observed Dirty.

Old Testament pulled out, Hank unlocks the cell door, and they all comes in.

And what follered kinda touched upon my heart-strings. It was Chuck's idea. I listened to Chuck, Hank and Liniment Lucas, as they unfolds what's on their minds. It has been said that every man has his price. Ours was one elephant, one camel and a tiger.

They wants us to steal them three animals for Paradise. All we've got to do is to hand 'em over to Paradise and all is forgiven. But they're square about it, at that; they will pay Wick Smith what he paid for 'em; and give us a hundred apiece.

"And Piperock ain't treated you two square," says Chuck.

"Thassall right," says I, "but yuh can't get away with anything like that, Chuck. It wouldn't be hard for Piperock to prove that they owned 'em, 'cause they're all there is of the species in Yaller Rock County."

"We've fixed that all up," says Chuck. "Don'tcha worry about that end of it. You fellers go back home, feelin' sore at Paradise, and nobody will expect yuh to raid the zoo; *sabe*?"

———◆———

When we went home, after swearin' to do our little best, and we finds Magpie in the shack, composin' some more stuff. We don't say nothin' about his kind note to us, and he don't mention it to us.

"Still tryin' to uplift Piperock on paper?" I asks.

"Combatin' an evil influence, Ike. We are the pioneers—others foller. Some one is tryin' to steal our thunder."

"You got plenty of it," declares Dirty. "They could swipe a lot of it from you and still leave enough for a dozen men."

"Sarcasm is the weapon of the ignorant," says Magpie. "What heard ye in Paradise?"

"Nothin' much."

"No? Huh. Did yuh know that Paradise is emulatin' us—or is goin' to?"

"All fools ain't dead yet," opines Dirty Shirt.

"They've ordered a elephant, camel and a tiger," says Magpie. "They're payin' a big price for 'em, just to keep Piperock from leadin' the procession. Telescope Tolliver and Muley Bowles told us about it today. Telescope said he thought we ought to know about it."

"Yeah, we heard about it," says Dirty Shirt, kinda off-handed like. "It didn't mean nothin' to us."

"Well, we're holdin' a indignation meetin' tomorrow night," says Magpie. "We aims to protest openly against such practice. It ain't ethical. You and Ike be there, will yuh? Up in the Mint Hall. The ladies auxiliary will be there, et cettery. We don't wish for blood to be spilled. It's ag'in our principles and regulations; but, by grab, they'll go too far pretty soon—and have to get helped back."

The next day is kinda quiet in Piperock; but when Piperock is quiet she's dangerous. Wick Smith ain't at the store, and Mrs. Smith ain't got much use for me and Dirty; so we keep away. After samplin' some wobble water we pilgrims down to the livery-stable to see how Hassayampa is comin'.

But we don't find Hassayampa in charge. Wick Smith meets us at the door, and he looks as wise as a owl.

"Whatcha want?" he asks.

"Whatcha got?" asks Dirty.

Wick clears his throat kinda hoarse-like.

"I've got civic pride, by —!"

"You've showed it, Wick," says I.

"Uh-huh. If I had more sense and less pride I'd be better off. Hassayampa Harris hands me a bill for thirty-six dollars' worth of feed—and I got so — full of pride that I kicked him out and took charge.

"My —, that elephant is jist like a hay-baler. Yuh can't fill it up, I tell yuh. And he was feedin' Cleo-patree meat! Can yuh beat that? Cleo-patree is the tiger. That son of a gun has cost me one hundred dollars per stripe."

"Wick," says I, "wouldst be rid of 'em?"

Wick looks at me for quite a while, spits painful-like and nods slowly.

"Wouldst."

"I can get yuh a thousand dollars for the layout."

"Ike, I hope yuh ain't lyin' to me."

"C. O. D.," says I.

"That's the joker," says he kinda wailin'. "C. O. D., eh? How in — can yuh deliver a thing like these, I'd ask you? Half of Piperock is guardin' this here stable. Over across the street is Pete Gonyer. Farther down the street is Mighty Jones, and up the other way is Olaf Hansen. One of them three has his eye on this place. They're watchin' to see that Paradise don't come and take them things away.

"And at night they're guardin' this place with sawed-off shotguns. They heard that Paradise was goin' to take away the menagerie; that's what they heard."

"It's kinda easy to see why Paradise wants to shift the job to me and Dirty Shirt Jones," says I. "Can't yuh do as yuh want to with yore own animals?"

"I can't," wails Wick. "Magpie got me drunk, Judge Steele wrote out a option—and I signed it. I can't sell until thirty days after Labor Day. By that time I'll be in the poor house."

"What do these here animals look like?" asks Dirty.

Wick leads up back in the stable and makes us used to the dangdest lookin' trio of animals I ever seen. Cleopatra is in a cage on wheels, and if there ever was a meaner-lookin' tiger I've never seen it. She's jist skin and bones and a big mouth full of teeth.

The camel opens his mouth and grins at us, kinda asthmatic-like. His name is Sahara, and he looks like —. If it wasn't for his humps he'd look like a moth-eaten burro.

"Here's the *e pluribus peritonitis*," says Wick, pointin' at the next stall. "There stands Gunga Din. I tied the son of a gun up a while ago."

We steps over and takes a close look. It's kinda dark in that stall.

Whap!

Somethin' hit me in the face and I done a foot-race backward plumb to the rear door, where I hits my shoulders first, followed by the rest of my anatomy, makin' a sound like the couplin'-up of an engine on a train of cars. Kinda *clunkety, clinkety, clank!*

Through the haze I sees Dirty Shirt fade out through the front doorway, and I seen Wick Smith climb up a post, where he hangs harness. He got hold of the harness peg and tries to lift himself up; but the peg busted and he landed back on the floor under two sets of heavy harness.

I got up and went weavin' down the stable, feelin' kinda light and airy. I seen Wick come up from under that harness and go gallopin' out of the place with a horse collar around his neck and a set of tugs sailin' out behind, holdin' a hame in each hand, like a man carryin' two flags.

I fell down twice before I got outside, where I found Dirty and Wick. Wick got a tug caught in the sidewalk and ain't got sense enough to let loose of the hame. There he is, yankin' and haulin', while Dirty is standin' in front of him, legs wide apart, wavin' his hat in Wick's face and yellin'.

"Whoa! Whoa! Whoa, you — fool!"

I fell over the tug and sat down on the edge of the sidewalk. Dirty manages to get Wick calmed down, and we looks each other over. Dirty has got a pair of sleeves on, but no shirt. His jiggly eye does a lot of cavortin', as he looks at me.

"I never expected to see any of us alive," says he.

"You don't need to start cheerin'," says I. "What in — was the matter, Wick?"

"Ignorance!" snorts Dirty. "If I didn't know any more natural history than that I'd hang my head in shame, Wick. You tied him up, did yuh? Well, by golly you ort to find out which is the head end of a elephant. You tied him by the tail."

"Well, I-I-I-I tut-tied him," wails Wick. "Ends don't mean nothin' to me. They both hang down. The only danged way I can tell which is which is to give it some hay and see which end turns toward it. He didn't kill either one of yuh, did he?"

"Don't give Gunga Din any credit," says I. "If that back door hadn't been shut I'd be in Canada right now. Go back and make pets of them things, if you must, but spare me from havin' anythin' more to do with 'em."

We helped Wick back into the stable, stole a bottle of horse liniment and went home to recuperate. Dirty walks like his rudder was cramped just a little, and I'm kinda reared back to take the strain off my shoulders, hips and ankles.

It was kinda late that evenin' when me and Dirty limped up to the Mint Hall and found Piperock assembled. Magpie is on the platform, and the argument seems to be gettin' warm. On the platform with him is Mrs. Wick Smith and Miss Jasmine Greenbaum. When she sees us, she hops off the platform, comes and leads me and Dirty up to the front of the room and asks us to sit down.

"These two gentlemen have offered to help me in this," says she. "They have the interests of Piperock at heart. I know they are brave and full of courage, and for that reason I have selected them."

"Brave and full of courage!" snorts Yuma Yates. "Full of rheumatism, from the way they walk."

"I'm goin' to remember most everythin' I hear said here," says Dirty. "That's remark number one, Yuma."

"My list shows number one for Yuma Yates," says I.

Magpie hitches up his belt and moves to the edge of the platform, where he glares at me and Dirty Shirt.

"Threats are out of order," he tells us. "Piperock is passin' from such things. From now onward we are promoters of brotherly love—not battle. Heed this and save yourself trouble. We welcome both to the fold, and thank yuh for of- ferin' yore assistance to Miss Greenbaum. Sincerely yours, Piperock Chamber of Commerce."

"In reply to yore letter of today," says I, "I can say that yore fold don't appeal to us; so am sendin' it back by return mail. Sincerely yours, Ike Harper and Dirty Shirt Jones. P. S. And if you don't know what I mean—ask us."

Magpie glares at us for several moments and then turns to Miss Jasmine.

"Miss Greenbaum," says he, "I told you that I was sure them two jiggers was drunk when they offered to help yuh. Probably they'll deny ever sayin' it now."

Dirty Shirt hops to his feet.

"Magpie Simpkins, yo're a—a—exaggeratin' things. By golly, we said we'd help Miss Greenbaum, and we'll do it. Anythin' she asks us to do is jist the same as done. Ain't that right, Ike?"

"Well," says I, "I hate to have anybody doubt that I don't know what I'm sayin'—drunk or sober. I'm with you, Dirty."

"I knew it," says Miss Greenbaum. "I knew they would do it for me. It isn't often that I make a mistake in human nature. When I first saw these two gentlemen, something told me that they were to be depended upon. Mr. Harper and Mr. Jones, I thank you."

"Yo're welcome," says Dirty. "You sure are awful welcome."

"Well, now that we've settled that part of it, I move that we adjourn. Tomorrow will be spent in preparin' things. We've got a lot of work to do. 'Scenery,' you'll bring yore autymobile in tomorrow?"

Scenery Sims admits that he will. Scenery is a little, thin son of a gun, with a E-string voice, and owns the only horseless vehicle in Yaller Rock County.

"The ladies will be busy on their costumes," says Magpie, "and there will be much decoratin' to be did. The time is kinda short to complete all the details; but it is goin' to be the biggest thing ever pulled off in the West. Our grandchildren will be proud of us."

"Yours won't be," says Dirty Shirt.

It's kind of a mean remark, bein' as Magpie never was married. Nobody laughed, but those directly behind us kinda eased themselves aside out of the line of fire.

Magpie shook his head and polished the nail of his trigger finger on his right ear.

"We've got to be meek," says he. "'The meek shall inherit the earth.'"

"That won't be a — of a lot of fun, if there ain't nothin' but meek ones left," says I.

"There'll be a — of a lot of earth to divide, too," says Dirty Shirt.

And that's all we knew about the meetin'. I've got a hunch that Dirty spoke up too quick. I told him that they've been arguin' about me and him before we got there, but he don't care. There ain't a chance to steal them animals for Paradise, even if we was so inclined—which we ain't—so we decided to let nature take its course.

Early the next mornin' we finds Magpie paintin' a big sign. He ain't noways artistic, but readable. At the top is one word, in letters two feet high—

PAGEANT

And just below that is two more big words—

OF PROGRESS

"What's that, Magpie?" asks Dirty Shirt.

"Depictin'," says Magpie, wipin' some black paint out of his mustache, "the progress of Piperock. Pageant means a high-toned parade. There has been parades before, but this is the first pageant. If you two fellers will go up to Wick

Smith's house you'll prob'ly find Mrs. Smith and Miss Greenbaum workin' on yore costumes. They was goin' to make 'em first thing today."

"Our costumes?" I asks. "Whyfor costumes for us, Magpie?"

"Have to have 'em, Ike."

"Oh, well, if we have to have 'em."

Me and Dirty spells out the next thing on the list:

WHEN EAST MEETS WEST
THE EAST IS AMAZED AT THE PROGRESS OF THE WEST
THEY MINGLE LIKE BROTHERS
THE COMING OF THE WHITE MAN VICTORY
THE SPIRIT OF PIPEROCK—PROGRESS
DON'T FORGET THE BIG DANCE AT THE MINT HALL□
THATCHER'S COMBINED ORCHESTRA□
WILL FURNISH THE STRAINS AND SCENERY
SIMS WILL DO THE CALLIN'□
COME ONE AND ALL
TWO DOLLARS PER EACH WILL COVER THE PAGEANT AND
DANCE

PIPEROCK CHAMBER OF COMMERCE
MAGPIE SIMPKINS, President

We found Wick Smith at the store. He hoodled Hassayampa into takin' charge of the animals again and is runnin' his own store; but he ain't cheerful.

"Tomorrow is Labor Day," says he with tears in his voice. "I ort to be happy, I s'pose, 'cause the proceeds of the pag-unt is to help pay me for them animals; but somehow I can't seem to rend the veil, as Old Testament says, and see the silver linin'."

"Aw, it'll be all right," says Dirty. "Parades ain't much to worry about."

"Thasso?" Wick squints at Dirty. "You've survived some of our parades, ain't yuh, Dirty?"

"Yeah, but you've got to figure that Piperock is civilized. It ain't noways what she used to be, Wick. Right now Piperock is meek and mild."

"I'll betcha," nods Wick. "Well, I still has hopes, but—I dunno. I can't quite figure out my wife lookin' like a statoo of Victory, nor I can't figure out Mrs. Pete Gonyer and Mrs. Mighty Jones depictin' Progress. My —, my wife don't look like Victory."

"You ain't never won a battle from her yet, have yuh?" I asks.

"No, that's a cinch. Well, mebbe it'll be all right. You fellers ain't got no easy chore yoreselves."

"We ain't?" I asks. "What have we got to do with it, Wick?"

"You two depicts the East, Ike. Anyway, that's what they've proclaimed for yuh."

"—, I don't look like no East!" snorts Dirty.

"I don't think I do either," says I. "Anyway, I ain't seen nobody from the East that looks a — of a lot like me. How does she come that we're inflicted with this idea, Wick?"

"Don't ask me. My —, it ain't none of my doin's. I've got all the grief I can stand. You better ask Magpie or Jasmine. They fixed it all up between 'em."

"Do we wear costumes?" asks Dirty.

"Search me. My wife does. Mosquito-bar! My —, can yuh see my wife in a mosquito-bar dress?"

"I'd like to," says Dirty.

And then we left. Wick hadn't ought to be so finicky. His wife is about five feet four inches tall and weighs two hundred and fifty. She also wheezes considerable in her talk. Mrs. Gonyer is six feet two inches tall, and so danged thin that she rattles when she walks. Mrs. Mighty Jones ain't no taller than Mrs. Smith, and she don't weigh a hundred.

Me and Dirty don't get much satisfaction around that town. Magpie goes to Paradise to advertise the affair, and to probably do a lot of braggin' about himself. We runs into Scenery Sims, who has his eyes focused on the wine when it is red, and he ain't exactly what you'd call coherent.

"I—I ain't much," he tells us tearful-like.

We agrees with him, which don't help him none.

"I can't do nothin'," he tells us.

"—, that ain't news," agrees Dirty. "Everybody knows that."

"In the pay-jint," says he. "I want to be somethin'."

"All right," says I. "You be a hump in the road for the wagons to run over."

"That's all right f'r you two pelicans," says he. "You've got things to do. I've been shoved aside, that's what I've been done to, by gosh. Mebbe Piperock is progressin', but I'm right where I was a week ago. Have a drink?"

We would. In fact we had several. We got to a point where Dirty gets to braggin' about bein' East. He orates that he's also effete. Magpie comes back from Paradise, all swelled up over himself, and invades Buck's place.

"They'll come," he tells the world. "Paradise will be here in copious gobs. From Curlew we'll poll a big majority, and there'll be a sprinklin' from Yaller Horse. I prognosticate that Piperock will hold about all there is in Yaller Rock County. We has spread the gospel of progress, and the world responds."

"Has Paradise got her animals yet?" asks Buck.

"Not yet. Mike Pelly tells me that they're on the way. It's goin' to be nip and tuck between us towns. Well, I've got to go and see how things is goin'. Is Pete and Yuma workin' on that float?"

"All day," says Buck. "It'll be a dinger."

"Float?" says Dirty. "My God, they're ignorant, Ike. There ain't water enough in this town to float a cork. We've done give our word to see that this here pe-rade is a howlin' success; but after it's over, me and you starts a pilgrimage. I sicken of the flesh-pots, jack-pots, et cettery. Long may she wave. Let's have another libation to old man Bacchus."

And that's the way she went. Bill Thatcher and his orchestra showed up a little later on—a bull-fiddle, a squeeze-organ and a jews-harp. Bill's boy, Ham, is the squeeze-organist, and old "Frenchy" Deschamps is doin' the moanin' on the harp.

"Kinda wanted t' know what kind of music Magpie wanted us to play," explains Bill. "We've got all kinds."

"You fellers graduated from 'Sweet Marie'?" asked Dirty.

"That's good music," says Bill kinda indignant-like. "If yuh don't like that, we can play it any old way you want it."

Some of Paradise comes that night, and among 'em is the gang from the Cross J. Chuck gets me aside and asks how we're comin' on the animal stealin'. I points out the difficulties, showin' him how close Piperock is guardin' their zoo.

"Get 'em durin' the parade," says Chuck. "Everybody will be interested in that, don'tcha see?"

"Can't be did," says I. "I'm part of the parade."

"What part are you, Ike?"

"I'm half of the east end," says I. "Now you know as much as I do."

"Who's guardin' 'em now, Ike?"

"I ain't sure, but I reckon Hassayampa is on duty."

Chuck goes away, leavin' me to nod at the bartender and lean against Dirty Shirt. Then cometh Polecat Perkins and his pack of high-class mongrels. He's got eight of 'em, all on ropes, and they proceeds to tangle themselves around our legs.

"Greetin's, everybody," says Polecat. "Lay down, dogs!"

Polecat joins our convention and gets enthusiastic over the fact that tomorrow is Labor Day and that we're goin' to have a jollification.

"Take them dogs outside," orders Buck. "My —, this ain't no doggery, Polecat. Take 'em away so folks will have a chance to git to the bar."

Just about that time Hassayampa Harris comes into that saloon. I dunno how far he jumped from the outside, but I know he scraped his head on the top of the doorway and landed plumb in the middle of the room

"Yeeow-w-w-w! Look out!" he yelps.

Right behind Hassayampa comes Cleopatra. She comes among us, like a striped streak, hits in the middle of the room, lands on the pool table and goes plumb out through the back door, which has just been opened by Mighty Jones. Mighty's feet flip up where his hat had been, and over him goes Polecat's flock of dogs, each one tryin' to yell louder than the rest.

"That's our tiger!" explodes Buck.

"You—you can huh-have it!" pants Hassayampa.

"How did it get loose?"

"Go and ask it. I—I was talkin to Chuck Warner at the front door of the stable when all to once I hears somebody yell, and here comes Cleopatra."

"Somebody yell?" snorts Buck. "By golly, I'll bet some of that Paradise gang turned her loose while you was at the front door. Git down there, everybody, before they turn 'em all loose."

They all went down there, except me and Dirty and Buck. They could turn 'em loose as far as me and Dirty are concerned. A few minutes after they're gone Old Testament and Muley Bowles comes in. Testament ain't got no hat and his coat is split up the back. Muley don't track very well and he's got a swellin' over one eye.

"'In the midst of life we are in death,'" says Testament, indicatin' that he don't want his lemonade straight.

Buck looks 'em over.

"You two been fightin' each other?" he asks.

"It—it was a mistake," says Muley, drinkin' the water and pourin' his liquor in the cuspidor. "I thought Testament was a—a—"

"He thought I was a door," finished Testament, "and tried to go through me. Perhaps we had better go home, Muley."

"Yeah—and stay home," says Muley painful-like.

They went out just before the crowd came back. It seems that Gunga Din and Sahara are all right, but they left five guards in the stable.

"We found a hat," said Mighty. "Hassayampa said that they ain't fed that tiger for two days, and I'm kinda scared that we won't never find the man to put under that hat."

I'm goin' to draw a veil over the rest of that night. It will be sufficient to say that mornin' came apace, the sun came up in its usual way, and among us was brotherly love and the sweet spirit of progress. Civilization is sweet to the civilized.

Magpie found us the next day. He looks us over, tells us what he thinks of our ancestors, takes our guns away and leads us down to Wick Smith's home. I'm kinda hazy on just what happened to us, but it seems that me and Dirty went to sleep on a bed.

I dunno what time I woke up, but I suppose it was afternoon. I sets up on that bed and looks at the dangest person I ever seen. He was settin' there, lookin' at me. He's kind of a dirty, brown-complected *hombre*, with somethin' white wrapped around his head, and his body is covered with a striped gown of some kind.

I bats my eyes a couple of times, but he don't disappear.

"I'm dead and in Hell," says the apparition.

It has the voice and eye of Dirty Shirt Jones, but the rest of it don't look like him. Right then and there I marks an X after my name for a temperance vote.

"Yessir, I'm dead," says the person. "I've had delirium tremens enough times to know that this ain't it."

I looks across the room and sees another jigger of the same brand. Then I starts to get out of bed, intendin' to head for the door and this second dirty-faced thing moves right along with me. I've been lookin' in a mirror. Then I lifts one hand to my face, and it comes away the color of chocolate. There's a strong odor of turpentine in the place.

"What in Hell has been happenin'?" I asks.

"Are you Ike Harper?" he asks, kinda awed-like.

"If that's a mirror, I ain't," says I. "Who are you?"

"I used to be Dirty Shirt Jones."

I starts to scratch my head and finds it all wrapped up in cloth.

"Did we get hurt, or somethin'?" I asks.

Before he can answer me, Wick Smith, Yuma Yates and Mighty Jones come in. They looks us over, and Wick Smith says—

"Thank gosh, they're sober enough to ride."

"Who done this to us?" asks Dirty. "I'll kill the man that painted me this-away!"

"There was six of us done it," says Yuma. "It sure is one good job. By golly, nobody will know yuh, that's a cinch. Haw-haw-haw-haw!"

I got off that bed, intendin' to maul somebody; but Yuma pulled his gun and backed me onto the bed again.

"The worst is over, Ike," says he. "Be docile and gain great fame for yourself—you and Dirty."

"We better be goin'," opines Wick. "The crowd is anxious for us to get started. C'om, you East Injuns."

"East Injuns?" says I. "Is that what we look like?"

"Accordin' to the book," nods Yuma. "C'mon."

What could we do, I ask yuh? We went out with them, wearin' bandaged heads, house-paint and mother-hubbards. That paint is beginnin' to dry on my face, and the turpentine stings like a lot of bees. I opened my mouth and I can't get it shut.

"H'rah for —!" wails Dirty. "Who's 'fraid of fire?"

We follers 'em up to the corner of Holt's hotel, and there we finds Gunga Din and Sahara, which are bein' held by Pete Gonyer, Olaf Hansen, Hassayampa Harris, Scenery Sims and "Half-Mile" Smith.

"Gunga Din is broke to ride," stated Hassayampa, "but I dunno about Sahara. Ike can ride the elephant, 'cause he's the biggest, and Dirty Shirt can mount the camel."

"Just a short moment," says I. "Nobody asked us. When I ride, I choose a horse; *sabe*? I ain't no elephant scratcher."

"Ain't yuh?" asks Yuma. "You swore to do what Miss Greenbaum asked yuh to, Ike. She asks yuh to ride the elephant."

"But what for?" I asks.

By golly, I ain't got no idea what it's all about. I can hear folks yellin' out in the street, and when they start to yellin' in Piperock, I don't wish to be there.

"Here's what yuh got to do," says Yuma. "You two ride down the street. About in front of Wick's store yuh will meet old Chief Cod Liver Oil and old Runnin' Dog. They'll have on their war-bonnets, et cettery, and they know what to do. They represent the old West; *sabe*?

"They give yuh the peace-sign, and it seems like yo're all talkin'. That's the part of it which is knowed as the West meetin' the East. Then comes Pete in an old covered wagon. That is the comin' of the white man. The Injuns act surprized. Behind his wagon comes Scenery Sims' autymobeel, which has been made into a float, and on it is the three figures, which represent Victory and the Progress of Piperock; *sabe*?

"Then that's about all, I reckon. I dunno what else there's to be done, Ike. Magpie explains that much to me. Thatcher's orchestra will be playin' all the time, I reckon. Anyway, it'll be good. Hassayampa, you and Half Mile help Ike up on Gunga Din."

"It'll be good all right," grunts Mighty. "Cod Liver Oil and Runnin' Dog done split a quart of lemon extract and a bottle of perfume between 'em."

I let 'em put me up on the back of that India-rubber ox, which ain't wearin' saddle nor bridle. Behind my animal is Dirty Shirt, settin' on the hump of Sahara, his face twisted kinda funny. He's got a pair of reins to hang on to.

Just then Gunga Din starts ahead. There ain't nothin' I can do but set there and let things go. We went surgin' around the corner and into the main street. Yaller Rock County sure was there. Every hitchrack is packed with horses, and between the racks and the middle of the street stands the population of a county, waitin' for us to show up.

They lets out a cheer when we showed up, and we ain't more than halfway to 'em, when up the street comes old Cod Liver Oil and Runnin' Dog, both of 'em decked out in war-paint, nose-paint, war-bonnets, and ridin' painted ponies.

I reckon it was a sight worth seein'. Honest to gosh, I sure did feel aboriginal. I was stoical, too. The only emotion I can show is with my right leg—the left one has gone to sleep. Then the East met the West.

We got within twenty feet of each other before them pinto horses got a good look at Gunga Din and Sahara. Cod Liver Oil's pinto just spread its legs, bawled like a calf—and fell down, sendin' the old buck into a somersault almost under Gunga Din. Runnin' Dog's pinto turns around on one hind leg, shuckin' old Runnin' Dog, and went past us like a streak.

Gunga Din reached down, wrapped his trunk around Cod Liver Oil, and stood the old boy on his head twenty feet away.

"Yee-ow-w-w!" yelps Liniment Lucas. "Some show!"

And into it all comes Pete Gonyer, drivin' a team of broncs hitched to a covered wagon. He is the Comin' of the White Man. He came—I'll say that much for him. The yellin' is too much for that team of broncs, and here comes Pete, feet braced against the front-gate of that wagon, haulin' short on the lines, while behind him billows that wagon-cover, like a anchored balloon.

Runnin' Dog has got to his feet, with the war-bonnet over one eye and blood in the other one.

"*Whoo!*" he screams. "*Hyas masahchie mokst la tet!*"

It was the first elephant he ever seen, and he called it a big evil with two heads.

There ain't no chance for me to move Gunga Din out of the path of them two broncs; so I sets supine and lets death rush down upon us. But it don't rush all the way.

About twenty feet away, them two broncs get their first look at the East, and they don't like it. They dig their heels into that hard street, set down in their harness, and out of that cloud of dust comes Pete Gonyer, all spread out like a flyin' squirrel, and he lands all spraddled out on the head of Gunga Din, still hangin' onto his lines.

As old Judge Steele might say—"Pandyammonium reigns."

The two broncs regains their equilibrium, ducks sideways and tries to go around us. They were goin' pretty good when they took up the slack on them lines, and Pete Gonyer lifted right off the dome of Gunga Din, sailed off through the air and butted Dirty Shirt plumb off his camel. He not only butted him off, but took him along.

Then Gunga Din lifted his trunk high in the air and bugles loud and free—
"Ra-a-a-a te ta-a-a-a ta ta-a-a-a!"

———— ◇ ————

Right then I want to get down. I don't reckon that any Harper ever lived that wanted to get down as badly as I do; but there ain't no safety on the ground. Every horse at them hitch-racks are heavin' and surgin, folks yelpin'. I want to yell, but that darned paint has set, with my mouth half open, and all I can do is say—

"Hoo, hoo, hoo!" like a darned owl.

Then cometh Victory—and Progress. Pete Gonyer has made a riggin' to fit over the top of Scenery Sims' automobile, kinda like a platform, and there's a railin' all around it, decorated with flags and colored cloth. The driver ain't in sight, and the danged thing looks like a runaway raft.

On the front of the arrangement stand Mrs. Wick Smith, all gauded up in cheese-cloth and a silver crown, which is settin' down over one ear, kinda rakish-like. One hand is grippin' the rail, while the other hangs to a big banner.

Behind her stands Mrs. Gonyer, dressed in white, tryin' to hold up one hand, like an Injun givin' a peace-sign, and hangin' onto her is Mrs. Mighty Jones, wearin' a nightgown and a pair of paper wings, one of which has climbed up on her shoulder, makin' her look like a broken-winged duck.

I seen all this in a lot less time than it takes to tell it. The thing is comin' too danged fast, I *sabe* that much, and I know that an automobile don't scare at elephants. A runaway horse goes past me, hits its rump against the platform of Victory and Progress and skids the thing aside.

Mrs. Smith goes down in a lump, and Mrs. Gonyer lands on her knees, with that one hand still up in the air. Then Victory and Progress hits the East.

They knocked Gunga Din loose from the street, but they didn't remove him. I got Mrs. Smith in my arms, but Mrs. Mighty Jones went past me so fast that I didn't have no chance to make a collection. Then Gunga Din got his four feet on to the terry-firma agin' and started out.

He bowed his head, put it against that float and started for Buck's saloon front. I seen Magpie's head come up from among the wreckage and he starts hammerin' Gunga Din over the head with a piece of two-by-four, but he might as well 'a' kissed him, for all the good it done.

Wick Smith comes gallopin' alongside of us, yellin'—

"Leggo my wife! Leggo my wife! Dang you, Ike—leggo her!"

"Tell it to her!" I yelps back at him. "You damn fool, I ain't doin' the holdin'."

The rear wheels of that equipage hits the sidewalk, lifts up real sudden, and we begins to shove that whole works plumb through Buck's saloon front. It was then that I managed to get loose from another man's wife, and proceeds to fall backward off that elephant.

I dunno what in Hell Sahara was doin' right behind Gunga Din, unless he was supposed to be there; but I do know that I lit kinda folded up across his long neck, and he starts to run with me. We went around in a circle three times before I fell off, and that damn camel walked all over me.

Then I sets up in that dusty street and tries to see what is goin' on. Horses are runnin' around like they was in a circus ring, and some of 'em are draggin' wagons and buggies behind 'em, which makes the street a dangerous place for to be. One wagon circled the street twice before I notices that Dirty Shirt is standin' up in the wagon, kinda balancin' himself, with his arms spread out wide.

Then the wagon hit the sidewalk and Dirty turned over twice before he landed sittin' down on the sidewalk. I managed to limp and crawl over to him. His good eye is plumb closed, and the bad one won't keep still.

He's singin' soft and low, and kinda beatin' time with that jiggly eye. I has to listen real close, but above the roar of destruction I hears his singin'—

"Littul birdie in the tree, in the tree, in the tree;
Littul birdie in the tree-e-e-e-e, sing a song for me-e-e-e-e."

"There ain't no tree, Dirty," says I.

"Ain't there?" he asks soft-like. "There ort to be—there's so — many birds."

Over around Buck's place there's folks yellin' to beat four of a kind, and some misguided jigger starts shootin'. I can see that there ain't no regular doorway left in Buck's saloon—just an openin' about ten feet wide.

Just about that time Gunga Din comes around the corner. He ain't got nobody on his back now, but he's got a chair hooked around one hind leg. He runs into the hitch-rack, tried to go under it, and lifts it plumb out of the ground. This kinda makes him sore; so he wraps his trunk around one of the posts and starts for us, packin' and draggin' it along with him, while on the far end of it is tied a piebald bronc from Paradise.

The most of the crowd stampeded for the Mint Hall, Wick's store and other places of safety, and it sure don't take long to clear the street of spectators. I *sabe* that Gunga Din is on a regular bust; so I picks Dirty Shirt up in my arms and staggers toward Buck's place.

I ain't in no shape to pack anybody, 'cause my right leg acts too short, which makes me circle a little to the right and I'm close to Gunga Din before I realize it.

There's just a *whap* and a *rip*, and outside of Dirty's headgear he's as naked as the day he was born. Gunga Din shucked him like an ear of corn. But Dirty don't know it, and I don't care; so we staggers on through the haze.

We fell into Buck's place, and it don't take a normal man to see that everythin' ain't right in there.

Old Testament Tilton is settin' up on what used to be the back-bar, squattin' there like a wise old owl, lookin' over the world; settin' there like a statue, sayin' nothin'. Piled up against the bar is what is left of the float. Buck is flat on his back, with his feet up over the pool-table, which has been moved over against the wall.

All to once that mass which used to be the float begins to heave upward, and from among the busted two-by-fours, twisted wires and colored cloth, cometh Sahara. How in — that camel got mixed up in that float, I don't know, but there he is.

He comes out of there, plumb decorated, and hanging to his tail like grim death comes Magpie Simpkins, the president of Piperock's Chamber of Commerce.

Magpie has still got on one boot, a suit of red underwear and the crown of his hat, and in his eyes is a stern resolve. And behind him, pawin' out of the wreck, comes Wick Smith. They all gets clear of the wreck and Sahara stops. Wick has a two-foot piece of two-by-four in his hands, and he braces his feet far apart.

"Mum-Magpie," says he kinda thin-like. "You has made me a widder man, gol ding yuh."

But Magpie don't hear it. His mind is far behind that pageant of progress. He bows and kinda smiles, as he says:

"The wheel of progress is turnin', and woe unto him who gits under the tire. The people of Piperock has risen in their might, unleashed their bonds which has held them in darkness—"

Tunk! Wick Smith's two-by-four ended the speech.

"You didn't have to blame him entirely, Wick," says I.

He turns and looks at me, kinda weavin' on his feet.

"You?" he whispers. "You come bub-back? Where's my wife?"

"I dunno, Wick."

"You had her, dang you! I seen you huggin' her!"

I seen that piece of scantlin' comin', but didn't have flexibility enough to dodge. I distinctly heard it clank against my head, and then I finds myself out in the street again. I can hear a lot of dogs wailin', and I wonders if I can hear this because I've gone to the dogs. Ain't it funny what a feller will think about in a case like that?

A lot of folks are yellin' at somebody or somethin'; so I sets up and concentrates on the present. A bullet digs into the dirt beside me, but I don't mind. I kinda wonders why they're shootin' at me, of course. Then somethin' hooks me off the ground and begins to give me a ride.

I managed to get one eye open and finds that I'm on one end of that hitch-rack, and the motive power is furnished by Gunga Din. They've picked me up in the angle between one post and the top-pole, and the friction on that part of me which wasn't on the pole was somethin' awful.

Then Gunga Din let out another of them awful bugles, shucked the hitch-rack and headed for Buck's place again—and hangin' to the slack skin of Gunga Din's rear end was Cleopatra. Behind them came Polecat Perkins' pack of hounds, run to a frazzle, but still able to stagger on and wail plenty loud and long.

Them dogs has run that tiger all night, and it ain't no wonder that the tiger is huntin' for somethin' to climb on to. Right into the wreck of Buck's place they went, while the crowd, which is located in places of safety, yelled, shot and generally decided that Hell was havin' a recess.

It's only about five minutes since East met West, but there has been several things come to pass. Gunga Din has gone back into Buck's place, tryin' to get rid of Cleopatra, when here comes Chief Cod Liver Oil, packin' an old Sharps rifle. The old war-whoop sure must 'a' been fortified against fear by much flavorin' extract, 'cause he heads straight for Buck's shattered entrance, soundin' his tribal war-whoop regular.

I got to my feet. I reckon they were my feet. There ain't no feelin' in 'em, but they hold me up; so they must be mine. An armless man could count all the Harper heroes on the fingers of his hands, but just the same I goes pawin' toward Buck's place to see what I can salvage from Gunga Din, Cleopatra and Cod Liver Oil.

I don't quite get there, when Cod Liver Oil comes out. He came out of there, end over end, missed me about a foot, and stood on his head and shoulders in the street. His Sharps lit just outside the doorway; so I picked it up and went in.

Cleopatra is settin' on what used to be the end of Buck's mahogany bar, her mouth wide open and her eyes shut. Gunga Din is standin' in the middle of the room, with one hind foot on Magpie's pant-leg, and Sahara is half-in and half-out of a rear window. And every time Gunga Din weaves the whole building shakes.

Dirty Shirt has got to his feet, and there he stands, plumb out of clothes, kinda rockin' on his feet and grinnin' foolish.

"Dud-do somethin'!" whispers Magpie. "Ain't nobody goin' to do somethin'?"

"Call on the Chamber of Commerce," says I.

From under a smashed card-table, Wick Smith shoves up his head. He's got the brim of his hat in his teeth, but manages to work it loose with his tongue.

"I give up," he wheezes. "I know when I've got enough."

Old Testament is still settin' on the back-bar, but now he shakes loose and falls into Cleopatra. He kinda takes that big striped cat into a lovin' embrace, but Cleopatra yowled once, kicked Testament backward and jumped straight at me.

I throwed up that old Sharps, took a wing-shot at Cleopatra and then a great weight settled upon me. I ain't no fighter. None of my family ever won any diamond belts; but there never was a Harper that wouldn't fight to save his own life. And I sure went into a clinch with that tiger.

My eyes are too full of dust and pain for me to see just how the battle is comin'. We just kept on fightin', thassall. Once we got separated and it takes us quite a while to get together again, but we did. I can't see a danged thing and I don't reckon Cleopatra can either; so we locates each other by sense of smell.

I dunno how long we fought. Scientists would probably differ as to how long a man and a tiger can fight without one or both of 'em dyin'. I ain't got no feelin' left within' me. I reckon I'm kinda primitive just now, and I fights with tooth and claw. I hears voices around me, kinda cheerin'; so I puts up a supreme effort, as it were, and feels the tiger go limp.

"My God!" I hears Dirty gasp hoarse-like. "They're still at it."

"I licked him—her," says I.

I ain't got more than enough breath to say that. And then I kinda passed out.

It seems like I heard somebody say:

"Let him alone, dang yuh! He done jist what I've wanted to see done for a long time."

It was probably quite a some time before I woke up again. For quite a while I can't figure out just where I am and what's goin' on. I seem to be layin' across somethin' that heaves and surges a heap. I manages to get one eye open and discovers that I'm on my stummick across a saddle.

Out in front of me and the horse is a queer-lookin' figure. It's got on a pair of overalls, which won't stay up, barefooted, bareheaded. It looks back at me, and I recognize Dirty Shirt by his jiggly eye.

Then I slides off and sets down beside the trail.

"Where we goin'?" I asks.

Dirty comes back and sits down beside me.

"It don't make no difference, does it?" he asks. "They said that we was mostly to blame; so I took you away from 'em and went away. It wasn't our fault, Ike; but they have to blame somebody."

"Magpie was mostly to blame," says I. "We done the best we could. I dunno what you done, Dirty, but I know I saved Piperock from a lot of heartaches."

"You sure did, Ike," says Dirty.

"That critter would 'a' been the ruination of Piperock."

"That's a cinch, Ike. But the worst of it is, you only stops the plague temp'rarily."

"Thasso?" says I. "I done my best, Dirty Shirt. I wish I had the hide for a souvenir."

Dirty looks queer-like at me.

"I dunno," says he kinda sad-like. "A shock sometimes causes a feller to jerk back to his cannibal ancestors."

I dunno what he's talkin' about, but I'm too bunged up to care much, and my face is beginnin' to crack.

"How in — did it finish?" I asks.

"All right, Ike. The animals all hived up in the livery-stable, and Wick Smith sold 'em to Paradise."

"The — he did!" I exclaimed, or as much of an exclamation as I can use in my condition. "And didn't the Piperock Chamber of Commerce stop him?"

"There was only one to vote agin' it—and he was too danged near death to even squawk. They never even give him credit for tryin' to save the tiger. I seen it all, Ike. When you lifted that old Sharps to shoot Cleopatry, Magpie got loose from Gunga Din and fell into yuh."

"Uh-uh-huh," says I, feelin' weak. "And then what did I do to the tiger, Dirty."

"Nothin' a-tall. The wheels of progress got to turnin', and Magpie got under the tire, thasall. In the language of Magpie Simpkins, I wouldn't be surprised to see Piperock one of the big cities of the world."

"Well," says I, "in the language of Ike Harper, whose spirit, liver, lights and gizzard has been busted to make a Piperock holiday, let's get to — out of here, before the place grows too big. I don't want to even be seen in the suburbs."

But she hasn't grown any since.

BY ORDER OF BUCK BRADY

BUCK BRADY WAS ALWAYS whittling. Thin shavings were an obsession with Buck. He would sit for hours, tilted back in a broken chair against the shady side of his little office, knees almost touching his chin, his long, thin face serious over the task of reducing a piece of soft pine to thin shavings.

Buck was the sheriff of Mojave Wells, and Mojave Wells was a heat and sand scoured, false-fronted town in Road Runner Valley. The town was invisible from a distance, because even the painted signs on the business houses had been sand-blasted until they were unreadable.

It was the end of the roundup in Road Runner Valley, and Buck knew that before night the town would be filled with thirsty cowboys, whose overall pockets were lined with money, and that when whisky met cowboy there might be plenty of work for the sheriff.

The first to arrive was Ben Dolan, a thin faced, gaunt sort of cowboy, astride a weary looking roan. Instead of heading for a saloon, Ben dismounted in front of the sheriff's office, dropped his reins in the dirt and sat down beside the sheriff.

"Hyah, Buck."

"Purty good," drawled Buck squinting at his handiwork. "Whatcha know, Ben?"

"Not much."

"In kinda early, ain't you?"

"Yeah."

Ben made a few marks in the sand with a lean forefinger.

"Had a reason t' come in early, Buck. Some of the boys said it wouldn't do no good, but I thought I'd tell you how it was. 'Long about an hour from now Bud Hickman will ride in. He'll have his gang with him and they'll imbibe real freely. Mebbe 'long about that same time Pete Asher'll ride in with his gang. They'll also imbibe freely, and some of 'em will likely get kinda drunk. The boys are all thirsty, you know. I expect it'll be kinda wooly around here t'night, Buck."

"Uh-huh."

Buck cut a particularly long shaving, looked at it critically and nodded with satisfaction.

"You shore rode in early to explain all this to me," he said. "If you're all through, you might tell me the rest."

"It's thisaway," explained Ben seriously. "You know what a feud is, Buck?"

"Yea-a-ah."

"Well, that's what she amounts to right now. And it's all over a danged girl!"

"I'm glad there's a reason, Ben. Mostly allus them feuds starts over nothin'. Go ahead and tell me the details."

"Rosie Smith."

"Huh?"

"That's what I said. You know how Bud and Pete kinda shined around her a month ago. I don't guess she knowed which one to pick. Of course, Bud thinks it's him, and Pete thinks it's him. And there you are. It's been kinda achin' both of 'em, I reckon. Anyway, Chuck Lester makes a remark the other night that he supposed Bud wouldn't be with us in Mojave Wells at the finish of the roundup, 'cause he'd stop along a picket fence before he reached the main street, and head straight through the gate.

"Pete was there, and I reckon it hit him in a sore spot, cause he chips in with a remark, which didn't set well with Bud. There wasn't much said, but it took all of us to take their guns away. We didn't want no killin' in camp. Bud was reasonable. He says to Pete, 'We'll settle this in Mojave Wells.'"

"Pete was agreeable. He says, 'That suits me. We'll make a truce until sundown, both agreein' to keep away from her. When that sun goes down, all truce is off, and we shoot on sight.'"

<hr />

Buck sliced another shaving, laid the stick aside and began whetting the blade on the counter of his left boot.

"And one of them damn' fools is goin' to get killed," added Ben.

"It's kinda hard to git straight grain stuff these days," said the sheriff seriously. "I 'member when I was runnin' a tradin' post down Yuma way, I used to git the best danged boxwood for whittlin'. I don't suppose it runs so good these days."

"Ben and Pete are both friends of yours," said Ben thoughtfully.

"Uh-huh. I like 'em both."

"A killin' might start trouble. The boys has kinda took sides."

"I s'pose."

"Bud and Pete are both good shots."

"Yea-a-ah—purty good shots. Awful damn' fools in lotsa ways, but good shots. Uh-hu-u-uh. Well, I've got to write me some signs, Ben. It's two hours till sundown."

"I thought you'd like to know about it, Sheriff."

"Yeah, I do. Thank you kindly."

"You're welcome."

Ben took his horse and headed for a saloon, while more cowboys came racing in, their horses covered with lather and dust. The sheriff watched the first contingent arrive. It was Bud Hickman and his gang from the Tumbling K. Bud was a likable looking cowboy, about twenty-five years of age, tall, lithe, swarthy as an Indian, with curling black hair and a white toothed smile. His crew was a wild-riding lot of hard bitten punchers, ready for fun or fight at a moment's notice.

They noted that Pete Asher and the J88 boys had not arrived yet; so they all headed for the Desert Well Saloon, the biggest place of its kind in Mojave Wells. The sheriff stood on the edge of the sidewalk for a while, cogitating deeply. He had been sheriff of that particular county for nearly two terms, which meant that Buck Brady was pretty much of a man. Finally he went into his little office, and after a search he found an old paint brush and a few ounces of almost dried paint in a battered can. He kicked the ends out of a soap box, drew out the nails and sat down at his desk.

Pete Asher and his crew rode in from the J88, tied their horses farther up the street and entered the Prospect Saloon. Asher was a heavily built, hard faced cowboy, about the same age as Bud Hickman. His hair was almost a neutral shade, his eyes deep set and blue. There was little to choose between his gang and the one which came in with Bud Hickman, and in numbers they were about equal.

There were more outfits to come, but they were not connected with the feud. Rud and his men were at the bar when the sheriff came in, and they greeted him noisily. He was carrying a box end and a hammer, and without any leave from the proprietor he proceeded to nail his sign to one of the walls. It read:

FROM NOW ON EVERY MAN MUST TURN HIS GUN OVER TO
MY OFFICE UNTIL HE IS READY TO LEAVE TOWN.
BY ORDER OF
BUCK BRADY

Some of the men laughed; some swore. Bud Hickman strode over to the sheriff and glared at him belligerently.

"You tryin' to kid somebody, Buck?" he asked.

The sheriff looked steadily at Bud for several moments.

"I ain't in the habit of kiddin' anybody, am I?"

Bud flushed quickly, but he recognized the fact that Buck Brady would back up his sign. That was why Buck was their sheriff.

"Kinda sudden, ain'tcha?" asked Bud.

"No-o-o. I've been thinkin' this out quite a while, Bud."

"Is this the idea?" queried Bud. "We all turn our guns over to you, and you turn 'em back when we're ready to leave town?"

"That's what the sign says, Bud; and I wrote the sign."

Bud laughed and turned to his men.

"It's all right, boys. Shuck your guns. I reckon we can stand it, if the others can." And then to the sheriff, "You might have a little trouble with Pete and his gang."

"I hope they'll be reasonable."

The men put their guns on a poker table, and the sheriff picked them up, putting some in his pockets, some inside the waistband of his overalls.

"You'll have to remember your own guns, boys," he said.

"I reckon I can spot mine," said Bud. "I made them handles."

The sheriff thanked them kindly and went back to his office, where he locked the guns in his desk. Then he went over to the Prospect Saloon, where he nailed up his other notice. Asher and his men didn't take so kindly to the idea. Some of them were openly belligerent, and it seemed for a few moments that the sheriff had a tough job, but Asher took the matter out of their hands.

"I suppose this thing only applies to me and my men, eh?"

"You're supposin' wrong, Pete; I've already collected from the Tumblin' K."

"You've collected from Bud Hickman?"

"Why not?"

"Oh, I jist wondered. But suppose we don't give you our guns?"

The sheriff considered Pete calmly. Then:

"I've allus liked you, Asher. You've been a damn' fool in lotsa ways, but you're jist human like the rest of us. I've posted my notice, and I wrote it myself."

"But jist suppose we refuse to give up our guns?"

"That," said the sheriff calmly, "would be jist too damn' bad."

"Oh—" softly—"and if I should happen to want to leave town, you'd give me back my gun?"

"Jist like the sign says, Pete."

"All right; here's mine. Take 'em off, boys. We don't need 'em—now."

The sheriff looked over the guns as he deposited them about his person; he walked out, swinging the hammer in his hand.

"Don't that beat hell?" laughed Pete.

"I'll betcha somebody told him somethin'," said a cowboy.

"I don't like the idea of a moth eaten old sidewinder takin' my gun away," complained a cowboy who was new to the country. "We'd 'a' had some fun, if we'd refused."

"You've got a sweet idea of fun," growled Pete. "That moth eaten old sidewinder is jist thirty-two years old, and if we hadn't turned them guns over to him he'd jist about ruined the whole gang of us with his pet Winchester. When you see 'By order of Buck Brady,' you better read the upper part of it and act accordingly."

<hr />

All the cowboys went back to their drinking, and the sheriff was forgotten, but both Bud and Pete kept track of the sun. The sheriff, humped in his chair, still whittling, saw Pete come out, saunter to the hitching rack, where he could view the sun. It was still an hour high.

Ben Dolan, fairly well filled with liquor, came over again and squatted on his heels beside the sheriff. Ben was as hard bitted as the rest of the cowboys, but he liked both Bud and Pete so well that he hated to see either of them wounded or killed. And Ben was wise enough to understand that both men would claim their guns at sundown.

They saw Bud leave the Desert Well Saloon, walk halfway across the street, as if heading for a store, stop and look toward the west. He too was keeping cases on the sun. Then he turned and went back to the saloon. Ben made meaningless marks in the sand with a forefinger, while the sheriff whittled thoughtfully.

"You shore collected a lot of guns, Sheriff."

"Yea-a-ah."

"Almost sundown."

The sheriff shut one eye and considered Ben. Then he looked toward both saloons, and went on whittling.

"The boys are gettin' nervous," said Ben.

"I notice."

Several cowboys were standing in front of the Prospect Saloon now, and one of them essayed a clog dance. His boots sounded loud on the old wooden sidewalk. Another beat time on a porch post with the end of a quirt. It was like the beating of a tomtom, and he kept it up for a time after the dancer had stopped. The beater was swarthy, with high cheek bones.

Some of Bud's gang came from the Desert Well and stood around in front of the building. One of them, a little drunker than the rest, started across the street toward the sheriff's office, but the others stopped him and, after an argument, persuaded him to desist.

"It's kinda sultry," said Ben, rubbing his forehead.

The sheriff nodded and looked at the sun, only half of which was visible now. He blinked from the strong light and cut several shavings, which did not suit him at all. A couple of dogs met in the middle of the street; town dogs, fat and with a friendship of long standing. But now they growled ominously at each other, as they circled, looking for an opening.

"Sic 'em!" hissed a cowboy from in front of the Desert Well.

"Take him, Tige! Shake his fleas loose. Four bits on the yaller one."

"You've done made a bet, cowboy. Choose him, Ponto."

But the dogs only circled and growled, and finally separated.

"Mebbe they're waitin' for the sun to go down," whispered Ben.

The sheriff shook his head.

"Got more sense than men have."

———◦———

The sun was down. Only the tip was visible, and the crests of the broken hills showed a golden highlight. It was very still in Mojave Wells. The shadows were gone now and the street glowed with a yellow light, which would not last long. Twilight was unknown in Mojave Wells. Sundown, a streak of gold, would quickly fade to blue, and then darkness.

Bud Hickman came from the Desert Well and went straight to the hitch rack, where he untied his horse and swung into the saddle. Simultaneously with Bud's move, Pete Asher came riding from the rack beside the Prospect. It was not a casual move. They intended to deceive nobody, not even the sheriff of Mojave Wells. The cowboys of both outfits were in the street, watching intently.

Bud came straight to the sheriff, and fifty feet behind him was Pete. Bud's face was grim, his mouth set in a thin line.

"I'm pullin' out, Buck," he said softly. "Would you mind handin' me my gun?"

The sheriff stopped whittling, tilted forward in his chair and got slowly to his feet. He looked closely at Bud, but said nothing, as he turned and went into the office. Pete moved in closer, but he and Bud ignored each other. Ben sighed and leaned against the wall.

The sheriff came out, carrying a gun in each hand. For several moments he looked at the two men rather sorrowfully.

"I reckon you're pullin' out, too, ain'tcha, Pete?"

Pete nodded quickly and held out his hand for the gun. They had been friends, these two, until a woman had come between them. Bud holstered his gun, swung his horse around and rode slowly down the street, looking straight ahead. Pete accepted his gun, glanced at it to see that it was fully loaded, snapped it down in his holster and swung his horse around, riding back to the center of the street.

Ben swore softly under his breath. Both of these men were good revolver shots.

"Goin' to be a funeral around here—mebbe two," he muttered. "Why don'tcha stop it, Buck? Gawd A'mighty, this ain't right! Look at Bud—he's turnin'!"

"You didn't expect he'd run away, didja?"

The contestants in this desert town drama were two hundred feet apart, facing each other, both horses moving slowly. They had both played a square game. There was no advantage now. Two hundred feet is a long shot. Both men had drawn their guns. Bud's horse was dancing a little, and he spurred it viciously.

Pete waited.

Ben's hands were gripping the wall beside him. He had seen gun fights before, but they had all been unpremeditated affairs. This one was too much like an execution. The groups of cowboys were as immobile as dummy figures. Even the horses at the hitch racks had ceased moving.

Bud and Pete were closing the gap between them, closing it slowly, each waiting for the other to make the first move with a gun. They were only a hundred feet apart now. It was close enough. But neither of them made a move to lift his gun.

Ninety feet; thirty yards. Either of them could hit a tomato can at that distance. Eighty feet! Horses walking slowly, Seventy feet; sixty feet. Twenty yards now. They were almost in front of the sheriff's office. Ben laughed foolishly. It would be a double funeral. He had seen Bud shoot the head from a prairie dog at that distance.

"It's a nice evenin' for it," said the sheriff rather inanely.

And then it happened!

Both guns came up at exactly the same instant. Ben's eyes snapped shut and he turned his head aside.

Came a tiny ping, hardly louder than the mere snapping of a revolver hammer. Another and another. Bud's eyes jerked open. The two riders were thirty feet apart, leaning forward in their saddles. Not a shot had been fired.

With a swift movement, Bud Hickman swung out the cylinder of his Colt and emptied the cartridges in his hand. Every primer had been dented. There were marks on the bullets, marks made by the jaws of a pair of pliers.

Pete was swearing viciously, as he drew cartridges from his belt and started to stuff them in his gun.

But the sheriff halted him with a sharp word.

"Damn you, you pulled the powder on my shells!" snarled Pete.

"Yeah; and I'll pull somethin' else out of you, if you make one more move," said the sheriff calmly. "C'mere, Bud."

Bud rode up to him, still holding the empty gun in his hand. Pete had quit trying to load his gun. They looked coldly at each other.

"You boys hadn't ort to fight," said the sheriff calmly. "Both of you goin' off kinda half cocked, as you might say."

The men from both outfits had moved in close now, trying to understand what it was all about, their enmity all but forgotten in this queer turn of events.

"I pulled them bullets," admitted the sheriff. "I don't reckon either of you showed any yaller streak. You played the game square, and I like you both for it. Personally I kinda enjoyed it. It was like lookin' at a show. I was the only one that knowed how it would turn out."

"Was it any of your damn' business how it turned out?" demanded Pete hotly.

"In a way, it was, Pete—" calmly. "Barrin' my friendship with both of you, and my position as sheriff, it still was my business, in a way. Now, you two boys was aimin' to kill each other over a woman. Yeah, Ben told me about it. You might thank Ben instead of glarin' at him.

"He liked both of you, and he didn't want no killin' done; so he told me about it. I don't think for a minute that this Smith girl would care to have you killin' each other over her. Most girls don't. Anyway, it was a sucker idea, because there ain't no Smith girl around here any more; so you was tryin' to kill each other for nothin'."

"What do you mean?" blurted Bud.

"The Smiths ain't moved away," offered a cowboy.

"If you hadn't had so much killin' on your mind, you might have found out that me and the Smith girl was married over a week ago. You boys better go back and have your spree, as soon as you give me back them guns, 'cause I've got work to do."

"Whittlin'?" asked Bud blankly.

"Lookin' for somethin' to whittle on."

RANCH OF THE TOMBSTONES

Two men swung their horses through the tumbledown gateway of the Half-Moon Ranch and rode slowly toward the old, rambling ranch-house.

The man in the lead was a tall, thin, unshaven cowboy, with a long, sad countenance and a pair of bright, grin-wrinkled eyes. He rode standing straight in his saddle, with the brim of his sombrero pulled down over his eyes.

The other man was shorter, heavier, with a heavy-lined face and half-shut eyes. A few strands of roan-colored hair straggled from under the brim of his hat, which rested on the back of his head.

They drew rein and looked the place over. The tall one nodded toward the side of the house, and they both rode around to the rear, from whence came the sound of a voice raised in anger.

"Cook!" exclaimed the voice scornfully. "You? Huh! Do yuh think the Half-Moon outfit wear steel bills and digests their food through a gizzard? Why, dang yore hide, yuh can't even burn stuff decently. Set yoreself up to cook fer an outfit, do yuh? Where'd you learn to cook? Cook, damn you! Yo're fired! No, I don't want to hear yuh explain how yuh got drunk on one li'l drink and forgot which way home was. No sir! Pack yore war-bag and drift. I've got enough troubles without annexin' a lot of bad stummicks around here. Yo're fired; sabe? If you can't understand English, I'll write it out in Swedish and mail it to yuh."

The tall cowboy's face wrinkled into a grin, and he started to say something to his companion, but just at that moment a woman opened the kitchen-door and looked out at them.

She was a tiny wisp of a woman, dressed in faded calico. About fifty years of age, with a mild, sweet face and soft, blue eyes. She stared at the two cowboys for a moment, and a flush crept into her tanned face.

"Ma'am," said the tall cowboy, taking off his hat, "I plumb betcha that cook knows where to head in at about now."

"Did—did you hear—me?" she faltered.

"Yes'm. I'm 'Hashknife' Hartley and my pardner's name is 'Sleepy' Stevens. Nod to the lady, Sleepy."

"I am Mrs. Snow," said the lady. "'Frosty' Snow is my husband. He owns this Half-Moon Ranch."

"T' meetcha," bowed Hashknife, and then seriously, "Ma'am, if that cook ain't took the hint yet, I'd admire to repeat yore words to him."

"The—there ain't no cook here now," confessed Mrs. Snow.

"Ain't? Why—"

"He won't quit, don'tcha see? His name's 'Swede Sam,' and if God ever made a more ignorant person than Swede Sam he sure kept him under cover for loco-seed."

"Didja ever try firin' him?" asked Hashknife.

"Sure. But he won't quit. Every day I practise on a new style of firin' him. And what you just heard was what I'm framing up to tell him when he shows up again. We've done everythin' except kill him outright, but he just grins and says:

"'Das goot yoke. Ay am de cook, you bet.'"

Hashknife laughed joyfully. He liked Mrs. Snow because she could see the humor of life.

"Where is he now?" asked Sleepy.

Mrs. Snow shook her head slowly.

"I dunno. A few weeks ago he cooked up a big mess of prunes and forgot where he put 'em. Yesterday he drank the result, and lit out for Caldwell; singin' somethin' that didn't sound like a Swedish church-hymn. I reckon he's asleep in Casey McGill's saloon now. He thinks Casey's a Swede."

"Much stock runnin' in this Lodge-Pole country, ma'am?" asked the practical Sleepy.

"Ye-e-es—I reckon you'd say there was."

"We're lookin' for jobs, ma'am," explained Hashknife. "Me and Sleepy are what you'd call top-hands."

"Never seen a puncher that wasn't," declared Mrs. Snow. "Frosty says there's been a epidemic in the cow-country, which has made top-hands out of every danged buckaroo what has two legs to wear chaps."

"They do get graduated fast, I reckon," agreed Hashknife grinning. "Me and Sleepy earned ours. Do we get the job?"

Mrs. Snow smiled and shook her head. She liked the looks of these two bronzed, practical-looking men, but the Half-Moon was full handed.

"We're runnin' full of help, boys. Frosty said he'd likely have to cut down pretty soon."

"Well, that's too danged bad," observed Hashknife. "I'd sure like to work for you, ma'am. Know any ranch that might be honin' for two more to feed?"

Mrs. Snow smiled and shook her head, but sobered as she squinted at them.

"Might try the Tombstone Ranch."

"Sounds right cheerful, ma'am," observed Hashknife. "Do they raise 'em already carved?"

"Kinda," admitted Mrs. Snow seriously. "Place belongs to old Amos Skelton, the meanest old son-of-a-gun that ever pulled on a boot. Everybody hates him."

"Must amount to somethin' then," observed Sleepy.

"What does his iron look like—his brand?" asked Hashknife, reaching for the cigaret makings.

"It's the old 33 outfit. Folks named it the Tombstone about a year ago. Bill Wheeler owned the old 33 and he let Caldwell put their graveyard on his ranch. It was a kinda nice spot, where the grass stays green most of the time. Then old Amos comes along and buys Bill out. Amos is a danged old blow-hard and most everybody starts in hatin' him at the drop of a hat.

"Long comes Halloween Eve and some brainless cowpunchers goes down to the graveyard, swipes the tombstones, and when old Amos wakes up the next mornin' his front yard is set full of them epi-tafts.

"It was a good joke on Amos, don't you think?"

"Did he laugh?" queried Hashknife.

"Not so's you could notice it," smiled Mrs. Snow. "He took a plow and harrer up to the graveyard, and when he got through cultivatin' it would take a higher power than exists in the Lodge-Pole country to tell where all them tombstones belonged. Yessir, he sure did remove all the brands. Them tombstones are all in his front yard yet, and I reckon they'll stay."

Hashknife and Sleepy laughed immoderately. Mrs. Snow looked severe for a moment, but joined in the laugh.

"Any punchers workin' for that outfit?" asked Hashknife, still laughing.

"One—'Quinin' Quinn."

"Why for the medicine cognomen?" asked Hashknife.

"Bitter. Quinn ain't smiled since he was born. Fact. Ain't got no grin-wrinkles on his face—not one. Nobody plays poker with him, 'cause of his face. Him and old Amos makes a good pair—to let alone."

"Well, we're sure much obliged to you, Mrs. Snow," said Hashknife. "We'll mosey along to Caldwell, I reckon. If you can't make your cook understand anythin', send for me. I sure *sabe* one word he'll jump for."

"Tell it to me, will you?"

"*Skoal.*"

"Shucks!" Mrs. Snow laughed shortly. "I *sabe* that one. It's like sayin', 'Here's my regards.'"

"Yeah, that's true," admitted Hashknife solemnly. "But yuh might yelp it just before you hit him with the ax."

They turned their horses and rode back around the house, heading toward Caldwell.

Ahead of them the dusty road circled through the hills, as though following the lines of least resistance.

There was little flat land in the Lodge-Pole range, but it was ideal for cattle; the breaks giving protection for feed in Summer and for stock in Winter. Cottonwood grew in abundance along the streams, and every cañon seemed heavily stocked with willow. The hills were scored with stock-trails, leading from water to the higher ground.

"Don't like this country," declared Sleepy after they had ridden away from the Half-Moon, "too many places to shoot from cover."

"Sleepy, you ought to have been an undertaker," said Hashknife. "Death sure does have an attraction for you, cowboy. To me this looks like a land of milk and honey."

"Milk and honey, like Hell! More like strong liquor and hornets."

Hashknife laughed. He and Sleepy argued continually, swore affectionately at each other and shared the blanket of a cowboy's joys and woes.

"Look at the doughnut," grinned Hashknife. "Consider the rim of brown dough instead of lookin' through the hole all the time. Nothin' ever looks right to you, Sleepy."

"I said 'strong liquor'," declared Sleepy, leaning forward in his saddle, "and here comes the proof."

A horse and rider had topped a rise just beyond them, and there was no doubt but what the rider was sitting drunkenly in his saddle. The horse was going slowly, and in anything but a straight line, as if trying to balance its rider.

"Drunker 'n seven hundred dollars," declared Sleepy. "Ho-old fast!" he grunted, as the rider almost toppled from the saddle.

The horse stopped as they rode up, standing at right angles to the road, snuffing at the dust. The rider swayed sidewise and Hashknife grabbed him by the arm.

"Drunk!" snorted Hashknife. "This man's been shot!"

"My Gawd, yes!" gasped Sleepy, dismounting and going around to the other side.

"More 'n once, too," declared Hashknife, "or he's smeared himself with the blood."

They took the man off his horse and laid him beside the road. His flannel shirt was soaked with blood, and an examination showed that the man had been shot twice. One bullet had struck him high up in the left shoulder, while the other had torn its way through his body on the right side, about midway between shoulder and waist.

He was unconscious from loss of blood and his breath came jerkily.

"There ain't a danged thing we can do for him," said Hashknife, getting to his feet. "Looks to me like he'd been hit with a thirty-thirty."

Sleepy nodded as he looked up from an examination of the man's face.

"Betcha forty dollars that this here is Quinin Quinn. Didja ever see such a sour face in your life?"

"'F you got two thirty-thirties through your carcass, I reckon you'd kinda sour, too," retorted Hashknife. "'F we knowed where the Tombstone Ranch was, we'd take him there."

"Must be between here and Caldwell. This feller likely headed f'r home and missed the gate. If we don't find the ranch, I reckon we can find the town."

"And that," said Sleepy, as they draped the man over his saddle, "is the first danged thing I ever suggested that you didn't argue about, Hashknife."

"First time you ever spoke sense, Sleepy."

"Glad you give me credit for this once."

"I'll give you credit, when you got it comin'. Get your lariat, Sleepy. We've got to tie this jigger kinda tight."

Sleepy got his rope and proceeded to tie his end of the man to the saddle.

"Lots'a times I never get no credit," grunted Sleepy. "Lots'a times you takes all the credit."

"Givin' you credit now, ain't I, Sleepy?"

"Yeah—this time—I could tell you a lot of times—"

"Shall we set down and argue and let this man die, or would you rather shut your face and give him a chance?"

"Who's arguin'?" demanded Sleepy, swinging into his saddle.

"'F I ever open my mouth—"

"You expose your ignorance," finished Hashknife. "Ride on the other side and see that he don't slip loose."

"Yeah, I'll do that, too," agreed Sleepy, suiting his action to the word. "But," he added, looking across the body of the wounded man, "don't think you've got all the brains, Hashknife—nor a big part of 'em. I never did see a tall man what had any too much *sabe*. Caesar was a short man, and Napoleon was small and—"

"And look what happened to Napoleon," grinned Hashknife. "They pastured him on an island all alone."

"How about Caesar, eh?"

"I dunno a damn thing about him," admitted Hashknife. "What happened to him, Sleepy?"

"I dunno f'r sure, but—betcha forty dollars that's the Tombstone Ranch."

They rode around the point of a hill and below them was a ranchhouse, sprawled in a clump of cottonwoods. A long feed-shed, its roof twisted out of a straight line, stretched from a series of pole corrals along the bank of a willow-grown stream.

A thin streamer of smoke was drifting from the crooked stove-pipe. Between the gate and the ranch-house the ground was dotted with white slabs, seemingly laid out in orderly rows.

"That's her," agreed Hashknife. "Graveyard and all."

They rode down to the gate and up past the graveyard to the front door. There was no sign of an inhabitant, until Hashknife dismounted and started for the door, when the door was suddenly flung open and Hashknife faced the muzzle of a double-barreled shotgun. The man behind the gun was as gray as a rabbit, slightly stooped and with a face as hard as chiseled granite.

"Hook your feet to the dirt and keep your hands above your waist!" he growled.

Then he saw Sleepy.

He peered closer and the muzzle of the shotgun came down.

"Your name Stevens?" he asked.

"Hey!" gasped Sleepy. "You're 'Bliz' Skelton! Well, you danged pelican! Whatcha know about that?"

Sleepy fairly fell off his horse and bow-legged his way up to the door, where he and Skelton shook hands.

"This is Hashknife Hartley, my pardner, Bliz."

"Ex-cuse m' scatter-gun," said Skelton, as he shook hands with Hashknife.

"Danged old dodo!" Sleepy grinned widely. "Ain't seen you since you owned the O-Bar-O in Eagle River. You ain't changed much, 'cept to get homelier 'n Hell. Mrs. Snow said that Amos Skelton owned this ranch. Never heard nobody call yuh anythin' but Blizzard."

"Christened Amos," grunted Skelton, squinting out at the horses.

"Plumb forgot the wounded man!" grunted Hashknife, leading the way out.

"Hellfire!" gaped Skelton. "That's Quinin! He's my hired man. What happened to him, anyway?"

Sleepy and Hashknife unfastened the ropes, while they told Skelton of how they had found Quinin. The old man's face grew tense and he spat viciously, but said nothing. They carried Quinin into the house and placed him on a bed. Hashknife took hold of a limp wrist and squinted down at the man. Then he took a tiny mirror from his vest pocket and held it to the man's lips. The surface remained unclouded.

Hashknife slowly replaced the mirror and looked at Skelton.

"He was your hired man—not is, Skelton."

"Dead?"

Hashknife nodded and reached for the "makings."

"Got any idea who threw the lead?" he asked.

Skelton shook his head.

"Trouble hunter, Bliz?" asked Sleepy.

"No!" Emphatically. "Quinin minded his own business."

Hashknife lighted his cigaret and looked around the room. It contained a box-stove, a table, littered with cigaret papers, two bunks and a few chairs.

"Me and Quinin lived in here," said Skelton. "Built our bunks in here so there'd only be one room to clean."

"What's the trouble around here?" asked Hashknife suddenly.

Skelton stared at him.

"What trouble?"

"Folks don't like you, Skelton. Feller don't get disliked for nothin'. Either you're wrong, or folks see things wrong. Me and Sleepy are danged good listeners."

"That's a fact, Bliz," nodded Sleepy.

"I'm damned if I know," admitted Skelton. "I've had this ranch about a year and a half and I ain't made a cent—nor a friend."

"Mebbe they're sore about the graveyard," said Sleepy.

"I don't blame 'em," agreed Skelton. "It was a dirty trick, but I didn't have a thing to do with it."

"You plowed out the grave-mounds," reminded Hashknife.

"I did, like Hell!" snapped Skelton. "I tell you I'm gittin' tired of denyin' that charge."

"Oh!" grunted Hashknife softly.

"I left them tombstones where somebody planted 'em; but I sure didn't smooth out them mounds, y'betcha. I'm wonderin' that somebody ain't killed me over it, 'cause it's sure a killin' matter to obliterate ancestors thataway."

"'S a wonder yuh never sold out," grunted Sleepy.

"Been asked to." Skelton grinned for the first time. "Yes sir, it has been hinted at considerable."

"You're bull-headed, Bliz," grinned Sleepy. "I'd sure as Hell sell out if I was you."

"Yeah? Mebbe you would, Sleepy—I dunno. They laid that tombstone job on to me, and everybody hates me fer it; and m' cattle disappears reg'lar-like, and once in a while somebody takes a whang at me with a rifle. But outside of that—"

Skelton spat and shook his head.

"What price do you hold on the ranch?" asked Hashknife.

"One hundred thousand dollars."

"Oh Hell!" gasped Hashknife weakly. "You're old enough to know better than that, Skelton."

Skelton nodded seriously and scratched the palms of his hands on his hips.

"Age don't cut no ice, Hartley. This danged ranch ain't worth more 'n eight, nine thousand, with them tombstones throwed in to boot; but I'm damned if anybody's goin' to run Bliz Skelton off the place! I ain't the runnin' kind, y'betcha. And as long as I've got a shell left for that old sawed-off shotgun, I ain't goin' t' run; sabe?"

"Tha's all right," mumbled Hashknife. "You know your own capacity. What'll we do with the dead man?"

"Take him to Caldwell, I reckon. I'll hitch up to the wagon. I suppose Jake Blue and Doc Clevis'll have a Hell of a lot of questions to ask now."

"Who're they?" asked Sleepy.

"Sheriff and coroner."

Skelton stopped in the doorway and looked back.

"I'm damned glad yuh came along when you did. 'F I had to take him in alone I'd sure be stackin' m'self agin' a lot of misery."

"I betcha," nodded Hashknife. "As it is, we'll split the misery three ways."

"Takes somethin' powerful to stir me in this damn heat; but right now I grows excited."

"Pinch" Johnson leaned back against the doorway of Barney Stout's black-smith-shop and spat explosively. Barney lifted a perspiring face and ceased rasping on the hoof of a piebald bronco. His rasp fell to the floor with a clatter, and he came to the doorway, rubbing his horny hands on his leather apron.

"Ol' Amos bringin' comp'ny to town," grunted Pinch.

"One's that Half-Moon Swede," observed Barney, "and he's drunker 'n Hell yet. Started out to walk to the ranch, and he was takin' up both sides and the middle of the road."

"And them ain't all!" grunted Pinch, getting to his feet.

"They's a pair of boots stickin' out the end of that wagon, Barney!"

Skelton drove up in front of Shipman's general store and tied his team to a porch-post. Several men crossed from the War-Bonnet saloon, and one of them was Jake Blue, the sheriff—a skinny, blear-eyed personage, of much self-importance and undoubted ability with a gun.

"Looks t'me like somebody done got hurt," observed Pinch wisely.

He crossed the street with Barney hurrying along behind him.

The sheriff and the other men looked over the sides of the wagon-box curiously.

"What'samatter?" asked Blue. "Drunk?"

"Dead," said Hashknife.

"Zasso?" Mr. Blue had a habit of speaking a whole sentence as if it were only a single word.

He moved to the end-gate of the wagon and looked at the body from that angle.

"Howdedie?"

"Quiet-like," said Hashknife, manufacturing a cigaret.

"Huh!"

Mr. Blue seemed to discover Hashknife for the first time. He masticated his tobacco rapidly and glanced at Skelton.

"Howaboutcha?"

Skelton told in a few words, while more folks came and looked at the dead man.

"Where'd you come from?" asked the sheriff, looking at Hashknife.

"Recently?"

"Yeah."

"Tombstone ranch."

"I mean—before that."

Hashknife snapped his cigaret away and leaned back in his saddle.

"I was borned in Pecos, Texas, about thirty-two years ago—"

"What in blazes do I care about that?" snapped Blue.

Hashknife looked surprised at the interruption.

"Pardner, you asked where I came from, didn't you? I'm tryin' to tell you."

"Zasso? Well, we'll let that slide fer now while we talks about other things. Will somebody find Doc Clevis?"

A man from the War-Bonnet signified his willingness to find the doctor, while the crowd waited and grew to greater proportions.

Doc Clevis was easy to find, and a few minutes later he arrived on the scene, bustling with importance. He was over six feet tall, dressed in a loose-fitting, rusty-black suit and short boots. A thin fringe of hair circled his otherwise bald head and surmounted a face which was a mixture of unutterable sadness and no little evil.

He climbed into the wagon and sat humped on the edge of the wagon-box, while he examined the body. Finally he nodded sadly and looked at the circle of onlookers.

"He's dead," he announced solemnly.

"My God!" marveled Hashknife. "You're a wonder, Doc."

"Been dead quite a while," said the doctor.

"Wonders'll never cease," grinned Hashknife.

Doc Clevis squinted at him, as if wondering if this tall cowboy was in earnest or not.

"Where does the Swede figure into this?" asked Pinch.

"We found him settin' beside the road," explained Skelton. "He's too drunk to know anythin'."

"Lemme look at that rifle," ordered the sheriff.

Sleepy handed down the rifle, and the crowd moved in to look at it. The sheriff levered out three cartridges and slipped a white cigaret-paper into the breech.

"Been shot lately," he announced, peering down the barrel.

"It was beside the road," said Skelton.

"Yeah?"

The sheriff looked quizzically at Skelton. "You found the Swede beside the road, too? 'Pears to me that you found a lot of things beside the road. Was the rifle near the Swede?"

"'Bout six feet from him."

"How far from the Swede did yuh find Quinin Quinn?"

"'Bout two miles."

"That don't mean nothin'," said Barney Stout. "Quinin was still pluggin' along when they found him. Anyway, that Swede never shot him."

"Zasso?"

Mr. Blue fastened his watery eyes upon Barney and lifted his sparse eyebrows.

"Mebbe you know who shot him," he said.

"Well," faltered Barney, "I dunno who shot him, but that damn Half-Moon cook was so drunk—"

"Yo're excused!" snapped Blue, and then to Skelton:

"This here is goin' t' need investigatin', Skelton. I dunno anythin' about these two strangers who horns in on this deal—do you?"

"This'n," nodded Skelton, indicating Sleepy. "I've knowed Sleepy Stevens f'r a long time; and when he takes a pardner, I kinda backs this here pardner. Know what I mean, Blue?"

"Gotcha. What do you make of it, Doc?"

"He was shot twice, and he's dead," replied Doc. "I ain't advancin' any theory who done it, sheriff."

"It's a damn good thing we called yuh, Doc," said Hashknife seriously. "I used to live in a place where we didn't have no doctor, and it sure was a bitch. Why, I've knowed times when we kept dead men propped up around town for weeks—waitin' to be sure they were dead. Lookin' back at them days, I'm wonderin' what killed 'em. Mebbe they was shot—I dunno."

"Are you plumb ignorant, or jist actin' smart?" asked the sheriff.

"That," said Hashknife seriously, "that is the secret of my success. Nobody ever found out, and I couldn't tell 'em, 'cause I didn't know m'self."

"Thasso?"

The sheriff's jaw muscles bulged, like twin walnuts, and he hooked his thumbs into the waist-band of his overalls, as he squinted at Hashknife's serious face.

"You came to a damn good place for to be found out."

"Well, that's right nice of you, sheriff. What do you reckon I ought to do for the information—kiss you?"

"Haw! Haw! Haw!" roared Pinch Johnson. "I'd admire to see you do it, stranger."

Mr. Blue's face did not belie his name, except that it went purple from the added flood of red. He opened his mouth, as though a ready retort burned his tongue, then he shut his jaws tightly and turned to the doctor—

"When'll you hold a inquest, Doc?"

"T'morrow, I reckon," said the doctor, rubbing his bald head with a rotary motion, as if polishing it. "Take that long to git evidence, won't it?"

Blue nodded and turned to Hashknife—

"You two fellers ain't aimin' to pull out soon, are you?"

Hashknife shook his head.

"No-o-o. We're plumb stuck on your town."

Blue grunted his unbelief. He might be ignorant, but not a fool.

"You ain't got no puncher now, have you, Skelton?"

Skelton shook his head.

"Ain't a lot of extra hands around this country," observed Blue. "Well, Doc, I reckon we better have Quinin moved into your place. Mind haulin' him down there, Skelton?"

Skelton did not mind. He turned his team around and headed for the doctor's office, with several men following. Hashknife and Sleepy rode across to a hitch-rack, tied their horses, and went into the War-Bonnet.

The War-Bonnet was a large place for a town the size of Caldwell, but it looked prosperous. There was not much activity during the day, so the place was nearly deserted when Hashknife and Sleepy came in.

A couple of girls were on the small stage-like platform at the end of the room, practising a few dance steps, while with one hand a pallid young man thumped out a melody on the piano.

A bartender humped his white-clad elbows on the bar, while he deeply perused a paper-backed novel. A "swamper" was scrubbing back of the bar. His activities seemed to irritate the bartender, who knew that sooner or later he would have to move and break the thread of his story.

Hashknife and Sleepy walked up to the bar and looked around the place. The bartender sighed, folded over a leaf of his book to mark his place, and came down to them.

"'Smatter over there?" he indicated the street with a jerk of his sleek-combed head.

"Feller got leaded up," said Hashknife. "Feller named Quinn."

"Quinin Quinn, eh? Dead? The son-of-a-gun! Whatcha drinkin'? Seen Swede Sam over there, too. He ain't mixed up in it, is he? Whatcha drinkin'? Know Quinn? Never smiled. No sir, that *hombre* didn't know how. Ain't no reason for killin' him off. Feller's got a right to look sour, ain't he? I'd sure have to have a good reason before I'd kill any man. Son-of-a-gun's dead, eh? Well, well! Whatcha drinkin'?"

"See-gars," said Hashknife grinning.

The bartender produced a well-worn cigar-box and disclosed a few dried-out perfectos.

"Ain't many cigar smokers around here," he volunteered. "Don't pay to keep a big stock. Them's real good Key Wests, y'betcha. I smoked one oncet. Got drunk and careless. 'F you lick them outside leaves, like you do a cigaret-paper, they'll stick. Them Key Wests allus kinda unravels thataway. I stuck 'em oncet, but they—"

Two very bad cigars went into a cuspidor, and the bartender looked sad.

"I didn't lick 'em," he explained. "I used glue."

"Tha's all right," grunted Hashknife. "A cigar ain't never good after the first drag or two."

The bartender turned and threw the two-bits into the till.

"Have a drink on the house?" he asked.

Hashknife shook his head.

"Feller that'd use glue on cigars is liable to put cyanid in his hooch. Who owns this ornate parlor?"

"'Spot' Easton. Didja ever hear of Spot?"

Hashknife leaned against the bar and admitted that he did not know the gentleman. Just at this moment a man came in the door, a frowsy looking man, with drink-bleared eyes and uncertain step. He slouched up to the bar and leered at the bartender; a leer which was intended to be an ingratiating smile, but which missed by a wide margin.

"Nossir!" The bartender shook his head violently. "Spot said to lay off givin' you liquor, 'Lonesome'."

"Spot did?" The old man seemed surprized to hear it.

He wiped the back of his hand across his lips and stared at the mirror on the back-bar. There was no question but what he needed a bracer; his whole nervous system cried out for assistance.

"You get the drink, grampaw," said Hashknife, tossing a two-bit piece on the bar.

"Spot don't want him—" began the bartender.

"Hooch!" snapped Hashknife. "What in Hell do I care what Spot wants?"

"He'll get sore about it," argued the bartender.

"Do I have to wait on him m'self?" asked Hashknife.

The bartender slid out the bottle and a glass. The old man seemed unde-cided whether to take it or not, but Hashknife settled the question by pouring the drink for him. The old man drank nervously and upset the glass as he put it back. He steadied himself on the bar until the liquor began to percolate and then sighed with relief.

A man came from the rear of the place and halted near the end of the bar. He was rather flashily dressed for the range country. His black hair was slightly tinged with gray. His features were narrow and he wore a small mustache, which was waxed to needle-like points. He scowled at the bartender, who got very busy wiping glasses.

The old man considered Hashknife and Sleepy for a moment, and began to search his pockets. He drew out a crumpled envelop and held it close for inspection.

"M' name's James B. Lee," he announced thickly, "but ev'ybody calls me Lonesome Lee. Now, what in Hell do you reckon anybody'd write a letter to me for? This'n jist come on the stage."

He handed the letter to Hashknife, or rather he started to; but the flashily-dressed person had moved nearer and secured it. For a moment nobody spoke. Lonesome swallowed with great difficulty and tried to clear his throat.

"Right sudden, ain't you?" said Sleepy.

The man ignored his question and spoke directly to Lonesome Lee.

"Nobody ever wrote to you, Lonesome."

"Yeah, they did, Spot. I—I—" whined Lonesome.

"The envelop will show who it's for," said Hashknife easily.

Spot Easton turned to the bartender.

"'Windy,' how many times do I have to tell you not to let Lonesome have any more whisky?"

"Lay off the bartender," advised Hashknife. "I paid for the old man's drink, if you care to know."

Spot Easton seemed to see Hashknife for the first time, and the discovery did not please him.

"Who in Hell are you?" he growled.

"Me?" Hashknife grinned. "I'm the li'l jasper that's goin' to make you give the letter back to Lonesome Lee."

"Yeah?"

Easton's brows lifted in surprize, as he looked Hashknife over appraisingly.

"How are you goin' to do it, if I may ask?"

Hashknife turned his body toward the bar. It was a disarming move. Easton stepped in closer to Hashknife; stepped in just in time to be in reach of the right swing that Hashknife pivoted to accomplish.

It caught Mr. Easton flush on the left ear and the force of the smash knocked the gentleman's feet loose from the floor. The thud of his fall had barely sounded, when Hashknife leaned over him and took away the letter.

Easton did not move. The piano crashed a discord and stopped. One of the girls gave a throaty little squeak and stopped dancing. Hashknife turned to hand the letter to Lonesome Lee, but that worthy was going out of the front door as fast as his unsteady legs would carry him.

"Well, that kinda beats all!" grunted Hashknife.

The bartender had dropped the glass he was polishing, but continued the action on the bunched fingers of his left hand. He breathed on the fingers and polished harder.

Spot Easton sat up, holding his left ear. He looked around as if wondering what had happened. His eyes strayed to the ceiling, as if wondering that it was still intact. Then he got slowly to his feet and brushed the dust off his broadcloth raiment.

"You asked a question," reminded Hashknife seriously, "but I don't reckon you need an answer—not now."

Spot Easton did not express any opinion. He wadded a silk handkerchief against his bruised ear, turned, and went to the back of the room.

"I've got the letter and nobody to give it to," chuckled Hashknife, and then to the bartender—

"Whatcha polishin' your fingers for, pardner?"

The bartender, suddenly realizing that he did not have a glass in his hand, recovered the one from the floor.

"What'sa matter with everybody around here?" asked Sleepy. "The old man hummed out of here like a spike, and you got absent-minded. Ain't the War-Bonnet used to seein' trouble, or is all this honkatonk only a blind for a Sunday school?"

"That—that was Spot Easton," stammered the bartender.

"Who's he—the king?" asked Hashknife.

The bartender glanced keenly toward the rear of the place, where Easton had entered one of the built-in rooms. He leaned across the bar and whispered:

"You better look out for him, gents. Spot Easton's a sidewinder, y'betcha. He's quicker'n a flash with a gun, and he used to be a middle-weight prize-fighter. Glad it ain't me he's sore at."

"You don't reckon he's sore at me, do you?" Hashknife seemed penitent.

"Huh?" Such a foolish question amazed the bartender.

"Gee cripes! He must be touchy if he is," observed Sleepy. "Some folks wears their feelin' on their sleeves."

"Well, for God's sake!" wailed the bartender. "I dunno whatcha mean by that. If you got hit in the ear—"

"Aw, come on, Sleepy," said Hashknife. "Never seen a bartender or a sheep-herder yet that had any sense."

As they started to cross the street, a rider on a mouse-colored horse passed in front of them, going down toward the sheriff's office. The man was almost as tall as Hashknife; his features were hidden by the shadow of his low-pulled Stetson.

Bliz Skelton and the sheriff were coming away from the office, and the sheriff hailed this rider, who swung over to the board sidewalk beside them.

"Wears bat-wing chaps, beaded vest and a polky-dot shirt," observed Hashknife aloud, "rides with his stirrups a notch too short; all of which makes me feel that I know that *hombre*, Sleepy."

"Let's look him over," suggested Sleepy. "Looks a li'l gaudy to me, but mebbe he's all right."

The stranger was talking earnestly to the sheriff, as they walked up, and the conversation seemed to interest Skelton. The stranger turned and looked at Hashknife, but continued to talk.

"I dunno," said Skelton, shaking his head. "I'm much obliged to you, but I ain't made up my mind yet jist what 'm goin' t' do. 'F I sell out I won't need no hired help."

"And if you don't, you do."

The sheriff was a trifle ungrammatical, but sincere.

"Yeah," admitted Skelton.

"It don't make me no never mind," stated the stranger. "I'm just open f'r engagement. Jake'll tell you that I'm a top-hand, y'betcha."

"All of which makes it so," stated Hashknife.

Jake Blue squinted at Hashknife and up at the cowboy. The latter seemed surprized that any one might doubt his ability.

"Who 're you?" asked the cowboy.

"Names don't mean nothin'," replied Hashknife. "I don't know your name, but I ain't inquisitive. 'Pears to me that I've knowed you some'ers."

"Huh!"

The cowboy's eyebrows lifted slightly, but no sign of recognition crossed his features. He was not at all handsome—due partly to a crooked nose, a split lip and a week's growth of downy, blond whiskers.

"What are you cuttin' in here fer?" asked Blue angrily. "Mister Hagen's goin' t' work for Skelton."

"Zasso?" Skelton seemed surprised. "I ain't hired nobody yet, Blue."

"You ain't goin' to have work for three men, are you?" asked Hashknife, turning to Skelton.

"Three men?" queried Blue quickly.

"T-h-r-e-e," spelled Hashknife. "Me and Sleepy's done hired out to him."

The sheriff spat explosively and looked at Skelton.

"Zasso, Skelton?"

"Well, yuh—uh—might say it was," faltered Skelton.

"I'm goin' to be the foreman," stated Hashknife, "and if you got any top-hands, you might send 'em to me, sheriff."

"Hellfire!"

Mr. Hagen spoke very peevishly, turned his horse and rode back to the War-Bonnet hitch-rack. There he dismounted, kicked his horse in the belly, and went into the saloon.

"There ain't no question but what he's a top-hand," agreed Hashknife. "All top-hands kick their broncs in the belly thataway. Kinda makes the bronc respect you."

"Where's the Swede?" asked Sleepy.

Jake Blue had been staring toward the War-Bonnet, deep in thought, and Sleepy's question seemed to jar him awake.

"The Swede? He's in jail. Where'd you think he was?"

"In jail," said Sleepy.

"Then what in Hell did you ask fer?" Mr. Blue growled.

"You can't hook that killin' onto the Swede." This from Hashknife.

"Can't I?" The sheriff grew very indignant. "Well, mebbe I ain't goin' t' try very hard."

He stepped off the sidewalk as if to leave, but turned and added—

"'F I was you I'd be hopin' that it was hooked onto the Swede."

With this parting shot, the sheriff crossed the street and went into the Paris restaurant, banging the door behind him.

"You made him mad," observed Skelton seriously. "He was only tryin' to git a job for this Hagen feller."

"Who's this Hagen?" asked Hashknife.

"I dunno him. He's been with the 88 f'r a while, but he quit, or got fired or somethin'."

"Who owns the 88?"

"Lonesome Lee used t' own it, but he drank it mostly all up, I reckon. Mebbe Spot Easton owns it by now. Lonesome got t' drinkin' and playin' poker, and I reckon he's lost all the money he ever had. He stays at the ranch—when he ain't drunk—which ain't often."

"Big outfit?" asked Hashknife.

"Bigger'n mine," answered Skelton.

"With two top-hands your ranch ought to grow," stated Hashknife seriously. "You don't mind us hirin' out to you?"

"I dunno where your pay's comin' from, but I don't mind, if you don't. Want to go back to the ranch now?"

Hashknife shook his head.

"No-o-o. You see I knocked Spot Easton loose from the floor a while ago, and if we left now it would look like I was runnin' away."

"You did!" gasped Skelton. "Spot Easton? Well—"

Skelton scratched his head and squinted at Hashknife's serious face.

"Well, I—I reckon yo're a top-hand, Hartley. Come out to the ranch any ol' time you git ready. Whoo-ee!"

The old man slapped his hat back on his head and bow-legged his way back to the sheriff's office.

Hashknife took the letter from his pocket and looked at it.

"She sure belongs to Lonesome Lee, Sleepy. The epitaph proclaims it to be for James B. Lee, Caldwell, Montana, and the little doohicky in a circle says that she was sent from Boston."

"Now, whatcha reckon Mister Easton wanted this here letter for, Sleepy?"

"Don't glare at me!" complained Sleepy. "You act like it was my letter. How'd I know what Easton wants?"

"Where did the old man go?" asked Hashknife, paying no heed to Sleepy's question.

"There you go ag'in! Think I'm a fortune-teller? You saw him the last time I did."

"Well, I reckon the only way to find him is to look for him. Come on."

They went up the sidewalk, past the Hole-in-the-Wall feed-corral, and almost bumped into Lonesome Lee, who was coming out from the narrow alley between the feed-corral and general store. The old man's cheeks were streaked with tears and dust, and he was half-sobbing—drunkenly. He gawped at Hashknife and Sleepy and tried to avoid them, but Hashknife took him by the arm and drew him back.

"What's the matter with you?" growled Hashknife. "Ain't nobody goin' to hurt you, old-timer. Here's your letter."

Lonesome Lee stared at the letter, but made no effort to take it. In fact he seemed afraid of it.

"You ain't scared of Spot Easton, are you?" asked Sleepy.

Lonesome did not say, but his actions spoke volumes.

"Has that tin-horn got you buffaloed, old-timer? Snap yourself together! You've blotted up so much hooch that your nerves are dancin', but you're a damn good man yet." Hashknife's voice was encouraging.

"Th-think so?"

Lonesome wiped his lips with shaking fingers and moved his feet uncertainly.

"Better read the letter," urged Sleepy. "It might be good news; you never can tell."

"Wh-where's it from?" he stammered. "My eyes ain't worth a damn no more."

"She's from Boston."

Lonesome licked his lips and stared into space.

"Bub-Boston! Hell!"

He staggered off the sidewalk, almost fell in the dust, and weaved a crooked trail straight for the doorway of the War-Bonnet.

"'F that don't beat all, I'm a pigeon-toed fool!" grunted Hashknife foolishly.

"His ear-drums kinda shrink from Boston," observed Sleepy, as Lonesome seemed to carom from one side of the door to the other.

"Scared plumb to death," declared Hashknife. "It's a danged shame for a man to get in that shape. Somethin' has sure put the Injun sign on the old gent, Sleepy. This Easton's a bass-drummer among these canary-birds, 'cordin' to what I can get in my loop; so he must be somethin' besides a card shark."

"Let's go over and talk to the blacksmith," suggested Sleepy. "I've got to have some shoes put on my bronc' pretty soon, and maybe I can save about four-bits by gettin' real friendly. I have done it, by cripes."

Barney Stout was inserting a new felly into a wagon-wheel, and swearing mournfully over the fitting. He rubbed his nose with the back of a very dirty hand and nodded to Hashknife and Sleepy. They had squatted down against the wall and were rolling cigarets.

"How's tricks?" asked Sleepy.

"Tricks?"

Barney squinted at the rim of the wheel, as he felt of the joint with a thumb.

"There ain't no tricks in this trade; it's all damn hard work and disappointment. Hear they put the Swede in jail."

Barney rubbed his hands on his hips and, reaching for Sleepy's sack of tobacco, squatted down beside them.

"I dunno who killed Quinin Quinn, but it's a dead immortal cinch that Swede Sam never did."

"Where'd that .30-30 rifle come from, do you figure?" asked Hashknife.

Barney shook his head and puffed violently.

"I never seen the gun," he said. "Quinn tol' me that he'd been shot at three or four times in the last year. 'S far as that's concerned, so has old Skelton."

"Any idea why?" asked Sleepy.

"Nope. I heard Jake Blue say that it was likely that folks hadn't forgot what happened to their graveyard—but Quinin didn't have nothin' to do with that. He came here quite a while after that."

"Folks got kinda sore about it, eh?" queried Hashknife.

"Yeap. Can you blame 'em? They sure as Hell lost track of their ancestors. Ev'body tried to relocate their dead, but it was no use. M' wife had one of them Kodiak things that you take pictures with, and she photygraphed the graveyard one day; but it's kinda blurred-like. They took that along to try and figure out things, but it didn't help 'em a danged bit."

"Lots of folks buried there, eh?" queried Hashknife.

Barney nodded.

"All them markers in Skelton's yard indicates a body. The first corpse was old Billy Meek, who was some sanctimonious old whippoorwill; and the last one was a gambler by the name of 'Faro'. I never did know his name.

"Spot Easton shot him over a poker-table. Folks kicked about him bein' buried in the cemetery, and old 'Peg-leg' Smith refused to dig the grave; but Spot and Doc Clevis dug the grave, and I reckon Jake Blue performed the funeral oration—I dunno. Anyway, Faro never got a headstone, 'cause his grave-mound was lost with the rest."

"Did they bury this here Faro person right in with the rest?" asked Hashknife.

"Danged if I know for sure. Seems to me that somebody said they planted him off to one side; kinda between the others and the creek. I never seen the grave."

Came the sound of a boot on gravel, and they turned to see Doctor Clevis coming in the front door. He peered at Hashknife and Sleepy.

"Wanted to tell you that the inquest'll be held t'morrow afternoon 'bout two o'clock," he announced. "Likely need your testimony."

"We'll be here," nodded Hashknife.

The doctor walked out, and Barney got to his feet.

"Gotta git that damn felly fixed up, I suppose," he groaned. "Hope I never git sick and have to call Doc Clevis. Him and Jake Blue are thicker'n two drunks in one bunk. Besides, I never like to have any truck with a doctor who is the undertaker, too."

"Gets 'em goin' and comin', eh?"

"Gotta cinch," agreed Barney. "And Jake Blue ain't as particular as he might be, especially when the reward notice don't specify 'dead or alive.'"

"We'll see you again, pardner," said Hashknife, as he and Sleepy walked out the front door.

"Come in any ol' time," yelled Barney. "Mostly always I've got time to talk."

Hashknife led the way past the War-Bonnet and up to the hitch-rack where they got on their horses and rode back toward the Tombstone Ranch. Hashknife looked back and saw Hagen standing in the doorway, looking in their direction; but there was no sign of Lonesome Lee nor of Spot Easton.

"Do you reckon they'll hang the killin' onto Swede Sam?" asked Sleepy, as they poked off down the dusty road.

Hashknife eased himself in the saddle and reached for his cigaret material.

"I'll do everythin' I can to hook it onto him," he said.

"You will?" Sleepy's surprize was genuine.

"Sure will. Me and you and Skelton have got to lie like Hell to keep out of jail ourselves."

"But the Swede never killed him."

"Neither did we, Sleepy. I reckon Mrs. Frosty Snow can get along without Swede Sam for a while—and Swede Sam ain't got brains enough to mind bein' locked up."

"But they couldn't put me and you in jail," protested Sleepy.

"Thasso? They put Swede Sam in."

Which left Sleepy without an argument worth while.

Hashknife locked a long forefinger around his spoon and fended it away from his right eye, while he sipped thoughtfully at his cup of coffee. Finally he nodded slowly.

"Yeah, that's true, Skelton. Whisky does pe-culiar things to a man's nerves; but why does ol' Lonesome go hippety-hoppin' like a scared rabbit when he sees that danged letter?"

Skelton helped himself to more coffee from the old battered pot and reached for Sleepy's cup.

"Not any more, Bliz," said Sleepy. "You ought to grind that coffee before and after makin', 'cause she's sure hard to chew."

"Lonesome Lee's sure in tough shape," admitted Skelton, ignoring Sleepy's insult to his ability as a coffee maker.

Hashknife took the letter from his pocket and studied it closely.

"Steam," said Sleepy slowly. "Steam'll cut the stickum on an envelop."

Hashknife squinted hard at Sleepy.

"That's a crooked thought, Mister Stevens. Sometimes you surprize me."

"You say that Spot Easton wanted the letter?" asked Skelton.

Hashknife yawned widely and glanced around the room.

"Skelton, you ain't got anythin' like mucilage, have you?"

"Y'betcha, I have. Li'l bottle, with a brush attached. I dunno what it was used fer, and she's been here since before Heck's father went wooin'. Whatcha want it fer?"

"To make this danged letter look like it never was opened."

Sleepy grinned joyously.

"Gimme credit—"

"Fer nothin'," finished Hashknife. "That was a common thing before your great, great-grandfather was lynched for tryin' to tell folks what to do."

Hashknife held the envelop over the steam from the tea-kettle, until the flap was softened, and removed the letter. He spread out the single sheet on the table, and the three of them read it together.

Dear Dad:

I will arrive nearly as soon as this letter, but am sending it anyway. I hope that your injured arm is better now. It was very kind of your foreman, Mr. Easton, to write in your stead, and I shall thank him personally for his offer to meet me at Gunsight.

I can hardly wait to see you. Just to think that I have never seen you since I was old enough to remember, but we will make that all up, daddy. I have just money enough to take me to Caldwell, and I am coming as fast as I can travel.

Since mother passed out I have felt entirely alone in the world, and even if you and mother could not be happy together, I am sure we can. Loads of love and a big hug very soon.

Your loving daughter,

Jane.

P. S.—I will be with you in time to celebrate my eighteenth birthday.

Along the margin of the paper was written—

I am glad you liked the picture of myself, which I sent you, daddy.

Hashknife lifted his eyes from the paper and looked at Skelton, who was moving his lips slowly over the written words. Skelton straightened up and shook his head.

"I don't *sabe* that foreman stuff. Spot Easton never was foreman of the 88."

"Has Lonesome Lee been nursin' a sore arm?" asked Sleepy.

Skelton laughed shortly.

"'F he has, I never knowed it. That letter's sure got me pawin' m' head. I never knowed that Lonesome Lee had a wife or daughter."

"And," added Hashknife meaningly, "Spot Easton was kind enough to want to meet her in Gunsight. He was also doin' the writin' for Lonesome, 'cause Lonesome had a sore arm."

"Whatcha make of it, Hashknife?" asked Sleepy.

Hashknife pondered over the manufacture of a cigaret, and read the letter again before he spoke.

"'Pears to me that the lady done sent her picture, previous. Mebbe she's pretty, which would attract Mister Easton. It also appears that Mister Easton has got old Lonesome Lee where the hair's short and tender, and he's kinda runnin' Lonesome's business.

"Accordin' to signs, Mister Easton has lied to said lady, who thinks her paw is somebody. Paw ain't got no nerve left to object, and Mister Easton has likely told him that he has invited this here daughter to live at the 88. Paw ain't got the guts to howl against such things, and when he finds that the letter is from Boston he's plumb shaky that it tells about daughter's de-parture. Mister Easton naturally is wishful to know how his invite has worked out; which is the reason he grabbed at the letter. That's how she looks to me."

"'F that's a fact, I sure as Hell feel sorry fer her," stated Skelton sadly.

"Yuh might feel sorry for Lonesome, too," said Hashknife. "He's all shot to pieces with hooch, and he likely knows that she's comin' to find him."

"Figurin' she's goin' to be happy with him," added Sleepy mournfully. "Comin' to celebrate her eighteenth birthday. Damn!"

Hashknife got to his feet and walked over to the open door, where he leaned against the casing and contemplated deeply. The sun had already dropped behind the hills, which looked like blue silhouettes, with silver trimmings. Far away on the skyline drifted a herd of cattle; their outlines blurred from the back-light of the sunset.

From below the long sheds came a string of cattle, heading for the water-hole opening on the brushy stream; bawling softly, as they followed the deeply-worn trail. Magpies chattered sleepily in the cottonwoods.

"Makes a feller wonder how a man can live in a land like this and hate anybody," muttered Hashknife.

He turned to come back to the table, when—

Ping-g-g—Whop!

Skelton fell backward out of his chair, clawing at the coffee, which sprayed all over him. Sleepy threw himself sidewise out of line with the door, and from somewhere came the thin, whip-like report of a high-powered rifle.

Hashknife kicked the door shut and gawped at Skelton, who got to his feet, shook the coffee out of his eyes, and picked up the coffee-pot—or what remained of it.

The soft-nose bullet had hit it near the bottom and there was nothing much left to identify it as a coffee-pot, except the color and odor. Even the ceiling was dotted with coffee-grounds.

"Anybody hurt?" asked Hashknife.

Skelton gazed ruefully at the remains of the pot, and dug inside his collar after more grounds.

"Hell!" he snapped. "They didn't miss us very far that time."

"Common occurrence?" asked Hashknife.

"Periodical. Last week I was shakin' some stuff out of a fry-pan outside, and they nailed the ol' pan, dead-center. Wrenched Hell out of m' wrist, too. Never even saw where the bullet came from. I dunno whether they're hintin' fer me to move, or missin' their target."

"Got damn good eyes, if they shot at that pot," grunted Hashknife, "'cause that rifle wasn't closer than five hundred yards."

"Cat-eyes," added Sleepy. "Nobody could see into a house at this time of the day. That *hombre* wasn't aimin' to spill our coffee, y' betcha."

"Got a rifle, Skelton?" This from Hashknife.

"Dang right I have."

He walked over to one of the bunks and threw back the blankets. He ran his hand over them, dug under the straw-tick, and stepped back, looking curiously around.

"What do you know about that?" he grunted. "It ain't there!"

"Are you sure?" asked Hashknife.

"Lemme think. It was there yeste'day, 'cause I took it out when I made the bed. I know danged well—no, I 'member leanin' it agin' the wall."

He glanced around the room and shook his head.

"Don't make a damn bit of difference; it's gone."

"What kind was she?" asked Sleepy.

"Winchester.30-30."

"That wasn't it we found near the Swede, was it?"

"No-o-o—I'm damned 'f I know whether it was or not. I never looked at it. Fact is, I never used it. I'm not worth a damn with a rifle, but I sure do *sabe* the old shotgun and buckshot, or a six-gun. Never liked that idea of shootin' a man with a mushroom bullet."

"Does kinda unravel a man," Hashknife agreed. "When did you buy that .30-30?"

"I acquired it with this damn ranch, along with the rest of the misery."

Hashknife nodded slowly and considered the ceiling. A question had suddenly popped into his head and he wanted to consider it before speaking. The coffee-grounds were beginning to loosen from the ceiling, and some of them drifted into his eye. He dug them out thoughtfully and turning to Skelton said—

"You got any relations, Skelton?"

"Not a danged kin," grinned Skelton. "One of my kind is e-nough, ain't it?"

"'F you got killed," suggested Hashknife, "who'd get this ranch?"

Skelton scratched his head violently.

"Never thought of that, Hartley. Why, I reckon the sheriff would sell it to the highest bidder. But who would bid on it—I dunno.

"Shucks!" Skelton added. "It must be somethin' pers'nal. Nobody'd kill me to get a chance to buy this damn ranch. That ain't reasonable."

"Human nature is a queer thing," said Hashknife. "I knowed a feller who was sent to the penitentiary for stealin' Christmas presents, which were goin' to be given to him."

"Why didn't you add the fact that he knowed it?"

"I know when to quit lyin'," said Hashknife gravely.

He got to his feet, went to the door, and peered out.

"Gets dark quick around here," he said. "I reckon it's plumb safe to saddle up now. That bushwhacker likely went away as soon as he fired that one shot."

"Saddle up? What for, f'r gosh sake?"

Sleepy settled back comfortably in his chair.

"Me and you are goin' to Caldwell."

"What fer?"

"That inquest is tomorrow afternoon, Sleepy."

"Oh, I see," said Sleepy sarcastically. "'Fraid you'll be late if you don't start now?"

"You might put it thataway," admitted Hashknife. "We'll be back kinda late, Skelton, I reckon; so I'll call m' name when we come home."

Skelton nodded dubiously and said:

"'S your own business, Hartley, and I reckon you can take care of yourself. I dunno what you got on your mind, but I wish you well."

Hashknife grinned at Sleepy's disgruntled way of pulling on his chaps, and went out of the door. Sleepy swore softly as he followed him.

———◇———

Spot Easton was not in a happy frame of mind at all. His ear had swollen to twice its normal size and had assumed the shade of a pickled beet. It not only pained him, but it hurt his pride; he was not in the habit of getting the worst of a personal encounter.

The evening business of the War-Bonnet was beginning to be audible to Spot, who was sequestered in his little private room in the rear. A half-empty whisky bottle decorated the table beside him, and his jaws were clamped tightly over a badly frayed cigar, which smoked much from the wrong end. He jerked it out of his mouth, cursed and hurled it across the room where it continued to throw up a streamer of smoke.

Just then, without any warning, the door swung open and Lonesome Lee staggered in. The old man was gloriously drunk, but tried to brace up when he faced Easton.

"Sus-somebody said you wanted to shee me," he muttered thickly.

"Yes; you lousy old bum!" snapped Easton, kicking a chair away from the table.

Lonesome eased himself shakily into the chair and sprawled weakly.

"Where's that letter?" demanded Easton.

"Tha' letter?" Lonesome grinned foolishly. "Wha' letter?"

"The one you got today. The letter—oh, Hell!"

Lonesome had emitted a long-drawn snore and his head sank slowly until his chin was buried in his collar.

Spot Easton shoved away from the table and, going over to Lonesome, proceeded to go through the old man's pockets. He shook Lonesome, but the old man continued to snore loudly.

Spot caressed his aching ear, while he reviled Lonesome with every foul epithet his tongue could command. Tiring of that, he drank half of the remaining liquor, threw the bottle across the room, and sat down again.

Then came Jack Blue. He too was a privileged character and did not wait to knock on the door. He squinted at Lonesome and sat on the edge of the table.

"Why don't you have Doc Clevis fix up yore ear?" he asked, noticing that Easton was fingering the sore organ.

"That damn veterinary!" exploded Easton.

"Doc could take out the soreness."

"I'm damned if he could!" rasped Easton. "Only one thing'd take the soreness out of that ear, and that's to notch a sight on that long-geared misfit that hit me."

"He's a fresh whippoorwill, all right," admitted Blue. "Never seen anybody with the gall he's got. Somebody's due to make jerky out of his tongue."

"Y'betcha," agreed Easton, "and I'm him."

Blue jerked his head toward the sleeping Lonesome.

"Did he have that letter, Spot?"

"Naw!"

"That puncher still got it?"

Spot looked very disconsolate, but did not answer.

"What was in it, do you reckon?"

"How'd I know?"

Blue gnawed off an enormous chew of tobacco and moved to a chair.

"'F he's still got the letter I'll git it for you tomorrow, Spot."

"How?"

"Law requires that I search all prisoners, tha's why."

"Thasso?" Spot Easton grew interested. "You goin' to put him in jail?"

"I sure as Hell am. More'n that, I'm goin' to put the both of 'em in jail, along with old man Skelton."

"How you goin' to make it look right?"

Blue spat copiously and grinned at the ceiling.

"That was old Skelton's rifle which they found beside the drunk Swede."

"Skelton's rifle? And he brought it to you?"

"Nope. I went past there yesterday and I dropped in to call on Skelton—knowin' he was in town."

"And swiped his rifle?"

"Uh-huh. Belonged to old Bill Wheeler, and she's got a li'l 33 cut into the forearm. She's a cinch to hang it onto Skelton, and I can hold them other two—easy."

Easton laughed and got to his feet.

"You're clever, Jake. Let's go and get a drink."

"I sure am."

Blue was not adverse to applauding himself. Being a sheriff in Lodge-Pole county entailed too much danger for the remuneration; so nobody cared much about a sheriff's morals—or methods.

Easton gazed approvingly upon the amount of activity within the four walls of the War-Bonnet, as he led the sheriff to the bar. The click of dice, the rattle of poker chips and the droning voices of dealers was sweet music to Easton's ears.

A number of men were standing at the bar, but Easton and Blue ignored them. Two cowboys were shaking dice on the bar-top at Easton's right hand.

"'At's horse 'n horse," declared one of them. "One flop, Sleepy."

Easton shot a sidewise look at the speaker. It was the tall cowboy, who had hit him on the ear, standing elbow to elbow with him; intent on his dice shaking.

Easton slowly turned his head and looked at Blue, who was toying with his glass of liquor. The dice rattled.

"You're stuck!" exclaimed Hashknife.

Easton jerked his head around and looked square into Hashknife's face.

"How's the ear?" asked Hashknife.

The question placed Easton in an embarrassing position. He could not see Hashknife's right hand, and his own hands were on the bar. Blue squinted past Easton's shoulder at Hashknife, and Hashknife grinned at him.

Sleepy leaned forward on the bar and craned his neck around Hashknife.

"I hope to die, if I ain't terror-stricken!" he gasped. "We've been told that it's fash'nable to be plumb scared of Mister Easton; so we turns pale, politely."

Easton tore his eyes away from Hashknife's grinning face and looked straight into the back-bar. His mind worked swiftly, but got nowhere. He was being insulted in his own house. Jake Blue leaned away from the bar, as if to move into the crowd, but Sleepy stepped around behind Hashknife and Blue leaned back against the bar.

"Where's the old man—old Lonesome Lee?" asked Hashknife.

Easton turned quickly.

"What do you want of him?"

"Want to give him that letter," explained Hashknife.

"Oh!" Easton's grunt seemed to relieve him.

"'F he ain't around here, mebbe you could take care of it for him, eh?"

"Sheriff's nervous," interrupted Sleepy. "'Pears to have an itch on his hip. Likely comes from a callous caused by packin' such a heavy gun."

Jake Blue scowled, but said nothing.

"I'll give him the letter," nodded Easton, trying to not appear too eager to be of service.

Hashknife's concealed right hand flipped the letter to the bar in front of Easton and dropped back. Easton picked up the letter and started to put it in his vest-pocket, but Hashknife stopped him.

"Whoa, Blaze!"

Easton stared at him wonderingly, as Hashknife motioned for him to stop.

"Not in a vest-pocket, pardner. Put it in your side pants-pocket, if you don't mind. That's the only pocket where a tin-horn gambler don't pack a derringer."

Easton scowled and shoved the letter into the designated pocket. He wondered if this tall cowpuncher was a mind reader, and knew that he was going to use the letter as an excuse to get at the two-barreled derringer in his vest-pocket.

"'F you don't stop hankerin' t' scratch—" Sleepy's voice held a note of menace—"'f you don't, I'm goin' to get a piece of sandpaper and give you one good curryin', Mister Sheriff. Ain'tcha ashamed to scratch thataway in c omp'ny?"

"By Hell, I'm tired of this!" wailed the exasperated Mr. Blue. "Who're you, anyway, I'd like to know? What right you got to tell me when I can scratch and when I can't?"

"I'm just teachin' you how to act polite, ain't I?" complained Sleepy. "Gee cripes, you sure do act peevish over learnin' things. If I was you—"

"Don't tease the li'l gent, Sleepy," Hashknife said, chuckling. "His chilblains has likely extended up to his hips. You know how cold feet makes you itch."

Hashknife kept his eyes on Easton, while talking direct to Sleepy, and he saw a flash of relief come over Easton's face. A man had stepped in behind him, brushing against Hashknife's right elbow, and Easton's eyes had followed this man.

The conversation had been even lower than ordinary and had attracted no attention.

———————◦———————

It all happened in a few seconds. As the man brushed Hashknife's arm, Hashknife stepped quickly away from the bar; stepped away just in time to let Hagen, the ex-88 cowboy, crash into Easton.

Hagen had intended to bump Hashknife hard enough to knock him off his balance, but he had not expected Hashknife to move so quickly.

Easton whirled half-around and jammed his heels onto Jake Blue's toes, while Hagen half-fell to his knees. Like a flash, Easton struck at Hashknife, and his bare knuckles came in contact with Hashknife's heavy six-shooter.

Sleepy sprang in to prevent Blue from drawing a gun, and his knee caught Hagen just under the chin, knocking his head against the solid bar with a dull tunk! Easton's right hand went out of commission and he stumbled awkwardly over Hagen's legs, falling flat on the floor, while Sleepy pinned Blue's arms in a bear-like hug, swung him up bodily and backed to the door. Hashknife backed swiftly out with him, covering the surprized crowd, which had no idea of what had been going on.

Once outside they went swiftly to the hitch-rack, with Sleepy still carrying the cursing sheriff.

"What'll I do with him?" panted Sleepy. "I don't want him."

"Got his gun?" asked Hashknife.

"It's back in the War-Bonnet."

"Let him loose," laughed Hashknife. "We ain't collectin' knick-knacks."

Sheriff Blue sat down so heavily in the hard street that his tongue, for once, refused to function. Hashknife and Sleepy mounted swiftly and whirled back past the War-Bonnet, where men were crowding the doorway.

Spot Easton cursed bitterly as he saw them flash past the beams of yellow light, then he turned back to "Blondy" Hagen, who was still sitting in front of the bar, holding his head in his hands.

Easton's right hand was deeply cut and swelling rapidly. He cursed it fluently and turned to see Jake Blue coming in, covered with dust, his face badly scratched.

Blue had nothing to say. Men crowded around them, wondering what had been the reason for the fight, but none of the three victims seemed inclined to explain things. Hagen got to his feet and started for the door.

"You!" gritted Easton bitterly.

Hagen scowled blackly and shouldered his way out of the door, where he turned and glared back at Easton.

"Aw! You be damned!" he snorted, and went away.

"It's a large night," said Blue inanely.

———◦———

The coroner's inquest over the remains of Quinin Quinn caused little excitement in Caldwell. The fact that Quinin was dead was enough in itself; who killed him, was merely conjectured and Lodge-Pole county felt that it would remain so, according to precedent.

The jury listened patiently to Hashknife, Sleepy and Skelton, while Doc Clevis, puffing with his own importance, crossquestioned them. Swede Sam was there, blank-faced over the whole thing, and all that Doc Clevis could get from him was:

"Ay dunno. Ay am de cook."

Neither Easton nor Blondy Hagen was at the inquest, which was held at the doctor's home. Sheriff Blue glared silently at the floor during the proceedings, looking at no one.

"Sheriff," said Doc Clevis, turning away from Swede Sam, "you've got a little evidence to show the jury, ain't you?"

Jake Blue looked straight at Hashknife for a moment and then he answered—

"Nope."

"Why, I—I thought—"

Doc Clevis seemed surprized.

Blue shook his head.

"We-e-ll, I reckon that's all—then," said the doctor slowly, looking at Blue. He turned to the jury and added—

"You can think this over now, and—"

"It ain't goin' to require much thinkin'," said a raw-boned cattleman. "These two strangers tell a straight story, and Skelton sure never shot Quinn."

"What about the Swede?" asked the doctor.

"I reckon the sheriff ought to apologize to him for puttin' him in jail at all."

Blue scowled, but said nothing.

"It'll be the reg'lar verdict, Doc," nodded one of the jury. "We finds that Quinin Quinn demises at the hands of a party, or parties, unknown. And," he added, "that sure as Hell ain't settin' no new example around here."

The jury nodded and got to their feet.

"You're free, Swede," grunted Blue savagely.

"Das goot," nodded Swede Sam, getting to his feet. "Now Ay buy drink—for me."

Blue hurriedly left the room ahead of the rest, and went straight to the War-Bonnet. Spot Easton was near the door evidently waiting for news, but Blue silently headed straight for the private room, and Easton followed him.

Blue flopped down in a chair and bit savagely into a plug of tobacco. His jaws fairly quivered as he spat out the twisted piece of metal—the trademark on the plug.

"Hook it on to 'em, Jake?" asked Easton, easing himself into a chair.

"Hook, Hell!" Blue's vocal cords seemed to unhook with a bang.

"What do you mean, Jake? Didn't the jury—?"

"To Hell with the jury! They turned the Swede loose and said that Quinn was killed by parties unknown; that's what happened!"

"Damn!" grunted Easton. "I thought you was so damn clever."

"Thasso?"

Blue masticated rapidly as if trying to control his temper.

"How about that rifle?" asked Easton.

Blue spat explosively.

"You want to know, do you? So do I! I had that rifle in a rack in my office. I had three more rifles in that same rack. I went to git that rifle this mornin' and—"

"It wasn't there, eh?" interrupted Easton.

"You're damn right it wasn't! Neither was the other three."

"You're clever," admitted Easton. "Clever as Hell! What did you leave—"

"Lemme alone!" snarled Blue. "Don'tcha ride me, Spot! If you thought of that, why didn't you say so? You're so danged smart that you always see mistakes after they happen."

Easton made no reply to this, and a deep gloom seemed to pervade the little room: Blue chewed mechanically, his eyes closed, a picture of abject despair; while Easton considered his bandaged right hand, which ached badly. His knuckles still tingled from contact with that heavy gun.

"Hagen knows that tall jasper," he volunteered.

"Yeah?"

Blue spat and leaned back.

"Name's Hashknife. Hagen says he's a fightin' hound."

"My God!" exploded Blue. "D' you need to be told?"

After another long period of silence Easton said—

"I'm goin' to make a trip to Gunsight, Jake."

"Thasso? Whatfer?"

"Business. Leavin' pretty soon."

Jake Blue got to his feet and walked to the door, where he turned and squinted at Easton.

"what in Hell do I care where you go? I'm gittin' sick of havin' eve'thing goin' wrong all the time. If we're goin' to let that long-geared coyote run this country, let's both go and give him room. We ain't a damn bit better off 'n we w as."

"Takes time, Jake." Easton's tone was conciliatory.

Blue masticated viciously.

"Where's Doc goin' to bury Quinn?"

"I dunno, but I think Doc's goin' to start a new graveyard with Quinn. Said he'd picked out a spot back of town. Is that Hashknife person still here?"

"Damn him; I suppose so. If I was you I'd sneak out the back way, Spot—if you want to git away safe-like."

Jake Blue slammed the door behind him and went down the big room, half-grinning to himself. At least it was some satisfaction to goad Spot Easton, who was losing prestige about as fast as possible. Easton's reputation had been earned, but he seemed to be running into a series of hard-luck and mistakes. Jake Blue also felt that the god of luck had deserted him, but he blamed everybody except himself. He went out of the front door and ran into Doc Clevis.

"I've been lookin' for you," stated Clevis. "What happened to you, Jake? Was you afraid to produce that rifle?"

Blue cursed solemnly and told the doctor what he had told Spot Easton. Doc Clevis removed his hat and polished his bald head with his palm.

"Somebody," declared the doctor, "stole them guns."

"Didja think they walked away?" Blue said sarcastically, and added—

"Where'd Skelton and them two longhorns go to?"

Doc Clevis did not know. He was dry, and he offered to buy a drink, but Jake Blue refused.

"You better let me look you over," said the doctor. "Any time you refuses a drink, you're sick."

Jake Blue turned wearily away from the doctor and went toward the office. Spot Easton went to the livery-stable and in a few minutes he came out driving a tall, bay horse hitched to a top-buggy. He drove to the sheriff's doorway, where Blue leaned dejectedly.

"I'm goin' to Gunsight," said Easton.

"You've got my consent," grunted Blue, and as Easton drove out of town he added, "I hope t' Hell you run off a grade and never hit bottom."

Hashknife, Sleepy and Skelton had left town immediately following the inquest. Hashknife was standing in the ranch-house doorway when Easton drove past, headed for Gunsight—the terminus of a branch railroad.

Easton did not look toward the house, but Hashknife recognized him.

"There goes the foreman of the 88, Skelton," he said.

"Th' son-of-a-rooster!" grunted Skelton. "He's done read that letter and he's goin' to meet her in Gunsight."

Easton disappeared around a curve in a cloud of dust, and Hashknife rubbed his chin thoughtfully.

"How far's it to Gunsight?"

"Thirty miles—about."

"Huh!" Hashknife cogitated deeply. "If she comes in tonight, he'll likely make the return trip with her."

"Danged lonesome ride at night," observed Skelton.

Sleepy came up from the corral and sat down on the steps.

"What's the matter, long feller?" he asked as he noticed Hashknife's thoughtful expression.

"That's what Easton likely wants," mused Hashknife, ignoring Sleepy's question. "A feller don't lie in a letter without havin' some kind of an ax to grind."

"Lemme in on it, will you?" asked Sleepy.

"Spot Easton just went past in a top-buggy, and he's headin' for Gunsight."

"That's good. I reckon we can get along without him."

"But," said Hashknife slowly, "you gotta figure that the girl's only eighteen years old. She won't *sabe* Spot Easton."

"I dunno much about human nature," said Sleepy, "but I do know danged well that I'm hungry. Don't we ever eat on this new job, Bliz?"

"Y'betcha," grinned Skelton. "I'm goin' t' rustle some bull-beef and bakin'-powder biscuits right now. I was just wonderin' why that rifle never showed up at the inquest."

"Did your rifle have any mark on it, Skelton?"

"I dunno. I sure as Hell couldn't identify it."

"Thassall right then," grinned Hashknife. "Me and Sleepy examined 'em all before we sunk 'em in the crick—they all looked alike to us."

Skelton scratched his head violently and squinted at Hashknife.

"You—uh—oh Hell, yes! I know what you mean now. Top-hands, y'betcha—yes sir."

Skelton went into the house and in a few moments he was busy with biscuit-dough, while Sleepy and Hashknife humped up on the steps and manufactured cigarets.

"Thirty miles to Gunsight," observed Hashknife. "Right pretty little ride."

"Yeah, it is," admitted Sleepy.

"She sure is, Sleepy; nice li'l ride. We'll saddle up as soon as we folds the stummick around a little provender."

"Saddle up?" queried Sleepy. "You ain't—"

"We are," corrected Hashknife.

"Aw-w!" Sleepy protested softly. "You're the dangdest person t' hop into—"

"What'd you do, Sleepy?"

"Well, it ain't our business noways, Hashknife."

"Supposin' Spot Easton was goin' to meet your sister?"

"But she ain't my sister."

"'F you was Lonesome Lee's son, she would be. Suppose you was, Sleepy."

"I ain't—not even supposin', Hashknife."

"Gosh a'mighty! Thirty miles! I suppose you'd go if it was sixty. Sixty miles ain't much."

"I never been able to figure you out, Hashknife." Sleepy shook his head disconsolately. "You do the dangdest things I ever seen. Some day you're goin' to horn into things what don't concern you, and you'll meet a hunk of lead—face to face.

"You always kind of go out of your way to bother into other folks' troubles. Every danged place we go you gets into some dang kind of a mixup, and she's always because you feel sorry fer somebody. If it was only you I'd say for you to go to it and grab a tombstone but, blast it all, you always drags me into it."

Sleepy stopped for lack of breath and glared at Hashknife.

"Yes sir," nodded Hashknife slowly, "just suppose you was a brother to that girl. It's thirty miles; which is some ride in the dark."

"Hey!" yelled Skelton from the kitchen. "You jaspers like gravy with your spuds?"

"You spoke my daily prayer," yelled Hashknife.

Sleepy got to his feet and stretched his arms.

"I hope that train don't get in so early that we'll have to hold up Spot Easton on the road. I had a sister, Hashknife, and I know what you mean."

It was nine o'clock when Hashknife and Sleepy rode into Gunsight, and the night was as dusky as the proverbial black cat. Gunsight was quite a bit larger than Caldwell and a trifle more modern, owing to the railroad which made it a shipping point for the surrounding country.

They dismounted at a hitch-rack and tied their horses.

"Mister Easton will likely put his horse in a stable," stated Hashknife. "Especially if he aims to drive back tonight. We better kinda examine the livery-stable."

They jingled their spurs down the sidewalk to where a lantern swung over a wide doorway, from within which came the unmistakable odor of a stable. Two more lighted lanterns were hung at the sides of the room to light up the rows of stalls.

A stable-man came out of the grain-room carrying another lantern which he placed on a backless chair near the door, and squinted at Hashknife and Sleepy.

"Evenin'," he grunted. Cowboys usually made the stable their headquarters.

"Evenin'," greeted Hashknife. "How's business?"

"'S'all right, I reckon. The day man got drunk and I'm doin' two shifts. Got any Durham?"

Hashknife passed him part of a sack and he rolled a cigaret.

"Ain't much night business, is there?" asked Hashknife.

"Naw—not much; but just enough to make me miss a date with m' girl. Figured to close up early, but a feller drove in a while ago, and he's goin' out agin' tonight. Naturally I've got to linger around here 'till he starts travelin' agin'. I ain't no drinkin' person, but whisky sure does cause me a lot of misery."

"Can't he hitch his own horse?" asked Hashknife.

"Well, I reckon he could; but it ain't hardly good business to ask a feller to pay fer service and not git it."

"That's a fact," agreed Hashknife solemnly. "We was just wonderin' if we could bunk in the hay t'night. I don't admire to pay a hotel four-bits for a chance to read my shirt the next mornin'."

"Sure, sure. The loft's got plenty of room, or you can sleep in the grain-room. They's a bunk in there and some blankets."

"That's right kind of you," said Hashknife. "If we can help you— Say, if it ain't too late to keep that date with your girl—"

"Whatcha mean?"

"Well, is there any reason why I can't tend to that feller's horse? Ain't no trouble to cinch a hull on a bronc. Course I wouldn't take his money—"

"Thassall right, I got his money in advance. It ain't no saddle-horse, though. If you don't mind hitchin' a horse to a buggy —"

"Cinch," grunted Hashknife. "Show me the horse and buggy, pardner."

It took the man about a minute to point out the horse, harness and buggy. It was the tall, bay horse which Easton had driven from Caldwell. The stable-man was voluble in his thanks, and hurried away to keep his date. Hashknife and Sleepy grinned at each other as they sat down to wait for Easton's return.

Blondy Hagen, following his run-in with Hashknife and Sleepy, had come to Gunsight. His head was still sore from its crash against the War-Bonnet bar, and he proceeded to embalm his wounded feelings in very bad whisky.

And when Blondy got drunk, he got bad. Like an Indian warrior he sang his own praises—until he saw Spot Easton drive in and stable his horse. Blondy was not afraid of Spot—not in the least, but he knew that Spot would have something to say about what happened in the War-Bonnet.

Blondy was one of those peculiar characters whose gun was always ready for hire, and he could still feel the weight of Spot Easton's cash. He really wanted to see Spot and, if possible, get more money; but he felt that he really should do something to earn what he had already been paid.

He weaved out of the Ten-Spot saloon and balanced himself against a porch-post. Just to his left was a hitch-rack, partly lighted from the Ten-Spot window. He clung to the post and puzzled over the two horses, which looked familiar. Suddenly he remembered; and the memory caused him to straighten up and grunt softly to himself—

"Tha's their broncs! Whatcha know?"

Blondy gawped foolishly and grew inspired. It might be worth his while to find Spot Easton and tell him that those two gall-laden punchers were in Gunsight. He lurched away from the post and proceeded to cut himself a wide trail down the sidewalk. He hadn't the slightest idea where Spot Easton might be found; but Blondy hadn't the slightest idea where he was going; so it made no difference.

He almost fell into the doorway of a restaurant as a man was coming out—and the man was Easton. He grabbed Blondy by the shoulder to keep him from falling, and shut the door behind him. Blondy got a glimpse of a very pretty girl sitting at a table; and then Spot Easton shoved him past the restaurant and into the darkness of an alley.

"What are you doin' here, Hagen?" demanded Easton.

"Me? Leggo that arm! Whatcha think you are?"

"You know who I am," growled Easton meaningly. "When did you come to Gunsight?"

"Thassall right," said Blondy drunkenly.

"Don't paw me 'round, Spot. I was looking fer you. Mebbe you'd like to know that them two Tombstone punchers are here."

"Who?"

"You know; them two that kinda jiggered our play."

"Oh!" Easton grunted softly. "What are they doin' here?"

"I never seen 'em," admitted Blondy, "but their broncs are tied to the rack at the Ten-Spot, y'betcha."

"Are you sure, Hagen?"

"Betcha I am. I know that tall roan and the blue-gray."

Spot Easton thought rapidly. If Hashknife and Sleepy were in Gunsight, they had a reason for coming—and he might be the reason. He suddenly realized that they had opened and read that letter, and he swore softly for not having thought of that before.

"Are they in the Ten-Spot?" he asked.

"Wasn't," Hagen replied. "I come out of there and found the horses."

"The Ten-Spot is almost straight across the street from the livery-stable," mused Easton aloud. "I wonder if they—Hagen, is there another livery-stable here?"

"Uh-huh. 'Soapy' Evans owns kind of a stable."

"You want to earn your money, Hagen?"

"Tha's me."

"Go up to the livery-stable and find out if them two snake-hunters are there. Don't let 'em see you; do you understand?"

"Prob'ly git killed, if I don't," grunted Hagen. "Where'll I find you?"

"I'll be right here waitin' for you."

It was about two blocks to the stable, and the average was about six saloons to a block. Hagen knew that he had won back the good graces of his employer; so he went in and partook of good cheer. Easton fretted in the dark and waited for a report, while Hagen weaved in and out of the saloons; getting closer to the stable at each entrance and exit, but also getting more cocksure of himself.

The last saloon took away every vestige of cowardice in Blondy Hagen's make-up. He came out, balanced on the edge of the sidewalk, while he filled his lungs to capacity and then emitted a war-whoop that would have shamed any Indian on earth.

He stumbled off the sidewalk, gripped his six-shooter tightly, took his bearings from the lantern over the doorway of the stable and set sail.

He stumbled up the plank drive-way and into the dim light of the stable, telling himself hoarsely how very great he was and how Spot Easton depended upon him for everything. As he halted to inhale enough breath for another declaration, a rope seemed to descend from nowhere, tightened around his arms and body, and something threw him upside down with a great crash.

Strong hands picked him up and carried him away, and a moment later he felt himself hurled into space. He landed on something fairly soft, while above him came the crash of a closing door and the rasp of a padlock-hasp.

Hagen staggered to his feet and his head came in violent contact with the roof, and he sat down again. After much painful effort he secured a match and inspected his position. He peered all around, felt of his empty holster, and cursed wickedly when the match burnt his finger.

"I'm in the oat-bin," he told himself, "an' I ain't got no gun. Tha's pe-culiar, but 's a fac'."

And Blondy Hagen settled down in the oats and went to sleep, while Spot Easton cursed savagely and wondered if Hagen had run foul of those two unmentionable cowboys.

———◦○◦———

He had told Jane Lee that he was going to the livery-stable to get the horse and buggy. Peeking into the restaurant window he saw that she was nervously waiting his return. He prided himself on the fact that he had made an impression on her already and he knew that—well, he owned Lonesome Lee, and the girl did not know any one in Lodge-Pole county.

Hagen had had time to make several trips to the stable by this time. Easton began to worry. Finally he decided to take a chance. He hurried back into the restaurant.

"Just run into a feller who talked business, and it delayed me," he explained. "I reckon you might as well come along with me as to stay here."

He picked up her valise and led the way out to the street.

"It's only a little ways," he assured her, as he switched the valise to his left hand and slid his gun loose. "She's a nice night."

A cowboy came out of a saloon, braced his legs wide apart, whooped loudly and emptied his gun in the air. The girl drew back in affright, but Easton laughed and assured her that the shots meant nothing.

"You're goin' to like this country after you get used to it, Jane."

"I—I suppose so," she faltered. "It is all so new to me, and the houses seem so small."

Easton said nothing. They walked up the sloping sidewalk to the door of the stable and stopped. There was not a sound from the interior, except horses munching hay.

Easton looked up and down the street. He could see the hitch-rack in front of the Ten-Spot, but was unable to distinguish the color of the horses.

"Hey!" he called. There was no response. "I suppose I'll have to harness my own horse," he said to the girl.

He placed the valise on the floor and walked slowly inside. The door of the grain room was partly open, and he peered in.

Came the dull *chuck!* of a muffled blow and Easton disappeared inside. The girl was watching him, and wondered how he had managed to get inside by dragging both feet.

From inside the room came a creaking noise and a crash, as if a bin-cover had been slammed down. Then the door opened and Hashknife and Sleepy stepped out.

"Howdy, ma'am," said Hashknife politely. "Are you Miss Lee?"

"Why, yes. I—I—where is Mr. Easton?"

"Easton? O-o-o-oh, yeah. He's in the oat-bin, ma'am."

"I do not understand you." The girl seemed puzzled.

"Harness the horse, Sleep," commanded Hashknife. "This lady's got to find a place to sleep."

Sleepy gleefully brought out the horse and backed it into the buggy-shafts. Jane Lee stared at the tall cowboy beside her, and wondered at the mystery of it all.

"You drive the rig, Sleep," ordered Hashknife. "I'll bring your bronc along with me."

"But," objected the girl, "I—I—Mr. Easton is going to take me to my father's ranch."

"Was," corrected Hashknife. "He's goin' to sleep with one of his hired men tonight, so we made him let us take you home."

Hashknife shoved the valise into the rear of the buggy and helped her into the seat. She started to protest, but Sleepy chirped to the tall, bay horse and they rolled hollowly out of the doorway and headed homeward.

As Hashknife crossed to the horses, the stable-man came from down the street and went into the stable. He had seen the top-buggy going up the street, and he surmised that its owner had returned.

As he turned to go toward the rear he heard a muffled voice calling. He listened closely and decided that it came from the grain-room. He sneaked in and lighted a match. Some one was hammering on the inside of the oat-bin. The stable-man was taking no chances. He went outside, got a lantern, which he hung over the top of the bin, took an old shot-gun from behind the door and flipped the fastener loose from the lid of the bin.

A moment later the lid lifted and Spot Easton, very much disheveled, stood up and blinked foolishly.

"Wh-whatcha doin' in my oats?" grunted the stable-man hoarsely.

"Aw! To Hell with you and your oats!" groaned Spot, as he crawled painfully over the edge and rubbed his sore head.

He looked back inside and motioned to the stable-man to look. Cautiously the man looked down at the sleeping form of Blondy Hagen.

"This," said the stable-man seriously, "this here is my-steer-i-us, by Heaven!"

"Where did they go?" asked Easton, rubbing his head, on which appeared to be a bump about the size and shape of an egg. "Did you see the lady?"

"Was there a lady?"

"You damn fool!" exploded Easton. "I brought a lady here with me; *sabe*? I came to get that horse and buggy I left here."

The stable-man stepped outside and glanced across at the empty stall.

"The horse and buggy is gone," he announced. "If you know where you left the lady, you might look and see if she's still there or not."

But Easton exploded a number of vile epithets and staggered away down the street. The stable-man went back, looked at Blondy Hagen, blew out the lantern and went outside and shoved the sliding-doors together.

"Too damn much hocus-pocus to suit me!" he grunted, and went home.

It was in the small hours of the morning when Mrs. Frosty Snow awoke from a troubled sleep—wherein she had fired Swede Sam in three languages—and sat up in bed. Frosty was on a cattle-buying trip, and Mrs. Snow was all alone in the ranch-house.

Some one was knocking urgently on the front door. She crawled out of bed, picked up a heavy Colt six-shooter, and padded her way to the front door.

"Who's there?" she asked.

"This is Hashknife Hartley, Mrs. Snow."

"Kinda early, ain't you?"

"Yes'm," admitted Hashknife, "it is early. Can I talk to you?"

"If you don't mind strainin' your voice through the door."

"I don't mind," Hashknife laughed softly. "But this has got to be confidential, Mrs. Snow. It's about a girl."

"Thasso?" Mrs. Snow's voice was a trifle sarcastic. "I ain't in the habit of bein' woke up at four o'clock to pass out advice to the love-lorn, Mr. Hartley."

"Listen, ma'am," begged Hashknife. "This ain't nothin' matrimonial—honest to gosh. You know Spot Easton?"

"By sight and smell," she replied. Spot Easton's perfumery was not at all popular with the range folk.

"He lied to a girl," stated Hashknife softly. "I done stole the girl from him, and I've gotta have somebody to take care of her for a while."

"Well, why didn't you say so?" demanded Mrs. Snow, opening the door about four inches. "Where is she? Tell me about her."

Hashknife swiftly recounted what he knew about the girl, and about the situation at the 88 ranch.

"Bring her in," ordered Mrs. Snow. "I'll sure take care of her and nobody's goin' to know where she is. Prob'ly end up in a killin', but that ain't my affair. Say you're livin' at the Tombstone ranch? Yeah, that danged Swede came b ack."

Hashknife went back to the dim outlines of a horse and buggy and returned in a moment with Jane Lee and Sleepy. After thirty miles in a top-buggy, with a companion who only talked in monosyllables, Jane Lee was more than willing to stay any place. She did not have the slightest idea of what it was all about. It was not like the reception she had expected. In fact, it was like a nightmare.

"Just edge to one side, while she comes in," ordered Mrs. Snow. "Frosty Snow's old woman is kind of in the rough at this time o' day."

Jane Lee walked in and Mrs. Snow closed the door to a few inches.

"Come agin, cowboys."

"Yes'm, y'betcha," laughed Hashknife, and the two men clumped down the steps and back to their horses and buggy, while Mrs. Snow put her arms around Jane Lee.

"Whatcha cryin' for?" demanded Mrs. Snow. "My gosh, you're all right, honey."

"I—I don't know what it is all about," sobbed Jane. "I don't know what became of Mr. Easton, and—"

"Don'tcha worry about that sidewinder," Mrs. Snow said soothingly. "You brace up and quit worryin'. Mebbe it was danged lucky them two punchers kidnaped you, honey."

"But why did they?" demanded Jane with some heat.

"Didn't you ask 'em?"

"Dozens of times. The one who drove the horse wouldn't tell me anything. He kept singing something about being buried on the lone prairie."

Mrs. Snow laughed and patted Jane on the shoulder.

"You brace up, honey. You're danged lucky to ride all the way from Gunsight with a mournful cowpuncher, if you only knowed it. You snap into a nightgown and pile into my bed, and I'll bet you'll feel better. We're common folks here at the Half-Moon, and, outside of havin' an imported cook, we don't put on much dog."

"I suppose," said Jane softly, "I should be thankful that I am here with you."

"Yes, and you don't know half of it, little lady."

Hashknife and Sleepy took the horse and buggy back to Caldwell, and tied the horse to the rack beside the livery-stable. No one saw them come, and no one saw them leave, except one or two dogs, which barked sleepily.

They rode back to the Tombstone ranch, and stabled their horses just as the first light of dawn showed over the eastern hills.

They stopped in the porch of the ranchhouse as the sound of galloping horses came to their ears, and saw two riders swing around the bend, riding swiftly toward Caldwell. One rider was a little in the rear, and in the dim light he seemed to be a trifle unsteady in his saddle.

"Somebody unlocked the oat-bin," laughed Hashknife softly, "and the bloodhounds are on the trail of a top-buggy."

"They're welcome to it," yawned Sleepy. "Hope I never have to ride that far in one again. I sung all the time to kinda keep things cheerful."

"My God!" gasped Hashknife. "The poor girl!"

Spot Easton rode all the way from Gunsight with a blind, unreasoning rage in his heart. It had taken him quite a while to arouse the other stable-man in order to hire a saddle-horse, and then he had gone back to the oat-bin and made Blondy Hagen ride with him.

He did not have the slightest idea which way the horse and buggy had gone, until he rode into Caldwell and found it hitched outside the livery-stable. Hagen was still too drunk and sleepy to care how Easton felt, and listened indifferently while Easton polluted the morning air with profanity.

"'F I stole a horsh 'n buggy, I'd git hung," stated Blondy knowingly.

"And that's no damn lie, either!" snapped Easton. "Come on."

Blondy followed him down to Jake Blue's office. Easton hammered on the door with the toe of his boot. In a few moments Jake's tousled head appeared and he demanded to know what in the adjective did anybody mean by waking him up in the middle of the night.

Rapidly, and with many oaths, Easton explained that Hashknife and Sleepy had stolen his horse and buggy at Gunsight.

"Thasso?" Blue shivered slightly. "Got any idea where they went with it?"

"Brought it here!" snapped Easton. "It's tied to the livery-stable hitch-rack."

"Then it ain't stole a-tall." Blue seemed relieved over this statement.

"They stole it from me!" yowled Easton. "I tell you they hit me on the head and threw me into a damned oat-bin!"

"Thasso," nodded Blondy seriously. "I know, because I was in there, too."

Blue started to laugh, but managed to choke it back. It was no place to laugh, and yet he howled inwardly at the thought of Easton and Hagen being thrown into an oat-bin.

"I want you to arrest the both of 'em on a charge of horse stealin'," demanded Easton angrily, "and if you think there's anything funny about it—go ahead and laugh."

Blue grew serious. He did not relish the idea of going out to arrest those two men on such a serious charge.

"Are you sure they was the ones?" he asked. "Can you git up in court and swear that they stole your horse and buggy?"

"I'm damned 'f I can," said Hagen. "All I knows—"

"Of course I can swear to it!" snapped Easton. "Do you think I'd get up there and admit that I didn't know who done it?"

"If I had a good deputy-sheriff—" Blue expressed his thoughts in words. "Take Hagen with you, Jake."

"Like Hell!" exploded Hagen. "No sir! I ain't—"

"Since when did you break away from us?" queried Spot meaningly.

"Oh, awright. I ain't breakin' away from nobody, Spot; but when you monkey with them two jaspers there's a hoo-doo on the job, I tell you. If you lemme try agin' with the long-range stuff—"

"And miss again," sneered Easton. "All the good that's done is to make old Skelton more careful."

"We ain't had much luck, tha's a fact," said Jake Blue sadly. "Mebbe we went at it all wrong."

"You can't expect a fortune to come along and roost in your lap, can you?" asked Easton sneeringly. "We'll get these two punchers into jail and then we'll settle with old man Skelton."

"If we'd only tried to buy the damn place at first," argued Blue.

"Well, we didn't!"

"It was your idea to make old Skelton sick of his place, so's he'd be willin' to sell cheap."

"Yeah? How did I know that he was going to hang on in spite of everything? I done the best I could."

"I reckon so, Spot. Doc Clevis tried to buy it agin' from Skelton and the old son-of-a-gun made him a price this time."

"How much, Jake?"

"Hundred thousand dollars."

"That," said Hagen seriously, "is more'n it's worth."

"Aw, Hell!" exploded Easton. "If you're tryin' to be funny, Hagen—"

"Well, ain't it?" wailed Hagen.

Easton turned back to Blue.

"You slam them two jaspers into jail right away," he said. "If you need more help I can send in some of the boys from the 88."

"All right," Blue said dubiously. "You go and sleep f'r an hour or so, Hagen. This ain't no blear-eyed job, y'betcha."

"Make it longer'n that if you feel like it," agreed Hagen. "Make it a week, and see if I git impatient."

Easton and Hagen went back up the street toward the War-Bonnet. It was too early for Caldwell to be awake, and Easton wondered what old Lonesome Lee was doing out so early in the morning.

The old man was standing in front of the Paris restaurant, and for the first time in months he seemed to be sober.

"what in Hell are you doing around so early?" questioned Easton as they came up to the old man.

"Just lookin' around, thassall," Lonesome Lee's voice was very husky, but there was no trace of drunkenness left.

"Lookin' around, eh? What for?"

"Just for instance." The old man was a trifle belligerent.

This attitude did not please Spot Easton. He much preferred to have the old man whining for liquor.

"What's biting you?" he snapped.

"Not a danged thing, Spot. I'm sober today, if you take notice, and I'm lookin' for a letter I lost."

"Letter?" echoed Easton. "What letter?"

"I was drunk," continued the old man, "but I wasn't so drunk that I didn't know about that letter. Somehow I remember you tellin' me about other letters, Spot— letters that you wrote. I've been a damn old drunken bum, but I'm sober right now and I want to know a few things."

"That must 'a' been the letter that the long cowboy had," said Blondy unthinkingly.

Easton shot Blondy a withering glance and turned back to Lonesome.

"I dunno what you're talking about, Lee."

"I remember the tall cowboy," muttered Lonesome. "He was a stranger. But you got the letter, Spot."

Spot Easton's hand went mechanically to his ear as he shook his head.

"No, I'm damned if I did! You ask Windy who got that letter. Come on and let's have a drink, Lonesome."

Lonesome shook his head slowly, licked his lips and walked away. Easton glared after him and turned to Hagen:

"Will you ever learn to keep your danged tongue out of my affairs? Ain't you got sense enough to let me do the talkin'? Now, that damn old fool will likely talk to everybody and—aw, Hell! I hope you and Jake Blue will get your men today. I don't want Lonesome Lee to talk to Hashknife. It may take a killin' to prevent it."

"You don't let me in on anythin'," complained Blondy bitterly. "You talk about letters and cattle-brands and the Tombstone ranch, and you never let me know the why of anythin'. All I'm good fer is to bush-whack, somebody."

"You get paid for it, don't you?" demanded Easton.

"Yeah, I get paid for it."

"Then keep your mouth shut, Hagen. The less you know the safer you are—*sabe*? It'll pay you to keep still."

It was about noon when Hashknife and Sleepy woke up. Bliz Skelton was cooking breakfast for them and, though evidently curious, he asked no questions of what happened the night before.

"I went up to Caldwell last night," he volunteered. "Ain't been up there at night for a dog's age, 'cause it wasn't noways safe for me to be on the road after dark."

"Any excitement?" yawned Hashknife, as he tugged at a tight boot.

"No-o-o," Skelton twisted his face away from the spattering bacon. "Doc Clevis offered to buy this ranch again. A few weeks ago he offered me eight thousand, but last night he made it nine. Got kinda ruffed 'cause I wouldn't take his offer."

"You've had other offers, ain't you?" asked Sleepy.

"Yeah. Spot Easton offered me seventy-five hundred."

"That don't noways include the stock, does it?" queried Hashknife.

"No. Just the ranch-house and what fenced ground goes with it. When Spot made that offer I reckon I had about seven hundred head of 33 cows on this range, but right now a 33 critter is as scarce as vi'lets in Jan'wary."

"Well, gee cripes!" exploded Hashknife, stamping his feet on the floor. "You mean to stand there and tell me that you let somebody run off all your stock?"

"Well, I—I didn't 'let' 'em, Hashknife. 'Pears that you don't have to let folks rustle your cows."

"Ain't you complained none?"

"Who'd I complain to?"

"That's a question," admitted Hashknife. "I reckon you'll just about have to sell out, Bliz."

"Damned if I will! No gosh danged bunch of—"

Bliz let loose of his skillet and grabbed his short shot-gun from its rack beside the door. Some one had ridden up to the porch, and now was coming up the steps to the door.

Bliz stepped back out of line with the door and motioned to Sleepy to open it. Some one knocked loudly. Sleepy grasped the knob and drew the door open, keeping himself behind it, while Jake Blue and Blondy Hagen stood there and blinked into the muzzle of Skelton's riot-gun and wished they had postponed their visit.

"Put d-down that gun," stuttered Blue, trying to force himself to be brave. "You—you—"

Blondy Hagen's hands went up above his head, and he squinted dismally. His heart was not in this job at all.

"Whatcha want here, Blue?" asked Skelton.

Jake Blue tore his eyes away from the menacing gun barrels and squinted at Hashknife and Sleepy.

"I want them two," he replied. "I've got warrants for their arrest for hors-estealin'."

He started to reach for his pocket, but changed his mind. Such a move might be suicide. Hashknife walked over to the door and looked at Blue.

"Who swore out that warrant, sheriff?"

"Spot Easton."

"Yeah?" Hashknife seemed greatly amused. "You go back and tell Spot Easton to come and get us, will you?"

"I'm the sheriff!" snapped Blue.

"That's sure a deplorable fact," agreed Hashknife, "and one of the main reasons why we refuse to get ourselves arrested. We'd have a sweet time ever gettin' out of jail, whether we were innocent or guilty."

"If you could prove—" began Blue, but Hashknife interrupted him.

"Prove it? Why, we'd have a fine chance. I suppose we'd have to stay in jail until the first term of court, eh?"

"Unless the judge would turn you loose."

"Judge Pelley'd jist about do that," grunted Skelton. "He knows about as much law as my old pinto horse, and he'd send his mother to jail for a quart of booze. Him and Spot Easton are thicker'n thieves."

"I've got to do m' duty," wailed Blue. "I ain't noways responsible for what Judge Pelley would do, am I? You're resistin' an officer of the law, if you only know it."

"Ain't nobody resisted you—yet," Hashknife reminded him softly, "but if you don't crawl to your horses and rattle your hocks out of here, I'll nail your pants to the floor and leave you there to starve."

"Come on," urged Hagen. "There's a difference in bein' brave and bein' a damn fool, Jake. I never knowed a two-barrel gun yet what wasn't easy on the trigger. Come on."

Hagen turned and went down the steps to his horse, flexing his tired arms as he went. Jake Blue swallowed his pride, along with a lump in his throat, and followed him down the steps.

"This ain't the last of it, y'betcha," he called back to the open doorway. "There's more'n one count agin' you now."

Skelton stepped out on the porch and pointed to where the road wound around the point of a hill.

"Speakin' of counts, Jake; there's just twenty goin' to be said by me. If you ain't around that corner—"

Twenty counts is a short time; but Jake Blue and Blondy Hagen beat it by four. It was an ignominious retreat, especially for Jake Blue, who had a reputation to sustain, but he was wise enough to go while the going was good.

Skelton turned to go into the door, but stopped and stared at the man who was standing at the corner of the house.

"Lonesome Lee!" he grunted. "Whatcha doin' there?"

"Waitin' for Jake Blue and Hagen to pull out," replied Lonesome, and came up to Skelton.

"How'd you come, Lonesome?"

"Walked. I side-tracked for Jake and Blondy."

"Well," Skelton scratched his head and looked up at Sleepy and Hashknife, who were standing in the doorway. "Well, this seems kinda queer t' me."

Lonesome looked up at Hashknife.

"I reckon you're the man I wanted to see. 'Member me havin' a letter the other day?"

Hashknife nodded.

"I—I kinda wanted to know what was in it," said Lonesome slowly. "I sobered up 'specially for—"

Came the whining *pluk!* of a bullet and Lonesome Lee jerked back a half-step, threw one hand to his face and buckled forward at the knees.

Hashknife dove forward, grasped the old man in his arms and fairly fell through the doorway with him. Another bullet bit into the door-casing, and Skelton and Sleepy dove in behind Hashknife. Another bullet *pinged* in through the door and ricocheted off the cook-stove before Skelton kicked the door shut.

Hashknife picked Lonesome Lee off the floor and laid him on the bed. The old man's face was a mass of gore and he was cursing wickedly, deliriously; fighting to get back to his feet.

"Like a chicken with its head cut plumb off!" gasped Sleepy.

"Lay still!" snapped Hashknife, dodging Lonesome's kicking legs. "That bullet knocked, but didn't come in."

"Creased?" queried Sleepy anxiously, as he grasped Lonesome by the legs.

Lonesome ceased kicking, but his flow of profanity was undiminished. Skelton brought the water-bucket and a towel and washed the blood off the old man's face. The bullet had cut a furrow from just above his right eye to a spot over his ear and, in the passing, it had flicked a notch in the top of the ear. The wound was superficial, but the shock was considerable.

He sat up and looked foolishly around, while Skelton mopped off the gore.

"Wh-what happened?" he croaked.

Hashknife examined the wound and turned quickly to Skelton.

"You patch him up, Bliz," he said. "He'll likely have a sore head, but that won't hurt him. Me and Sleepy are goin' to Caldwell."

Hashknife was half-way out of the door at the finish of his statement and heading for the stable. Sleepy gawped for a moment and trotted after him. They saddled swiftly and galloped out to the Caldwell road.

"Whatcha goin' to Caldwell for?" asked Sleepy, as they hit a level stretch and shook up their mounts.

"They'll arrest us sure as Hell, Hashknife."

"Thasso?"

Hashknife spat out a half-burned cigaret and pulled his hat lower over his eyes.

"I'm plumb tired of bein' shot at, Sleepy."

It was about three miles to Caldwell, and they covered the distance in record speed. At the War-Bonnet hitch-rack they dismounted and went into the big saloon. There was no sign of Jake Blue or Blondy Hagen.

Windy, the bartender, gaped at ths sight of them and upset some glasses on the back-bar with his elbows.

"Seen Jake Blue lately?" asked Hashknife.

"Nope."

"Where's Spot Easton?"

"Dunno."

Hashknife leaned on the bar and studied Windy closely.

"You don't know very much, do you?"

"If I did," said Windy slowly, "I wouldn't be a bartender. I didn't lie about not knowin' where Spot Easton is, but Jake Blue and Blondy Hagen went through here a short time ago, headin' for the 88."

"Goin' after help, eh?"

"Mm-m-m."

Hashknife considered this. It was going to be very awkward if the sheriff brought the gang from the 88 outfit to help him serve the warrants.

"How many punchers on the 88?" he asked.

"Seven, I reckon."

"That makes nine, countin' Blue and Hagen. Odd number, ain't it? Wish it was ten."

"For gosh sake, why?" grunted Windy.

"I hate to fight odd numbers," said Hashknife seriously. "Kinda hoodoos me."

"Tryin' to kid me?" asked Windy.

"If you think so, come with 'em. Didja hear about Lonesome Lee gettin' killed?"

"Lonesome Lee! Whatcha mean?"

"Somebody shot him on Skelton's porch a while ago."

"Kill him dead?"

"Didja ever know a feller to get hit with a .30-30 and fail to grab a harp?"

"Whatcha know?" grunted Windy. "Who'd kill him?"

"Come on, Sleepy."

Hashknife strode back to the door and headed for their horses. They rode swiftly back toward the Tombstone ranch, with Sleepy demanding to know what in Hell they ever made the trip to Caldwell for, and what good it was going to do?

"Elimination and instruction, Sleepy," replied Hashknife, as they dismounted at the Tombstone corral.

"I had an idea that Hagen and Blue might 'a' stopped and took a shot at Lonesome Lee; but they wouldn't 'a' had time to circle back and still go through Caldwell much ahead of us. I was also kinda anxious to find out how many men Blue was goin' to bring back with him."

"Hell of a lot of good that'll do us," complained Sleepy, "except to know that we died fightin'. I'm sure ready and willin' to pull out of Lodge-Pole county."

They found Lonesome and Skelton discussing cattle over their pipes. Lonesome was not much the worse for his wound. Skelton had used up every available rag on the ranch to check the bleeding, and Lonesome's head looked like a turban.

"What kind of a bunch are workin' on the 88?" asked Hashknife abruptly.

"What kind?" Lonesome cogitated deeply.

"Not much good, I reckon. None of my old gang are there."

"Easton fired 'em, eh?"

Lonesome nodded slowly and wearily.

"I reckon so. He got a bunch from Arizona. I dunno anythin' wrong about any of 'em, but I know I wouldn't want that kind of punchers working for me. A feller by the name of Dell Blackwood is his foreman and he—"

"That's a plenty," interrupted Hashknife. "I know that horse-thief. Me and him worked on the Hashknife outfit and I know him from the belt both ways. Betcha he's got 'Holy Moses' Herman workin' for him."

"There is a Herman," nodded Lonesome. "Short feller, with a big nose."

"That's him!" exclaimed Hashknife. "Ought to 'a' been hung fifteen years before he got old enough to wear long pants. Say, how much of the 88 does Easton own?"

"I dunno. He kinda took charge, and—and—"

"You mean he's kept you drunk for a year or two and jist kinda nudged you out of everythin'. Shot your nerve all to Hell with hooch, and hoodled you out of every thing you own."

Lonesome stared down at the floor, but said nothing.

"Has he got a bill of sale from you?"

"I don't know," admitted Lonesome. "If he did, he got it from me when I was drunk."

"And he could 'a' got it from you any old time durin' the last year or so," declared Hashknife, "'cause you ain't been sober in all that time."

"What business is it of yours?" demanded Lonesome angrily. "It's my ranch?"

"What about Jane Lee?"

Lonesome jerked upright and stared open-mouthed at Hashknife.

"Jane?" he croaked. "What—who—"

Lonesome Lee spluttered over his own words, his hand trembled wildly as he tried to grasp Hashknife.

"Set down!" snapped Hashknife. "She ain't far from here, but I'm danged 'f she's goin' to see you in the shape you are now, old timer. She thinks you're a dandy old dad, instead of a broken old wreck. She thinks you own the 88. You're a Hell of a nice specimen for a young lady to pick out for a dad, ain'tcha?"

Lonesome bowed his sore old head on his hands and wept, while he swore feelingly at himself.

"You ought t' have a gizzard," said Hashknife, "and then you could eat with the chickens."

"I betcha," sobbed Lonesome. "I got it all comin' to me, young feller. Don't talk soft on my account."

"All right," grinned Hashknife. "I'll try and say somethin' mean to yuh. Can't remember givin' Easton a bill of sale, eh?"

"No."

Sleepy got up, and going over to a rear window, peered out, then drew back quickly.

"Here they come!" he said softly. "The whole damn works!"

Hashknife looked around quickly.

"Got a cellar, Skelton?"

"Damn right I have!"

Skelton hopped across the floor and lifted his table away from a trap-door. This he raised.

"Git down in there, Lonesome," ordered Hashknife, "and don't make a noise; *sabe*? Don't ask questions!"

Lonesome went down the short ladder, and the trap was closed and covered with the table, just as a crowd of men, led by Jake Blue, rode up to the front door.

Hashknife and Sleepy had closed the door as they came in, and now Skelton slipped the bar into place and picked up his shotgun.

"Come on," whispered Hashknife. "We'll go out the back window, Sleepy. Don't make any resistance, Skelton. Put down the shotgun and act natural."

He and Sleepy slid out the back window, and shut it behind them, just as some one knocked loudly on the front door.

They went cautiously around the house, walking sidewise, with their backs against the wall.

"'Bout a dozen of 'em," warned Sleepy, but Hashknife gave his warning no heed.

They could hear Jake Blue questioning Skelton, and the murmur of other voices.

"Where's the dead man?" It was Doc Clevis' voice.

"I dunno what you're talkin' about," replied Skelton.

Hashknife peered around the corner and stepped out, with Sleepy beside him. Jake Blue and Doc Clevis were on the porch arguing through the open door with Skelton, while the rest of the men were still mounted. The nearest man to them was a grim-faced person, with a heavy red mustache. Just beyond him was a heavy-set cowboy, with an enormous nose.

"Horse-thieves from the Hashknife!" snorted Hashknife loudly.

Every one turned quickly, and just as quickly they realized their disadvantage. Hashknife was standing with his legs far apart, his right hand resting on his hip just over the top of his holstered gun, while Sleepy stood with one elbow braced against the house and his hand swaying over the butt of his Colt.

"Don't move, Blue," cautioned Hashknife. "You and Doc just hold that pose or the picture is spoiled."

Hashknife did not seem to look at them as he spoke, but watched the two mounted men nearest him.

"Blackwood and Holy Moses," grinned Hashknife.

Blackwood moistened his lips.

"You!" he grunted with a great effort. "I didn't know it was you."

"Danged right you didn't," agreed Hashknife. "If you did, you and that elephantnosed horse-thief over there would 'a' fogged for Canada."

"Thasso?" retorted the big-nosed cowboy, and cleared his throat with great difficulty.

Hashknife appeared to size up the rest of the crowd.

"I dunno the rest of you, gentlemen, but you're in danged bad comp'ny."

"You two are under arrest," declared Blue loudly, "and we want Lonesome Lee's body."

"You don't need to watch these two," stated Skelton from the doorway, indicating Blue and the doctor. Skelton had them covered with his double-barreled shot-gun.

"You're under arrest, too!" wailed Blue nervously. "Better submit quietly if you know what's good fer you."

The big-nosed cowboy must have thought that the Sheriff's discourse had drawn Hashknife's attention, because he whirled quickly in his saddle.

Hashknife's right hand flicked down and up, and Blackwood flung himself forward to be out of line with the bullet that hissed past him and thudded into the big-nosed one. The latter's pistol discharged and broke a window. He jerked back, swayed sidewise and fell out of his saddle, while his horse whirled, kicked at the falling man, and trotted toward the gate.

"Oh, the damn fool!" complained Blackwood bitterly. "If he didn't know Hashknife Hartley—Gawd!"

The shooting had unnerved Blackwood.

"You seen how it was done, didn't you Blue?" asked Hashknife softly. "He went for his gun."

"By Hell!" swore Blue savagely. "Can't ten of us take two men?"

"Hop to it," said Hashknife. "Ain't no reason why you can't try it."

"Count me out," said Blackwood quickly. "I sure as Hell ain't lost neither of 'em."

He turned his horse and rode straight toward the gate and the rest of the horsemen followed him.

"Come back here and get Holy Smoke!" snapped Hashknife.

Blackwood and two of the men dismounted, and one of them put the wounded man on his saddle and rode away with him.

Blue chewed savagely on his tobacco and stared at Doc Clevis, who seemed indifferent to it all.

"Arrestin' folks ain't in my line," stated Doc, as if in self-defense. "I'm here to take charge of the body of Lonesome Lee."

"What's your line, Blue?" asked Hashknife, and the Lodge-Pole sheriff swore feelingly.

"If cussin' showed ability, you'd be Secretary of War," said Hashknife. "What's all this about Lonesome Lee bein' dead?"

"We-well!" snorted Doc Clevis wonderingly.

"He's in there," said Blue pointing into the house. "By Hell, I'm goin' t' find out about things."

He brushed past Skelton, who stepped aside at a nod from Hashknife, and they all went inside. Blue and the doctor looked around. The blood-stained blanket on the bed caught Blue's eye, and he pounced on it quickly.

"Whose blood is that?" he asked triumphantly.

"You can have it, if you want it," said Hashknife.

"What'sa idea of hidin' the body?" demanded the doctor.

"Looks mights queer t' me," swore Blue meaningly. "Man gets shot and his body hid. You fellers think you can do things like that? Huh!"

"Mebbe he's already buried," suggested Hashknife. "Mebbe we dug a hole and buried him."

Blue snorted in disgust and turned toward the door, as if to go outside, but whirled like a flash, gun in hand. Skelton, who was a trifle to one side, idly swinging the shot-gun in one hand, had seen Blue's move toward his gun, and as Blue whirled, Skelton threw the heavy riot-gun straight at his head.

It was over in a second. The breech of the shot-gun crashed into Blue's face, knocking him off his feet and tossing his pistol toward the ceiling, while the shotgun slammed into the wall and sent a handful of buckshot into the floor.

"Kerzowie!" whooped Hashknife.

Doc Clevis helped Blue to his feet and led him outside to his horse. Blue did not seem to have the slightest idea of what had happened to him, although his nose had shifted from its original mooring, giving him a peculiar lopsided, cock-eyed appearance. His right eye was also beginning to draw a dark mantle across his vision, but in spite of it all, Blue whistled through his teeth and obeyed Doc Clevis to the letter.

As they rode away Bliz Skelton shook his head and looked at Hashknife.

"It's all right so far, but this is the finish, I reckon. I don't like Blue and his gang, but they stand for the law. Everybody around here hates me, and it ain't goin' to stretch your imagination to see that Blue will have the whole country behind him. If I was you fellers I'd saddle up and pull m' freight, *muy pronto*."

"Not yet, Bliz. Shucks," Hashknife looked solemnly at several heifers, which had drifted up past the barn and were grazing among the tombstones. "I've got business to attend to, don'tcha know it. There's—"

Hashknife stopped and squinted at a spotted yearling, which had turned broadside to him, about fifty feet away.

"You brand on the right hip, Bliz?"

"Uh-huh."

Hashknife stepped inside the house and took a coiled rope from a peg in the wall. Quickly fashioning a hondo and running out a loop, he roped the yearling, which bucked and bawled, kicking over a number of tombstones in its gyrations, while Sleepy and Hashknife dug their heels into the hard ground and held it firm.

"Mebbe I'm wrong," panted Hashknife, "but I wish you'd take a squint at that brand, Bliz."

Skelton approached the half-choked calf and squinted at the 88 on its hip.

"Nothin' but an 88 calf," he replied.

"Look closer," urged Hashknife. "See if the front halves of the 88 ain't newer burn than the other."

"By Hell, it is!" exploded Skelton foolishly. "Whatcha know about that? Who in Hell done that?"

"Come on and let's put the critter into the corral," ordered Hashknife.

They led it into a gate and removed the rope while the rest of the calves scattered out through the main gate and into the hills.

"That's where your calves have gone to," said Hashknife seriously. "It's a cinch to use a runnin'-iron and make 88 out of 33. Some danged cow-men ain't got sense enough to make their brand fool-proof. How long has that outfit been knowed as the 88?"

Skelton masticated rapidly for a moment.

"Since Easton's been in control, I betcha. I've hear the place spoke of as the old Cross-L outfit. That was likely Lonesome Lee's brand. We'll ask him."

Lonesome Lee came painfully and cautiously out of his hiding-place and considered Skelton's question.

"Easton bought that brand from a feller over near Ross Mountains. He drove in a hundred head of feeders which was wearin' the 88, and he—aw, I'm danged if I know what he wanted to do it for, but he rebranded all of the Cross-L stock, and cancelled my registry."

"And the 88 brand made it a cinch to steal all of Skelton's stock," said Hashknife. "All they had to do was to burn on the other half of the 88."

He took a pencil and illustrated it to Lonesome.

"I—I didn't have nothin' to do with that," wailed Lonesome. "My God, I ain't no thief!"

"No, I don't reckon you are, Lonesome."

"I'll make it all up, Skelton," blurted Lonesome. "I sure will. I'll give him half of my own stock."

"Have you got any stock?" asked Hashknife.

Lonesome stared at the three men and turned away.

"I dunno," he said dully. "I ain't got no idea how I stand. Mebbe I've got a thousand head of cows, and if I have, I'd give 'em all for just one drink of liquor."

Skelton dug under his bunk and drew out a jug and handed it to Lonesome.

"I reckon you need a shot, Lonesome. If you're goin' to do a good job of quittin', you've got to—what'sa matter?"

Lonesome turned and walked wearily to the door.

"I ain't drinkin' nothin', Skelton—not today. I've had my share."

Skelton shook his head wonderingly and replaced the jug, while Hashknife went to Lonesome and put his hand on the old man's shoulder.

"Everybody in Caldwell thinks you're dead, Lonesome. Mind keepin' out of sight for a while, and let 'em go on thinkin' that?"

"What's the idea?"

"It's like this," Hashknife wrinkled his nose away from the smoke of his cigaret. "In an honest court we could make Easton and his gang hard to catch, for rustlin', but under the present conditions it's only an excuse to kill somebody. If you can keep out of sight I'm bettin' my hunch that we can wallop that gang. I ain't no Sherlock Holmes, but I sure as Hell have an idea.

"If you got an effect, you sure must 'a' had a cause. Know what I mean?"

Hashknife pointed at the tombstones.

"There's an effect, Lonesome."

Lonesome nodded as if only half-understanding and looked at Hashknife.

"Where's my daughter?"

"Never mind her, Lonesome. What you don't know won't hurt you, and dead men tell no tales. You're supposed to be dead, you know."

"All right. I ain't goin' to worry about her; but there's a danged lot of things I don't understand."

"We're all thataway, old-timer," said Hashknife.

———◇———

Nothing further happened that day at the Tombstone ranch. Everyone kept under cover for fear of another shot from the hills. Lonesome Lee asked no more questions. He seemed to be willing to let Hashknife engineer the whole thing.

It was about eleven o'clock the next morning when Mrs. Frosty Snow drove through the big gate and uprooted several of the tombstones in her mad haste.

Hashknife met her at the door, and she fairly exploded in her eagerness to tell the latest news.

"You fellers better hit the hills!" she panted. "You're accused of kidnapin' Lonesome Lee's daughter and killin' the old man, 'cause he tried to make you give her up!"

"Whatcha know about that?" Hashknife asked with a grunt.

"Shall I bring that girl up here?" asked Mrs. Snow. "It won't take me—"

"No," Hashknife shook his head. "Leave her stay where she is, Mrs. Snow. I kinda reckoned that somethin' like this was due to happen, but it sort of makes me work faster. How soon do you reckon they'll show up here?"

"Pretty soon. Jake Blue is organizin' the whole thing, and he says he ain't takin' no chances on you gettin' away. Goin' to surround the place."

"Jake's got a lotta good ideas," said Hashknife. "If he only turned his mind to honest endeavors he'd do well and last longer."

"Well," said Mrs. Snow dubiously, as she brushed the tumbled hair from her forehead and took a deep breath, "well, I've done my darndest. If you won't run—don't mind me. Maybe you don't realize what they mean to do to you."

"Ma'am, I sure thank you a lot. If you want to bring that girl up here in about an hour, it might be kinda opportune."

"I'll bring her."

Mrs. Snow went back to her team and climbed up on the wagon-seat.

"You fellers hang onto your necks until I get back."

As she whirled her team around and drove swiftly back down the road, Hashknife turned and grinned at Sleepy and Skelton.

"Whatcha goin' to do?" blurted Skelton. "Produce the old man and the girl?"

"They're comin' in a bunch this time," observed Sleepy, "and we can't out-smart the whole danged country."

Hashknife squinted out at the tombstones and turned quickly to Skelton.

"You got any wire, Skelton?"

"Wire? Yeah, I got a big spool of small wire—smaller than bailin'-wire, if that's what you mean."

"That's the stuff, Skelton. Sleepy, you find a pick and shovel."

When the desired articles were produced, Hashknife dug four small holes; spading up the top soil on each for a space of about three feet square. He got four stakes, which he drove into the ground, and fastened a wire to each; piling the dirt to cover the stakes.

These spaded places were in a semi-circle in front of the porch, and about ten feet apart. Hashknife worked swiftly, whistling unmusically between his teeth, while Skelton and Sleepy watched him curiously. When the work was all finished, Hashknife took the wires back into the house and fastened them to a chair.

"Looney as a shepherd!" exploded Sleepy. "Can you beat that? Whatcha think you are—a medicine man?"

"Now, come on—fast!" grunted Hashknife. "Skelton, you stay here with Lonesome, and we'll try and be back ahead of the procession."

He turned and raced for the corral, still carrying the pick and shovel, while Sleepy, protesting at the top of his voice, followed. Swiftly they saddled. Hashknife mounted, holding the pick and shovel across the fork of his saddle in front of him.

"Headin' for the graveyard, Sleepy!" he yelped.

"Y'betcha," grunted Sleepy meaningly as he spurred after him.

Skelton stared open-mouthed as they galloped past the house and headed toward town. It was beyond him. He studied the four wires, shook his head, and going inside he squirted some oil into the old riot-gun. That done he sat down to wait.

At the entrance to the obliterated graveyard Hashknife drew up and vaulted off his horse.

"Go to the point above that first curve, Sleepy," he ordered. "Glue your eye to the road, and when you see 'em comin'—yell like Hell and come runnin'."

"Aw-w-w!" protested Sleepy disgustedly, but Hashknife, with a shovel in one hand and the pick in the other, was already through the wire fence and running toward the creek.

Sleepy yanked his horse around and rode swiftly away. Hashknife's actions left little doubt in Sleepy Stevens' mind but that he was crazy. Still, Hashknife had never failed in an emergency—yet.

Hashknife stopped near the bank of the little creek and studied the ground. The graveyard had been most thoroughly obliterated, but luckily the destroyers had only harrowed the ground where the graves had been. Hashknife was able to find the spot where the gambler, "Faro," had been buried. Barney Stout had said that Faro was buried between the other graves and the creek.

Hashknife took off his coat and began digging. It was hot work, hard work. The ground was rocky and progress was slow, and Hashknife had a horror of digging into a grave. The old pick was dull and the spring was missing in the shovel. A rocky reef impeded his progress and he was forced to dig around it.

Suddenly he dropped to his knees and began an examination which made his eyes sparkle. Every few moments his head would pop up like a prairie-dog, listening for Sleepy's yell of warning.

Then it came—the long-drawn "Yee-hoo-o-o!" cowboy yell, and he saw Sleepy riding swiftly down the side of the hill toward the road.

Hashknife sprang to his feet and ran toward the fence, drawing on his coat as he ran. He was in his saddle when Sleepy galloped up.

"Everybody in the county comin'!" panted Sleepy. "And they're sure comin' in a hurry."

"Quite an honor," laughed Hashknife, as they spurred down the road. "First time we ever had 'em all callin' on us, cowboy."

"If you can see a joke in it, God knows I can't," grumbled Sleepy. "A big audience ain't goin' to bring no joy to my soul when I'm standin' on nothin', and lookin' up a rope."

They stabled their horses and raced for the house. Skelton met them with an unspoken question, but Hashknife only laughed and shut the door softly on the four wires.

"Lemme do the talkin'," he said, "and don't start no gun-play until I bust loose."

"Here they come!" exclaimed Sleepy, peering out of a rear window. "By cripes! They're surroundin' the place this time!"

"Wish 'em joy, Sleepy," chuckled Hashknife, licking the edge of a fresh cigaret.

"Skelton, you keep that danged riot-gun under control, will you. There's a lot of decent folks in that mob, and that thing scatters."

Beyond a doubt this time Jake Blue was prepared to make good. He had at least fifty men in his posse, fifty hard-bitten cattlemen, who were determined to help him uphold the law. Easton's tale of the kidnaping had been substantiated by the stable-man, at Gunsight.

The reported murder of Lonesome Lee did not stir them up, as did the kidnaping, but showed a clear incentive for the murder. Spot Easton had felt perfectly safe in elaborating his story considerably. He had spoken at length on the graveyard question, which was still warm in the minds of those who had friends or relatives buried there, and it appeared that Skelton was in danger of sharing punishment with Hashknife and Sleepy.

In fact, Easton and Blue had dwelt long upon the graveyard question, and there were some in the posse in whose minds this was of more interest than kidnaping and murder. Considerable liquor had also added to the general ill-feeling.

The Tombstone ranch-house door was closed, and there was no sign of life about the place. Blue detailed twelve men to circle the place and stop any chance of escape, while the rest of them, confident in their might, rode straight to the porch. Nearly every man held a rifle in his hands, ready for action, while Jake Blue swung onto the porch and approached the door.

Doc Clevis, Spot Easton and Blondy Hagen were in the main body of the mob, as were also Dell Blackwood and two of the boys from the 88. Blackwood's horse was at the extreme outer edge of the crowd, and Blackwood's eyes shifted around as he considered the safest way out. He knew Hashknife Hartley.

"Inside there!" yelled Blue, knocking on the door with the barrel of his rifle.

"Well, if it ain't Mr. Blue!" exclaimed Hashknife's voice. "Ain'tcha never goin' to have any sense, sheriff?"

"What do you mean?" roared Blue nervously. He did not trust Hashknife.

"Look at them four wires which runs across the porch, will you?"

Blue glanced down at the small copper wires and his eyes traveled their length. The rest of the crowd took them into consideration. A horse was standing with both front feet on one of the mounds, and its rider yanked back on the reins, half-swinging the horse around.

"We was expectin' you," stated Hashknife, "and we got all set. Now, everybody hold quiet or my pardner will slam on the battery. You came down here to kill us and, if we've got to pass out, we'll take a lot of company."

He opened the door and came out on the porch. The assembled company relaxed. They felt they were sitting over a volcano; and men do not argue in a case of that kind.

Jake Blue backed away from Hashknife, masticating rapidly, and his eyes flashed from the wires to the interior of the house, as if trying to see if it was only a bluff.

"Well," said Hashknife grimly, "we're all together, it seems."

"Do you think you can git away with this?"

Blue's voice was thin as a high violin note. Some one in the crowd laughed. Blue's nose resembled a beet, and one eye was almost swollen shut.

"I kinda thought I would," said Hashknife as he looked around at the crowd.

"Well, well! There's Mister Easton and Mister Hagen. And there's my old friend, Doc Clevis. I was afraid they'd disappoint me. If there ain't Dell Blackwood! My, my! The devil must be gittin' a laugh out of this."

Those indicated shifted nervously. They had no idea of what was to come next, but they were afraid to force the issue. Hashknife singled out a respectable-looking cowman and spoke directly to him:

"Pardner, you look honest to me. Talk a little, will you?"

"Sure will."

The man cleared his throat.

"Mebbe you can explain this here kidnapin' and murder charge. Lonesome Lee's daughter was stolen and old Lonesome was murdered. Anyway, that's how she's been told to me."

"You're damn right!" snapped Blue.

Hashknife looked at Blue, steadily and closely. Blue shifted nervously. He liked to be the center of interest, but not at a time like this.

Hashknife backed against the wall near the door, where he could include Jake Blue in his sweep of the crowd.

"Folks, this is kind of a long tale I'm goin' to tell you, and I ask you to set tight. One crooked move and my pardner, who is just inside the door, will jam down the little handle and we'll migrate together."

"We're listenin'," said one of the men.

"Why listen to him!" exploded Easton angrily. "We didn't come down here to listen to a lot of damn lies, did we?"

"Stuff your fingers in your ears then!" retorted the cowboy who had pulled his horse off the spaded spot. "I sure as Hell am willin' to listen. I know dinnymite, y'betcha."

"'Pears to me that the whole thing started over the graveyard," observed Hashknife slowly. "Somebody played a joke on Skelton, and he returned the compliment."

One of the men swore feelingly, and a growl came from several more. They agreed on this point, at least.

"It was a Hell of a joke," continued Hashknife, "but was it a joke?"

"Whatcha mean?" snapped Blue.

"Mebbe I'll tell you." Hashknife was quite at his ease. "Old Lonesome Lee owned the Cross-L outfit—and a big thirst—a very big thirst. Bein' drunk most of the time made it plumb easy for another man to hoodle him out of the brand, which was changed to the 88—for a reason."

"That's a damn lie!" snorted Easton. "Everybody knows that I—"

"About that time," interrupted Hashknife, "this old 33 outfit begins to dwindle. Their cows don't bring in no calves. Everybody hates Skelton, and he knows damn well that nobody is goin' to help him find out where they went to. Somebody tries to buy him out. I reckon there was quite a few tryin' to buy him out. About that time he gets shot at a few times. 'Pears to me that it's a damn bad shot, or shootin' to scare him."

"Now, wait a minute!" interposed Blue. "If Skelton was losin' cows and gettin' shot at, why didn't he come to me about it?"

"You?" Hashknife squinted at Blue and shook his head. "Mebbe you was busy at that time, sheriff."

The inference was plain, and it drew a mild laugh. The crowd was interested in Hashknife's story, and did not relish an interruption.

"Lonesome Lee has a daughter," said Hashknife. "She's a danged nice-lookin' girl, too. Lonesome was too drunk to *sabe* things much, and this girl writes him letters, which somebody else reads—and answers. There was a photygraph, too, I reckon. Pretty girls ain't any too plentiful.

"Then somebody killed Quinin Quinn, and a poor, drunken Swede cook was jailed for it."

"Yes, and if them guns hadn't been stolen—" wailed Blue meaningly.

"Outside of that you feel good, don'tcha?" asked Hashknife seriously. "I dunno who killed Quinn, but I've sure got a hunch. Anyway, this girl was sent for and came to Gunsight, where she kinda dropped out of sight, leavin' a certain party very peevish."

Hashknife glanced at Easton, who was sitting very straight in his saddle.

"Then Lonesome Lee sobered up," Hashknife continued, "and realized what a damned fool he had been. He comes down here to find out a few things, and somebody pot-shoots him at long range."

"That's your story," interrupted Doc Clevis. "You never let us see the body, so how do we know how he got killed?"

"The man that shot him didn't want him to find out anythin'." Hashknife ignored Doc's peevish statement.

"What'sa idea?" queried one of the cattlemen. "Who didn't want him to?"

"I'm leadin' up to that, pardner. The man who shot him was the man who was interested in this girl. He knew that Lonesome Lee was sober. He was the same man who bought the 88 outfit and changed Lonesome Lee's brand to the 88. Didja ever figure that a 33 is easy to change to an 88 with a runnin' iron?"

"You're a damn liar!" yelped Easton trying to draw his gun. But the man next to him, fearful of the buried dynamite, stopped him.

"Now," Hashknife swayed away from the wall and hooked a thumb over the top of his belt above his holster, "now, I'll tell you where it all started. Hold still, Blue! You're as close to your gun as you'll ever get. Listen, you damn coyotes are to blame for this Lodge-Pole trouble!

"Skelton did not wipe out your graveyard. He had nothin' to do with it. Accusin' him of that was a damn good scheme to git rid of him. It's a wonder that folks didn't lynch him for it. It was a good joke to plant them tombstones in his front-yard. Sure it was. It gave a damn good reason for him to go out and wipe out the graveyard and to stop any more buryin' there."

Hashknife stopped for a moment. Jake Blue had gone gray as ashes, but his eyes flashed wickedly. Doc Clevis hunched in his saddle, his face set in lines of wonderment and fear.

"Skelton told me he didn't do it," continued Hashknife softly, "and I believed him. I knew that somebody wanted to force him away from this country. Them white tombstones"—Hashknife pointed at the yard—"were only an effect.

"The last man to be buried in that graveyard up the road was Faro, a gambler. Jake Blue, Doc Clevis and Spot Easton buried him, 'cause the other folks didn't want him buried there.

"They dug his grave near the little creek. Right after that burial this graveyard joke was pulled off. Do you know why?"

Hashknife leaned closer to the crowd and his eyes flashed wickedly.

"No? You don't? Well, I do! Two feet deep, where that gambler was buried, is the cropping of a ledge of quartz that is so danged rich in gold that it scared me. Jake Blue, Easton and Doc Clevis moved your graveyard for fear they might never own that gold. They killed Quinin Quinn, either because he knew too much, or to try and scare Skelton into sellin' 'em the ranch!"

As Hashknife was finishing Skelton and Sleepy stepped out onto the porch beside him. Behind them came Lonesome Lee.

For a moment there was absolute silence, broken only by the slap of Jake Blue's palm against the butt of his gun.

—◦◦◦—

But, swiftly as he drew, Hashknife shaded him by a second and fired from his hip. Blue spun off the porch, splintering one of the porch-posts with his misdirected bullet.

Spot Easton had thrown himself sidewise and fired across his horse's neck, but his horse threw its head wildly, and the bullet buzzed through the door-way—doing no damage. A second later one of the cowboys crashed his horse into Easton's mount, knocking Easton from his saddle.

Doc Clevis, insane from the disclosures, and knowing what it would mean, drew a heavy pistol from under his coat and spurred straight at the porch, only to meet Skelton's riot-gun at close range. He was literally blown out of his saddle.

From the ground, among the milling horses, Spot Easton shot wildly at Sleepy, who was churning up the dirt around Easton's head with bullets. Hagen fired once, and his bullet ripped along Hashknife's forearm just as Hashknife shot. The jar of the bullet threw Hashknife's gun far enough aside to miss Hagen but caught his horse, which whirled wildly, unseating its rider. Hagen's foot hung in the stirrup.

Bucking and kicking, the bronco whirled into the tangle of tombstones where Hagen fell free. Easton's gun was empty and he tried to fight his way out of the milling horses, but Sleepy dove after him and, locked together, they rolled into the open.

Dell Blackwood forced his horse to the porch and held up his hands.

"I'm out of it," he yelled. "I'm admittin' that I stole some 33 calves for Easton, but I never shot nobody."

He tossed his reins to the ground and slid out of his saddle.

Came the rattle of a wagon, and Mrs. Frosty Snow and Jane drove into the yard. Two cowboys helped Sleepy rope Spot Easton, and then all eyes turned to the two women in the wagon.

"Lonesome Lee, here's yore daughter!" called Mrs. Snow.

Lonesome went slowly out to the wagon to meet Jane and held up his arms to her. The crowd watched them silently.

"I been waitin' for you, Jane," said Lonesome slowly as she climbed down over the wheel.

He held her in his arms for a moment and turned to the crowd.

"Hashknife, I want you to meet my daughter; you and Sleepy Stevens."

"Why, I know them!" exclaimed Jane. "They —"

"Know us?" grinned Sleepy. "My God, I sung all night to her once."

A grizzled cowman leaned over the shoulder of his horse and said to Hashknife—

"You can prove all the things you said?"

"Yeah," nodded Hashknife. "I sure can."

"What about him?"

The man pointed at Blackwood, who stood beside the porch, guarded by another cowboy.

"Him?" Hashknife squinted at Blackwood seriously. "Pardner, I—I dunno. He kept out of this. He admits that he mis-branded calves for Easton, and we could likely send him—" Hashknife shook his head slowly. "Lookin' at it from a cold-blooded angle, suppose we give him his horse and tell him to git to Hell out of here."

"But he's a rustler!" exclaimed another cowman.

"That's a fact," nodded Hashknife. "That sure is a fact. He admits it, don't he?"

Hashknife looked around at his listeners.

"How many of us would admit the truth?"

Somewhere in the crowd a man laughed and smiles began to appear. Hashknife had won his point. He turned to Blackwood, who could scarcely believe his ears.

"Blackwood, you're free to drift. I ain't preachin' to you, but kinda remember what might 'a' happened."

"You mean—" Blackwood licked his dry lips. "You mean, I'm free to—go?"

"You've got good ears, old-timer."

Blackwood swung into his saddle, looked at Hashknife for several moments as though wanting to say something, but was unable to begin. Then as he turned slowly and rode out of the yard, unbelieving that any man or men could be so generous.

The cattlemen roped Easton to a horse, picked up Doc Clevis and Jake Blue, and strung out in a long cavalcade toward town.

"What happened here?" asked Jane wonderingly.

"Well, ma'am," said Hashknife slowly, looking back at the tumbled tombstones, "you see, a front-yard ain't no place for a cemetery, so we held a meetin' today to start a new one some'ers else."

"And that ain't such a big lie, at that," said Mrs. Frosty Snow slowly. Then to Lonesome and Jane, she said:

"Pile in here and go back to the ranch for supper with me. I hope that danged Swede cook don't take the things to heart that I told him today, 'cause I need him for one more meal. You fellers better come along, too, 'cause I want you to tell me all about it."

"Please do," Jane pleaded. "Perhaps Mr. Stevens will sing for us."

Mrs. Frosty Snow turned the team around and headed for the gate, while Hashknife, Sleepy and Skelton stood together and watched them disappear around the bend. Hashknife went over to the porch and kicked loose the pegs and broken wires.

"Do we go over to Snow's to supper?" asked Sleepy.

"Uh-huh," grunted Hashknife. "I'd like to get used to Jane Lee, 'cause she's sure as Hell got a wide streak of humor in her system. You goin', Skelton?"

"After what you've done for me? My God, I'd even do a little singin' m'self, Hashknife."

"Thassall right," said Hashknife hastily as he wound a handkerchief around his scored forearm, where Hagen's bullet had left its mark.

"Your appreciation is accepted—but don't sing. There's such a thing as carryin' humor to excess, Skelton."

Skelton grinned widely and put his hand on Hashknife's shoulder.

"Cowboy, you shore made history in Lodge-Pole County today, and jist t' show you how much I appreciates it, I'm splittin' the 33 into three parts right now. From this here date, me and you and Sleepy own this place. No arguments a-tall—no sir. She ain't worth a Hell of a lot for cows, but if there's a gold mine—anyway, we're pardners; the three of us."

Hashknife looked closely at the old man and at Sleepy, who was busily rolling a cigaret. It was very quiet now. A string of dusty-looking cattle were coming down past the corner of the ranch-house fence, heading for the creek.

A magpie flew past the house, swerved sharply at sight of the three men, and perched on a corner of the corral, scolding earnestly. Fleecy clouds flecked the blue sky beyond the timbered ridges; from the hillside came the whistling bark of a ground-squirrel; down in the willows a cow bawled softly for her calf.

Hashknife turned slowly and took a deep breath, as he said—

"Whatcha say t' havin' a song by the Tombstone trio?"